FOAL

DEATH *of*
A NEW AMERICAN

ALSO BY MARIAH FREDERICKS

A Death of No Importance

YA Novels

The Girl in the Park
Crunch Time
Head Games
The True Meaning of Cleavage

DEATH *of*
A NEW AMERICAN

Mariah Fredericks

Minotaur Books
New York

This is a work of fiction. All of the characters, organizations, and events portrayed in this novel are either products of the author's imagination or are used fictitiously.

MINOTAUR BOOKS
An imprint of St. Martin's Press

www.minotaurbooks.com

Designed by Devan Norman

Library of Congress Cataloging-in-Publication Data

Names: Fredericks, Mariah, author.
Title: Death of a New American : a mystery / Mariah Fredericks.
Description: First Edition. | New York : Minotaur Books, 2019.
Identifiers: LCCN 2018049423 | ISBN 9781250152992 (hardcover) |
 ISBN 9781250153005 (ebook)
Subjects: LCSH: Murder—Investigation—Fiction. | GSAFD: Mystery
 fiction.
Classification: LCC PS3606.R435 D429 2019 | DDC 813/.6—dc23
LC record available at https://lccn.loc.gov/2018049423

Our books may be purchased in bulk for promotional, educational, or business use. Please contact your local bookseller or the Macmillan Corporate and Premium Sales Department at 1-800-221-7945, extension 5442, or by email at MacmillanSpecialMarkets@macmillan.com.

First Edition: April 2019

10 9 8 7 6 5 4 3 2 1

For my friends and neighbors who have come from around the world and landed in Jackson Heights, Queens

Acknowledgments

I am deeply grateful for Catherine Richards's editorial judgment, support, and sense of humor. And she is merciful, saving the life of one character in this book. (If you like this character, you have her to thank.) I also thank her terrific assistant, Nettie Finn.

I am also grateful to . . .

My agent, Victoria Skurnick, of whom I say roughly once a month, "Thank God she's my agent."

Sarah Schoof and Allison Ziegler for achieving the impossible and making publicity fun. David Rotstein for the beautiful cover on this book. Also thanks to production manager Cathy Turiano and production editor Chrisinda Lynch. And because copyeditors and proofreaders rule—huge thanks to Rachelle Mandik and Laura Dragonette.

As always, the ladies of the Queens Writers Group for their friendship and wisdom—especially at conference cocktail gatherings.

Several people and organizations were invaluable when it came to research. Among them:

The Italian American Museum on Mulberry Street, which was very helpful and gave me a chance to visit the pork stores I visited with my dad as a kid.

Lieutenant Bernard Whalen for directing me to sources on the police force at the time, including his own excellent book, *The NYPD's First Fifty Years*.

Newspapers—especially *The New York Times*—thank you and God bless a free press.

The excellent guides at Sagamore Hill in Oyster Bay, Long Island.

Stephen Talty for his book *The Black Hand* and Steven Biel for his terrific cultural history of the *Titanic, Down with the Old Canoe*.

This book has some lines in Italian, a language I do not speak. A sincere *grazie* to Anna Kushner and Anna Schivazappa.

An enormous thank-you to Pearl Hanig for her early read and for asking questions like, "Would they really have a morgue in Oyster Bay in 1912?"

Finally, I would like to thank everyone who read *A Death of No Importance*. Some of you wrote me, some came to bookstore or library events, some just weighed in on Goodreads. Writing the book is pleasure number one. Interacting with readers is the other great benefit of this job.

And so, 20,000 women paraded down Fifth Avenue to the sound of the trumpet and in the glare of electric lights. Did their leaders really think that any sensible man likes to have his wife, or his mother, or his daughter thus parade in the streets? It seems to me that this parade is one of the strongest arguments against universal suffrage for women that has yet been presented.

—A LETTER TO *THE NEW YORK TIMES*, 1912

They were monstrous and nebulous adumbrations of the pithecanthropoid and amoebal; vaguely moulded from some stinking, viscous slime of earth's corruption, and slithering and oozing in and on the filthy streets or in and out of doorways in a fashion suggestive of nothing but infesting worms or deep-sea unnamabilities.

—H. P. LOVECRAFT ON ITALIAN
AND JEWISH IMMIGRANTS

DEATH *of*
A NEW AMERICAN

A *wedding took place* on Long Island yesterday. This morning's newspaper informs me that the bride, sixty-seven, is the star of a popular television drama. The groom, twenty-five, was recently employed as a waiter. The two became acquainted at a clinic known for its success in treating alcoholics. It is the groom's first marriage, the bride's seventh.

The guests included many from the world of show business, as well as a presidential candidate who was also once an actor. A chimpanzee was the ring bearer. He performed his duties without incident. The actress's adult daughter was not in attendance; she reportedly disapproved of the match, first on the grounds of the groom's age, and second, that his résumé included employment at a place called FunKey Nuts, an establishment popular in the Florida Keys.

The bride was walked down the aisle by her personal psychic. The couple was to honeymoon in the South of France; proceeds from the sale of the wedding photos would be donated to a cause dear to the bride's heart: the safety and preservation of whales.

I happened to notice the story not because I was familiar with the bride or the groom—or even the chimpanzee—but because I recognized the house where the wedding took place. It is now a resort where a great deal of golf is played, but it once was a private home. I was there in 1912. I remember the year clearly because it was shortly after the *Titanic* sank, taking more than fifteen hundred lives with her. It was a memorable year for other reasons as well. It was the time of the Bull Moose, when Teddy Roosevelt came roaring back to the political arena he had so recently quit. Eleven candidates fought for the favors of the small percentage of the American public able to vote—and women wondered if that fraction should not be enlarged. The arthritic Ottoman Empire was struggling to hold on to its European riches and three thousand cherry blossom trees arrived in Washington as a gift of the Japanese people.

And there was a wedding.

Then as now, there was a wealthy bride. Then as now, an eager groom, disgruntled relatives, and a suspicion that the match was more economic than romantic, although we were not so fussy about such distinctions back then. Then as now, the wedding was to be a glittering society occasion, an alliance that would result in prestige and wealth for all concerned.

But death intervened.

1

"*I don't suppose we'll* be invited to the best funerals. Only the second-rate ones."

"Charlotte!" Mrs. Benchley and Louise stared in horror at the younger Benchley daughter, who was reclined on a chaise lounge, her face obscured by *The New York Herald*. Under a banner headline—"*Titanic* Sinks!"—was a picture of John Jacob Astor and the words "*He gave his life so that women and children might live*."

We were in Louise's room, preparing for her visit to her fiancé's family on Long Island. In the silence that followed, I thought how foolish we had been two days ago when we first heard the news, imagining that the *Titanic* had sunk with no great loss of life. The earliest bulletins had said as much, stating that everyone had proceeded in an orderly fashion to the lifeboats and were now patiently awaiting rescue. It was only when *The New York Times* reported the abrupt end of the ship's distress signal that we began to feel uneasy. Then came the bewildering news that the *Carpathia* had only picked up seven hundred survivors. That was when we faced the reality: fifteen hundred people were dead, gone in a single night.

And the wealth and fame of those who had died! Astor, Straus, Guggenheim. People so blessed with the world's riches—how could they be lost, anonymous forms swallowed by the Atlantic? The unsinkable ship, wrecked upon an iceberg, pulled headfirst into the icy water. And there had been no orderly evacuation, just panic, desperation, screams, and death. Over the past two days, I had found myself dazed and short of breath, lost in contemplation of children who, separated from their parents, had gotten lost in the madness and were left to face their end in the rising waters alone.

"It's so awful," said Louise, who was also gazing at Mr. Astor's picture.

"You mustn't think about it, Louise," said her mother. "It's not a time to distress yourself. Think of the wedding."

"Yes, think of it," said Charlotte. "Don't the Tylers have a duchess coming over from England? Imagine—'I survived *Titanic* and the Tyler-Benchley wedding. Two disasters in a single month.'"

Louise went pale. Sinking onto her bed, she whispered, "I think maybe Charlotte's right."

Mrs. Benchley, who had been asking for the third time if I had packed Miss Louise's navy day dress, said, "Right about what, Louise?"

"Maybe we should postpone."

Mrs. Benchley's mouth dropped. "*Postpone?*"

"Just by a few weeks, or even months."

"Decades?" offered Charlotte, turning the page. Inwardly, I sighed. Kindness had never been one of Charlotte's more salient qualities, but her spite was growing worse as the wedding day grew near. Two years ago, the sisters' prospects had looked very different. Charlotte had made a dramatic debut in New York society by becoming engaged to one of its most eligible bachelors. But on the night their engagement was to be announced, he was found bludgeoned to death. Charlotte had fallen under suspicion, but another was found guilty and executed. (Still another person *was* guilty, but that's a story for another time.)

There had been hope that people would forget Charlotte's connection to the celebrated murder. Alas, society was not so willing to forgive. Charlotte found herself stranded among people who remembered her as the interloper who had destroyed the Newsome family. Oh, she was still received, but she was relegated to the far distant edges of conviviality, forced to survive on conversational scraps such as old Pierpont Jackson's discourse on the breeding of foxhounds or Melanie Derwent's chatter about the paranormal. The iron had entered into Charlotte's soul. The sweet dimpled smile made appearances when necessary. But I had the feeling that behind the smile, the teeth had grown sharper.

Louise gestured helplessly at the headlines. "I don't see how we can have an enormous wedding right after such a tragedy."

Mrs. Benchley's face was blank with incomprehension. "But dearest, just the other day, Mrs. Borcherling said how much she was looking forward to it."

Wringing her hands, Louise said, "Well, maybe we could, just this once, disappoint Mrs. Borcherling?"

"We certainly could *not*," said her mother with unusual vigor. "She's asked me to serve on a committee for a memorial to the men of the *Titanic*."

Frustration agitated Louise's body; her lip began to tremble and tears welled in her eyes. Shutting the trunk, I said perhaps Miss Louise should lie down; we would be leaving early and it was important she be rested. Mrs. Benchley hastily left the room, taking Charlotte with her.

Hand to her chest and gulping air, Louise said, "It's all going to go wrong, I know it. Completely, horribly wrong—"

"It will be fine, Miss Louise," I said soothingly.

"No, it won't. I can't do it. I can't."

A society wedding is a daunting prospect for even the most beautiful young woman. Louise Benchley was not a beauty, being somewhat deficient in chin and protuberant of eye. When I first met her, she had been a girl uncommonly affected by gravity; everything inclined downward. Her shoulders slumped, her arms dangled, her hair hung lank. I sometimes wondered if the midwife hadn't pulled too hard on the infant Louise and her newborn form, pliable as taffy, had been stretched several inches beyond a desirable length.

We had worked hard, Louise and I, to bring out her charms. Careful coiling had given her hair height and volume, improved posture an air of vitality. Stylishly adorned hats had lent their support, and she could now utter as many as three sentences in succession in the company of mere acquaintances. But nothing had improved her looks more than the glow that came the day she became engaged to William Tyler.

But the *Titanic* was only the latest obstacle to be placed in the way of Louise's happiness. William had returned from law school to propose to Louise in the summer of 1911, during a heat wave that drove people to sleep in Central Park, caused rail accidents due to melted tracks, and killed nearly four hundred people. When William told his mother of the engagement, Mrs. Tyler asked him if his wits had been turned by the heat. Had her son forgotten that she no longer spoke to the Benchleys, after Charlotte's snatching of his sister's fiancé? William's sisters Beatrice and Emily simply blocked out the information. Oh, was William getting married? To whom? Louise Benchley? No, not possible, you must be mistaken.

Several inspections over tea had persuaded Mrs. Tyler that Louise was pleasant and bullyable, and these were qualities Mrs. Tyler looked for in her relations. And there was the fact that the Tyler fortune was depleted, the Benchley fortune considerable, and Mrs. Tyler still had two unmarried daughters. So, Mrs. Tyler sighed and resigned herself to a wealthy daughter-in-law.

The couple had wanted a quiet wedding, preferably at the Benchley home. But here Mrs. Tyler would not give way. Her only son's wedding must be an occasion; there would be no comparison made to the embarrassment of the wedding of the Roosevelt boy to his cousin Eleanor several years back. (*Town Topics* criticized that affair for the "pathetic economy of the food," which was "supplied by an Italian caterer not of the first class." The flowers were arranged by a "Madison Avenue florist of no particular fame; and the narrow staircase of the house permitted only one person to ascend or descend at a time.") With complicit dithering from Mrs. Benchley, William and Louise had been overruled.

Months of searching, evaluating, arguing, and—in Louise's case, weeping—had followed. Everything grand enough for the mothers was terrifying to the bride. Finally, William's uncle, the celebrated Charles Tyler, had stepped in. The wedding would be held in a home, but at *his* home, the beautiful estate of Pleasant Meadows on Long Island. The space could match Mrs. Tyler's most fevered dreams of splendor, yet it was a place beloved by William, which in turn made it acceptable to Louise.

Of course, the involvement of Charles Tyler drove the newspapers into further frenzy and they pounced on the preparations. Everything about Louise—the size of her foot, the span of her waist, the enormity of her father's bank account—was detailed. To date, there had been twenty-seven articles on the wedding dress alone: was it to be Worth or Paquin? The veil cathedral length or floral crown? The state of her bridal underwear was speculated upon from stockings to corset. The identities of the bridesmaids, the shade of white of the shoes, the provenance of the caviar—everything made its way into papers. And all with a degree of malicious anticipation; one could expect nothing but fusty good taste from the Tylers, but of the newly rich Benchley clan, expenditures of splendid vulgarity might be hoped for.

None of this helped Louise's already fragile nerves. And she was not alone in her distress. I took some pride in this match; for all intents and purposes, I had made it. As a ladies' maid, it was a central part of my calling to see my employers securely established in society. As the plain, older sister of a woman suspected of murder, Louise's marital prospects had been grim. Her money would have ensured a suitor eventually, but not the sort of man capable of caring for a shy, desperately insecure young woman.

Handsome, well-bred, and poor, William Tyler had also been overlooked on the marriage market. Everyone knew he would marry in the end, but no one was fighting for the privilege. Here, I saw an opportunity. She was rich, he was socially connected. He was kind, she needed kindness. I was the one who suggested William call on Louise, but it hadn't been easy to put them together. Louise had a terror of being seen in public or speaking out loud, both of which are useful in courtship. William had the predictable affinity of the good-looking for the good-looking. And he was a romantic; his early calls on Louise had had the stale whiff of duty to them.

But that had changed as they discovered over walks in the park and pastries at the Hotel Astor that they had much in common, chiefly, being the deferential members of overbearing families. Furthermore, they were both enamored of an elderly basset hound named Wallace, who was walked frequently and unwillingly in the park by his owner, a Mrs. Abernathy.

So, I could now tell Louise with sincerity, "Everything will seem brighter once you and Mr. William are married."

She whispered, "I don't think so. I want to think so. But I can't quite believe it."

The only answer I had to this vague foreboding was: "Tea."

Going to the kitchen, I winced at a thump and thud from upstairs; the housemaid Bernadette was wrestling with the vacuum cleaner and presumably ruining the Benchleys' molding in the process. In the kitchen, Mrs. Mueller, the cook, was vigorously kneading a ball of dough; she was a mediocre cook but had a real enthusiasm for pounding things. Elsie, a hired girl, newly arrived from Idaho, sat, elbows on the table, reading the newspaper. After the last girl had quit—a Greek—Mrs. Benchley decided the fault lay not with her own communication skills, but in the candidates' lack of English, and instructed the agency to send her nothing but "good, plain American girls." Hence, Elsie. Tall and dark haired, she looked as if the plains winds had blown every bit of fat from her body, leaving her spindly and sharp jawed. But she had energy and willingness and so far, Mrs. Benchley's experiment in domestic nationalism seemed a success.

Like the rest of New York—indeed, the rest of the world—the Benchley staff was obsessed with the *Titanic*. Everyone had her particular part of the story. Bernadette was suspicious about the lack of lifeboats, the cook distressed over the fate of Baby Trevor, while Elsie anxiously awaited word of tennis champion Karl Behr.

Now she read, "'International Tragedy Rouses Sympathy of the French People. Kaiser William Sends Message of Condolence. Sir Ernest Shackleton Says, Abnormal Year for Icebergs.'" What was normal for icebergs, I wondered.

Elsie turned the page. "Oh, this is sad. 'The White Star office was be—besieged'"—she was an unsteady reader and she gave the word a hard *g*—"by weeping women, several of whom had sons on board. Among these was Mrs. William Dulles, who left the office in a state of collapse, supported by her friends."

Now there was another thud from upstairs, followed by a curse.

Looking up, Elsie said, "She hates that thing. Says it doesn't work."

"You take the rugs outside, you beat the rugs outside," opined Mrs. Mueller, giving the dough a good whack.

I said, "Progress, Mrs. Mueller. Would you make some tea for Miss Louise?"

Bernadette stomped into the kitchen and threw herself into a chair. She, Mrs. Mueller, and I were survivors in a manner of speaking, having lasted two years in the Benchleys' employ, a feat that had eluded every other domestic in the city and possibly the state. Not that the Benchleys were difficult to please; they were just impossible in every other way. There was also Mrs. Benchley's personal maid, an elderly woman who went by the name "Matchless Maude." But she kept to her room, preferring gin to company.

Bernadette was a stout young woman with red hair and small, watchful eyes. She had more wits than her job made use of, and she often exercised them at others' expense. Elsie, new to the city, was an easy target. When the country girl expressed sympathy for Madeleine Astor, Bernadette rolled her eyes. "Poor Madeleine Astor! She saved her maid and let her rich husband drown."

Elsie argued, "Well, she didn't have a choice, it's women and children first."

"The code of the sea," intoned Mrs. Mueller, flinging the dough onto the counter.

"If they'd had enough lifeboats, you wouldn't *need* a code," said Bernadette.

Wanting to diffuse the argument, I took up the newspaper. There was a fetching picture of a young woman hanging from a trapeze and I read: "'The Ladies of Barnum and Bailey to March for Suffrage!'"

But Bernadette could not be put off needling so easily. She asked Elsie, "Are you all signed up? Going to march for your right to vote?"

Elsie shrugged. "We've had the vote in Idaho since 1896. Maybe they just don't trust you New York gals. I guess *you'll* be out there."

"Oh, sure," lied Bernadette.

I smiled. "Wearing your thirty-nine-cent hat?" The suffrage marchers, wanting to project unity, were urging everyone to wear special thirty-nine-cent hats, and the papers were gleefully antici- pating the spectacle of well-heeled women sporting a cheap pa- rade bonnet with their white suits and tricolored sashes.

Then Elsie asked, "Who would you vote for, if you could?"

"None of them," snorted Bernadette. A neat way, I thought, not to admit she didn't know any of the candidates. True—there were a lot of them. In February, Teddy Roosevelt started what he called "the biggest fight the Republican Party has been in since the Civil War," and declared he was running against his former friend and protégé, President Taft, whom he now deemed a fathead with the brains of a guinea pig. Wilson promised a New Freedom, Roosevelt a New Nationalism. Someone named Champ Clark was keen to annex Canada. Everyone promised to end corruption and curb the abuses of big business. Republicans favored something called a protective tariff, while Democrats were in favor of free trade. I myself had no opinion on the matter.

"Are you going to march, Miss Prescott?" Elsie asked me.

The question surprised me. I was so preoccupied with the wed- ding, I had never even considered going. And I didn't think of myself as a . . . marcher.

"It's barely a week after Miss Louise's wedding. I'll still be asleep."

As Mrs. Mueller poured the water into the teapot and wrapped it in a cloth, I arranged the tray. Bernadette said, "I heard her crying again. I never saw a girl cry so much before her own wedding."

Elsie leaned in. "He's nice-looking, that William Tyler. Oh, say, there was something in the papers—"

She turned the pages, then pushed it to the center of the table so we could all see.

"I DEFY THEM!"
DEPUTY COMMISSIONER CHARLES TYLER STANDS
AGAINST THE BLACK HAND

"That's Mr. William's uncle, ain't it?" asked Elsie. "Where you're going tomorrow."

"Yes."

Mrs. Mueller said, "He saved that little boy that they kidnapped." Mrs. Mueller's children were grown, but she was not yet the grandmother she longed to be. Anything to do with children caught her attention.

"Now, *he'd* get my vote," said Bernadette, pointing to the picture of Tyler. "He's not all talk. He gives the dagoes what they deserve."

I winced. Dago was not a word I cared for—and I heard it a lot. A series of sensational (or sensationalized) incidents had many in the city feeling under siege from foreign criminals. Our last commissioner, Theodore Bingham, had made the startling claim that 85 percent of the criminals in the city were exotic. Russian Hebrews, he said, had cornered the market in crimes against property, such as burglars, firebugs, and pickpockets. Chinatown was a "plague spot that ought not to be allowed to exist." But the "Italian malefactor" was by far the greatest threat, and the most notorious of these was a group known as the "Black Hand." Their crimes were legion. Homes and shops were dynamited by blackmailers. Children kidnapped and held for ransom. Italian families extorted of their earnings. The body parts of those who ran afoul of the gang were strewn in city streets.

In response, Commissioner Bingham and Charles Tyler had created a special "Italian Squad," headed by Lt. Joseph Petrosino and staffed by other men of Italian extraction, who could go undetected through the Italian neighborhoods of the East Side and Upper Broadway. A string of dramatic arrests brought great acclaim to the squad—and of course, the men responsible for its creation. If there were some who felt Charles Tyler's war against gangs was a little showy, his cultivation of his own myth a little obvious, it could not be denied that he invested his work with all the considerable energy and wits at his disposal.

But it was the Forti case that had made Charles Tyler a national hero, winning him the hearts of American mothers so definitively that it was said that if women were given the vote, Charles Tyler could stroll right into the White House. The kidnapping of six-year-old Emilio Forti, who disappeared from his own street, had commanded Mr. Tyler's attentions because, as he told the papers, "I have sons of my own and the thought of their mother's heartbreak should they be taken from us is unimaginable."

The Fortis were a well-to-do family. Emilio's father was a lawyer. Emilio's mother had first become alarmed when he failed to come home from school that afternoon. When she checked, she was told her son never arrived. That evening, the family had received a letter, demanding payment of $15,000 for the child's return. The kidnappers warned that if the matter came to the attention of the police, "you will receive the body of your son by parcel post. In pieces."

Some people observed that there was little reason for Charles

Tyler to accompany "his" Sicilians on the Italian Squad, but accompany them he did. When they got a tip as to the whereabouts of the suspected kidnappers, Tyler, in disguise, tailed them from a saloon on Flatbush Avenue to a grocery on Eleventh Street. "I heard a child crying," Tyler later told reporters. "I banged on the door and demanded entrance. No one answered and so we broke into the room. There I saw a boy, who trembled and said, 'Please don't kill me, mister, I'm Emilio.' I picked the little fellow up and told him I was a policeman and that I was going to take him home to his people."

The Italian Squad managed to arrest two of the kidnappers; the police implied there were others, but these two were dim enough to get caught. One of them was Dante Moretti, son of the notorious Sirrino Moretti. Speaking with the newspapers, the senior Mr. Moretti, who described himself as a humble merchant, had suggested that as the charges were false the trial would not be in Charles Tyler's best interest. His reputation, worried Mr. Moretti, could "suffer." Tyler responded to these threats with characteristic bravado, and a war of words had ensued, much to the delight of the press. I just hoped that the battle would not escalate. At least, not before the wedding.

"Maybe that's why she's nervous," said Bernadette, tossing her head toward Louise's room. "You're walking down the aisle, all of a sudden, some guinea jumps out and tries to cut your throat."

I had seen too much of Louise's nerves to find this funny. "Miss Louise's wedding day will be perfect. Even if I have to cut someone's throat myself."

Bernadette narrowed her eyes. "And what happens to you after the wedding? What if her mother-in-law decides you're not good enough for the new Mrs. Tyler? Wants someone who's worked for royalty and speaks French?"

The question had occurred to me, but I wasn't going to admit it to Bernadette, who added, "It's not like you ever got along so well with Miss Charlotte."

I picked up the tray. "I'm sure when Miss Louise decides, I'll be the first to know."

"Future's uncertain, that's all I'm saying," said Bernadette. She nodded to the headline, ONE THOUSAND EIGHT HUNDRED SOULS LOST! "Tomorrow's promised to no man—or woman either."

2

The next day we set off for Pleasant Meadows. The purpose of the trip was twofold: the week would give the mothers-in-law the chance to see how their grand schemes would play out in the actual setting where the wedding was to take place, thus avoiding the last-minute embarrassments of caterers thwarted by narrow corridors or the bride tripped by a loose flagstone. It would also give Louise a chance to become acquainted with her hosts, the people William loved best in the world.

It was not a calm departure. Given the mission of the visit, Mr. Benchley decided his presence was not required—nor was Charlotte's. So, he dispatched her to Philadelphia, where she would visit with her aunt and then escort the older woman to the wedding. He himself would stay in the city. That morning, he announced he did not even have time to see the ladies to the station. This threw Mrs. Benchley into fits.

I don't think I am being indiscreet if I say that Mrs. Benchley was *not* a suffragette. To her, the world beyond her door was chaotic and bewildering, best navigated by a man who would tell you when and where to go and carry anything heavier than a handkerchief. The prospect of facing Pennsylvania Station without her husband was daunting; the news that O'Hara, the Benchleys' oft-inebriated chauffeur, would accompany her from the house to the station did not console her.

"William will meet us at the station, Mother," Louise reassured her. "He'll manage everything."

"Yes," said Mrs. Benchley, brightening at the thought of her son-in-law. "And we'll have Jane."

"Yes, we'll have Jane."

Both Benchley ladies were apprehensive about the journey through the new tunnel that now linked Manhattan to Queens under the East River. Up until two years ago, travelers had had to be ferried across, but now the train simply ran through a tube, submerging on the East shore of Manhattan and coming back out again in Long Island City. Mrs. Benchley had grave doubts about this tube and would not be reassured as to its soundness. What if there were a crack? What if the train got stuck? Would they have to swim? Because she wasn't a very good swimmer . . .

Much has been written about the glories of the old Pennsylvania Station, and I suppose it was magnificent—if you had nothing to do but look. Constructed of marble and pink granite, it was modeled on the glories of Paris and London as a signal to the world that America had its own great capital cities. The main waiting room had been inspired by the ancient baths of Rome, and the huge vaulted hall, guarded by eagles and unseeing maidens, was imperial in scale. Maps of the world covered the walls. The elaborate glass skylight commanded the gaze and made you feel dizzy to look up. You were at once in the center of the universe and the entry point of the entire nation. You might go anywhere, do anything.

But I wasn't in the happy position of sightseer. I had to find a porter to take the bags, shepherd Mrs. and Miss Benchley inside the station, then find a place for them to sit, as Mrs. Benchley was feeling faint.

"Mother, we're supposed to meet William under the clock," Louise fretted.

"You stay with Mrs. Benchley," I told her. "I'll go find Mr. William."

As I made my way through the crowds, I found myself brought up short by the newly completed statue of the president of the Pennsylvania Railroad, Alexander Cassatt. The bronze colossus stood in an archway, surveying the multitudes who scurried through his splendid creation like so many ants. In his hand, he held his hat and cane, as if still about his business. Mrs. Benchley had Mr. Cassatt to thank for her worries, as it was he who, Moses-like, had blasted through the New York bedrock and tunneled through two rivers to connect the island of Manhattan with New Jersey and Long Island. Hundreds of homes had been demolished, and fourteen men had died. Cassatt himself had not lived to see his vision realized—and so this tribute. I found myself strangely provoked by the statue. Its massive size and imposing demeanor spurred me to stand my ground and meet its eye—even if I had to look up twenty feet to do so.

Then I remembered the Benchleys and hurried on to find William.

I often thought if God gave me a choice of brothers, I would have picked William Tyler. He was the nephew of my first employer, Mrs. Armslow, and I had known him since I was fourteen. The Tylers had long been under obligation to their more well-off relations. While she was alive, Mrs. Armslow had paid for William's education and for his sisters' apparel. But when she died, she left her fortune to charity and the family had struggled. The stench of

charity accompanied them at social gatherings. People politely—
but pointedly—overlooked the fact that the Tyler girls wore
others' cast-off dresses and that their jewelry was "becomingly
modest." When it seemed Beatrice was about to marry Norrie
Newsome, everyone looked forward to the day they could stop ac-
commodating the Tylers' embarrassing condition. But she had
not and they could not. Until now.

William got the best of the family looks, being dark haired and
sweet natured. He was a little oversized—too tall, ungainly in his
gait, too sincere in his views. He had brought many a social gathering to stunned silence with his enthusiasm for the novels of H. G.
Wells or the brilliance of Robert La Follette. All his life, he had
worked to fulfill the expectations of his mother and aunt. And while
those expectations had not included a marriage with a family viewed
as the destroyer of his sister's happiness, he was at least now in a
position to restore the Tylers' financial fortune. His mother had arranged a position for him at a suitable law firm, which he would
take up after his honeymoon.

Being so tall, William was easy to spot; his head was lifted, his
mouth open in frank admiration of the station's wondrous skylight.
I explained that Mrs. Benchley was resting and asked if he could
come to where she was. As we made our way through the bustling
crowd, walking one behind the other, he called, "What do you
think, Jane? Have I done a good thing?"

Over my shoulder, I said, "I think you're marrying the finest
girl in New York."

"I think so, too." He caught up to me. "But don't you sell yourself short."

"Oh, no," I said mockingly.

We paused as a large lady in front of us paused, unsure as to
where she was going. Lowering his voice, William asked, "How is
Miss Louise?"

". . . Apprehensive."

We were within view of Louise and her mother. Gazing at his fiancée, William said, "I know certain things are hard for Louise. Talking to people, that sort of thing. But I think if I can build up her confidence, make her see herself . . . well, the way we see her, she'll be quite splendid."

"I pledge my complete cooperation." The lady made up her mind as to her direction and we moved on.

The mere sight of William improved Mrs. Benchley's spirits out of all recognition. William bestowed a kiss on Louise's cheek, listened patiently to her mother's complaints, and commandeered all of us to the train, where he found just the right seat by the window for Mrs. Benchley, then neatly arranged it so that he sat next to Louise. Seeing them settled in the first-class car, I started down the aisle, only to hear Louise call, "No, Jane, sit here with us!"

It was not the first time Louise had asked me to stay with her and William. I had "chaperoned" any number of walks in the park, trips to the Metropolitan Museum, and even a tea or two. I suppose it gave her courage, but it was not regular.

But William said, "Absolutely!" and gestured to the aisle seat opposite himself and Louise. A man having made the decision, Mrs. Benchley made no objection.

It was not the last decision William made either. His newfound stature as the savior of the Tyler family fortune had given him courage to go with his manners. When a pretty young woman came down the aisle burdened by a squirming Pekingese, William gallantly offered to hold the dog while she found her seat. An older woman was helped with her bags. Two giggling college girls were guided to their row, a kindness for which they showed such excessive gratitude that I felt it necessary to remind William that he had the tickets and the conductor would be by shortly. Louise, who had grown more and more pale the longer William was out of his seat, smiled in relief as he sat beside her.

Once the train had lurched into motion, Mrs. Benchley said, "Now, William, you must tell me more about your uncle. He sounds such an uncommon man, I'm sure I won't know what to say to him."

"He is an uncommon man," agreed William. "But you shouldn't worry; once Uncle Charles gets talking, you won't get a chance to say much."

The fact of Charles Winslow Tyler's uncommonness was widely known because Charles Winslow Tyler wished it widely known. He courted attention the way he did everything else: vigorously. He was the younger brother of William's father, a position some find trying, but which he saw as a liberation from convention. He had constantly sought out experience at its roughest and most wild. As a teenager, he had worked on a swordfishing vessel alongside Portuguese fishermen. Following the example of the celebrated mountaineer Mrs. Fanny Bullock Workman, he had climbed one of the Nun Kun peaks in the Himalayas and had come fifth in the Iditarod dog sled race (he currently owned a husky named Brownie who was a descendent of the lead dog in that race). There was a rumor that he had wrestled a grizzly bear in the Yukon, and while he never owned up to it, he did nothing to dispel it. He had gone west, serving in the US Cavalry, but he found army life too rigid, and so enrolled at Harvard. Those who might dismiss him as a barbarian were surprised when he excelled. They were further surprised when he rushed from graduation straight into politics in the New York State Assembly, a business no gentleman took an interest in. However, Charles Tyler found Albany rougher than even he could stand—grizzly bears, he said, fought you fair—so he returned to the city, where he joined the police department and threw himself into the fight against organized crime.

Now William said, "I know my uncle sounds rough in the newspapers, but that's just show. He'll do anything for his family."

Here William broke off, no doubt remembering his own father, who had come to a tragic end when William was young, falling prey to two ailments that strike many an old distinguished family: gambling and drink. When he died, he left his children very little beyond a resourceful mother and society connections that guaranteed they wouldn't starve. I had heard the story in whispered bits and pieces when I was at the Armslow house. Charles Tyler had tried to save his older brother, scolding him through letters, sending him to sanitariums, getting him the semblance of a job at a law firm, and paying off his debts on more than one occasion. When the poor man made his unfortunate exit out of his office window—it was always referred to as a fall—Charles Tyler took charge of his family. It was he who made sure William and his sisters were remembered by those who mattered, enrolling William in the right schools and writing to him at least three times a week, dispensing the kind of hearty, fatherly advice that would have otherwise been lacking in his life.

"But his career must make his poor wife very nervous," said Mrs. Benchley. "Those criminals he's fighting, they want to kill him, don't they?"

Here Mrs. Benchley was not entirely wrong. Last year, a car that was to take Charles Tyler to the mayor's office had been blown to pieces with him just twenty feet away; he had suffered a nasty wound to his arm from flying shrapnel, but was otherwise fine. "Thank God," he told the papers an hour later, "that I am never on time. Always running late. Drives my wife mad."

William laughed. "Most wives would probably be nervous. But my aunt Alva's very different from most wives."

As a young man, Charles Tyler had rarely been in one part of the world for long, and such a busy life did not lend itself to domesticity. Therefore, it was some time before he found a mate. But he had succeeded in this as he had succeeded in everything else—in a manner both triumphant and unorthodox. Alva Tyler, formerly Alva Van Ness, might better be described as handsome rather than beautiful, but at the time of their marriage, people spoke with envy of Charles Tyler's luck in marrying a woman who was "rich and a beauty besides." Her brown hair had a lovely red tint when it caught the light. She was not tall, slightly short in the waist, which made elegance a challenge, but elegance was not what she aspired to. Her reputation for looks rested almost entirely on her eyes, which were indeed spectacular: large and luminous blue-green. At one point, she had managed to sit still long enough to have her portrait done by Mr. Sargent; he captured her as the vibrant "New Woman," dressed in sports clothing, her overlarge mouth laughing, her glorious eyes alive with curiosity.

Having married one of the chief adventurers of the day, Alva joined him in exploring the world. The Charles Tylers shot in Africa with Frederick Russell Burnham, sailed on the Ganges with Lord and Lady Dumfries, and took a spin in a motorized airship soon after their debut at the 1904 World's Fair. I could remember the photo of her grinning and windblown next to the vast dirigible. She did appear in the newspapers more than was considered ideal. But she was that sort of singular personality who was allowed to break the rules—people felt she was so singular, few would be daring enough to emulate her.

Even the birth of their first two sons hadn't slowed her down much. But when she miscarried a third, the doctors recommended she adopt a quieter lifestyle. It was at that time that the Tylers took up residence in Pleasant Meadows and were rewarded with more children, a daughter and a son. Sadly, last year, the son had died just after his first birthday, and for a while, the newspapers had only pictures of a subdued Charles Tyler to show and none at all of Alva, whose grief was said to be great. But four months ago, the couple had welcomed a new baby boy and joy returned to the household. Mr. Tyler still worked in the city, staying at their house there during the week, but Alva Tyler stayed at Pleasant Meadows year-round, saying it was better for the children. I had glimpsed Alva Tyler a few times when I worked for Mrs. Armslow. I admired her enormously and was looking forward to seeing her again.

The rest of the train journey proceeded without incident; Louise clutched William's hand and Mrs. Benchley clutched mine as we went through the tunnel. We stepped off the train and into the fresh sea air of the North Shore—or as others were calling it, the Gold Coast.

Sometime around the end of the last century, New York's wealthiest families had become frustrated with the limitations of the square city block. Space, they needed space! And fresh air. So they decamped forty miles east to Long Island, where the likes of the Vanderbilts, Guggenheims, and Fricks could be free to build chateaux, cottages, and castles as sprawling as their hearts desired. Also to play. Long Island's great lawns and windy bays were the site of endless contests such as only warriors with great wealth and leisure time can afford. Ponies charged down the polo grounds of the Meadow Brook Club, horses leapt hedges in pursuit of fox, yachts vied for supremacy on the waves at Seawanhaka Corinthian Yacht Club, and motorcars thundered down the raceway at the Vanderbilt Cup. (Ostrich races had been tried, but in the words of a local paper, "the birds seem unreliable and not exactly fitted for track work.") Some found diversion at the newly open aeroplane schools or by tending their model farm or competing fiercely at cards. At the heart of all these battles of course was the ultimate fight: who could spend the most and most stylishly.

We were met at the station by a gentle breeze tanged with salt and the Tylers' charabanc. The chauffeur was a rotund little man, visibly harassed, and mopping sweat from his neck. He had a beaky nose, liverish lips, and the start of a double chin. But he brightened when he saw "Mr. William," and pumped his hand with enthusiasm. When he spoke, I was startled to hear a strong Italian accent.

Bringing Louise forward, William said, "Louise, Mrs. Benchley, this is my uncle's new chauffeur, Aldo. Aldo, this is my fiancée, Miss Louise Benchley."

Aldo intensified his performance of the earthy Mediterranean, throwing up his hand with an extravagant cry of welcome and dubbing Louise "Mrs. William." Round-eyed with shock, Mrs. Benchley flinched when Aldo raised his cap to her. Then, pulling William to one side, she whispered, "But he's *Italian*." William whispered back, "Yes, Mrs. Benchley."

I watched as Aldo loaded the luggage onto the charabanc. With the family out of earshot, he was less ebullient, raising his eyebrows in displeasure as he squatted to lift the first trunk. Shoving it with a grunt, he muttered to me, "She's rich, huh? Better be rich."

It was a few miles' drive from the station. The city's wealthiest families had made their presence known, but this was still farmland. Horses cantered behind split-rail fences. Cows lowed from the field. I lifted my face to the sun, breathed in the smell of freshly cut grass, and listened to the birds chitter overhead. We hit a small bump and I opened my eyes to see the dull pewter gleam of the ocean. As we approached the house, I was struck by the inadequacy of its name: Pleasant Meadows. The grounds were lovely, with wide swaths of grass and towering old trees. But the house, set atop a hill, had far too much wayward individuality for such a bland title. I had visited several estates and none of them had the ramshackle, boisterous design of the Tyler home. Fittingly, given its owner, it resembled a boy's paradise. A generous porch circled the front of the house; the second floor boasted an enclosed porch on its right side. A third, smaller floor had a row of windows overlooking the front lawn. A thirty-foot hall or gallery connected the main house to a small addition about the size of a guest cottage. The topmost floor was almost a tower; a flag fluttered from its roof, and I wondered if it were a skull and crossbones. One could imagine Charles Tyler barking at the builder, "Yes, let's put a balcony there, a picture window there, and a secret passageway in the library. Over there, I want a swing. Overlooking the pond. What do you mean, no pond? Put one in!" I could see why William loved it here.

But it was also hard not to notice the anonymous men who nodded politely as we passed through the gate. Or a sandy-haired man strolling the grounds in a coat far too heavy for the warm weather, hand fixed at his waistband. Charles Tyler might tell the papers he was unconcerned by the Black Hand's threats, but he was not unaware of them.

Charles and Alva Tyler were waiting for us on the lawn. Standing behind them was William's mother, Florence Tyler, looking as settled and imperious as an abbess. A little behind the official welcoming party stood a young dark-haired woman who held a sleeping baby in one arm and a little girl by the hand. The little girl kept rising on tiptoes, twisting her head to see around the adults.

I had seen Charles Tyler in person on a few occasions and many times in the papers, but even I was struck at how much he was himself, vivid, full of life, arms outstretched to embrace anything in his path—in this case Louise, who was knocked breathless when he wrapped her up in a massive hug. Mrs. Benchley all but swooned when he took her hand and intoned, "Welcome to Pleasant Meadows, my dear Mrs. Benchley. This is a happy house!" Alva Tyler observed her husband's performance with good-natured restraint; she had seen it all before, but could appreciate its effect on a new audience.

Aldo was taking his time with the luggage, so I had begun to take down some of the smaller pieces when I heard a booming, "Jane! Little Jane Prescott. I want to have a look at you."

Startled, I turned to see the great man himself standing next to me. Grasping both my hands, he lifted them and crowed, "Why, you're splendid! Do you remember, Alva, my old aunt's little thing of a maid? All eyes—saw everything. Figured out it was my rotten cousin Dicky filching Aunt Laura's earbobs. And now look at you!" He grinned, a happy beam that had no condescension in it, only genuine pleasure, as if my maturation were proof of a prosperous America where all things were done right.

"Alva," he said, "look at her!"

"I can't, dearest," said his wife. "You're hiding her behind the charabanc."

Mr. Tyler gave a shout of laughter and led me out. Alva Tyler advanced, hands outstretched, and said in her lovely, deep voice, "It's very nice to see you again, Jane."

I smiled. "Thank you, Mrs. Tyler. It's very good to see you."

If Alva Tyler wasn't quite the woman I had remembered, it was to be expected that age and motherhood would stake their claims. She had grown thicker through the waist, and her vivid hair was leached of brightness. There were sharp lines around her mouth and bruised shadows under her eyes. The hands that held mine were sharply boned, almost brittle. But the miraculous blue-green eyes were still luminous.

There was a brief shuffling sound and Mrs. Tyler looked over her shoulder. "And this is my daughter—"

A girl of about six stepped forward with broad steps and swinging arms. She had inherited her father's looks, which did not sit so well on a female child, but I couldn't help thinking here was the energy that had deserted her mother.

She forthrightly held out her hand. "Mabel Tyler."

I shook it. "A pleasure to meet you, Miss Tyler."

"And how are the fair Sofia and the magnificent Frederick?" William approached the nanny, who offered him a shy smile.

"Very well, Mr. William." She was, by her accent, also Italian, and quite lovely, with sloping dark eyes, and olive skin that, although mildly pockmarked, glowed with youth and health. William spoke nonsense to Frederick, but his eyes stayed on Sofia. Seeing Louise fuss unhappily with her reticule, I decided I would have to tell William that it would be better if he did not notice other women existed for the foreseeable future.

Alva Tyler said, "Jane, I'll take you to Mrs. Briggs, our housekeeper. She can help you get settled. Sofia—"

The dark-haired girl broke her gaze with William, eyes apprehensive. I sensed she had not had this job long.

"I think you should take the children inside. I feel rain coming." I glanced at the sky. It was clear blue.

Sofia said doubtfully, "They have been inside all morning . . ."

"I think it's better," said Alva Tyler.

The party began to move indoors, Sofia gently herding Mabel to the door. Aldo had taken the bags inside. This gave Mrs. Benchley the opportunity to say what she had been dying to since we got off the train.

"I am surprised, Mr. Tyler, given your work, that you see fit to hire people of Italian extraction."

"Nothing wrong with Italians," said Mr. Tyler firmly. "They're a fine people. It's the criminality I despise, not the race."

"And I suppose you know who all the bad ones are," said Mrs. Benchley.

Mr. Tyler decided to take this foolishness in good humor. "Indeed I do, Mrs. Benchley, indeed I do."

3

Mrs. Briggs was a small, bustling woman in her early fifties. Her dark brown hair was touched with gray like whorls of ice on a frozen pond. Her face was appealing, with an upturned nose, short upper lip, and prominent front teeth; she put one in mind of a pig—but of all the very best qualities of that animal. She was efficient but welcoming, sweeping me into the house with instructions on how to find my way around alternating with instructions to herself: have the day girl fold the sheets, put up the spring curtains, bring up the Bordeaux, logs in the fireplace, it was warm now, but could turn cold . . .

"I'm sorry, Miss Prescott," she explained as we reached the third floor. "But if I don't run through the day's list every hour, it goes out of my head."

"Now, this house"—she set her fists on her hips as she launched into a speech I sensed she had given many times before—"is an unusual house. Twenty rooms. Easy to get lost. The tower at the top is for the younger children and their nanny, but I don't suppose you need to know that. Third floor, servants' quarters at one end for those of us who live in, which is only myself and visiting staff. Mr. Grimaldi the chauffeur sleeps above the garage. Mr. Tyler's study at the other end."

Seeing my surprise at the proximity between servant and employer, she said, "Mr. Tyler's not fussy about those things. As he says, 'I'm just a man, Mrs. Briggs, not a duchess.' The boys' bedrooms are on the second floor. The master bedrooms are through the gallery at the far end of the house."

The guest cottage I had noticed when we arrived. The parenting style in vogue at the time dictated a certain amount of distance between parent and child. The nursery was, if possible, far from the parents' bedroom, and the children's rearing left chiefly to professionals.

"Mr. William is in one of the boys' rooms. Your Miss Louise and her mother will be in the second-floor guest quarters on the right."

"Thank you, Mrs. Briggs."

"Now, one thing *you* need to remember—doors are closed and locked at ten o'clock. Mr. and Mrs. Tyler have keys, I have keys. Other than that, no one has a key." She smiled. "So, if you're the type that likes to wander at night, all I can say is I'm not a nice woman after ten."

"I'll remember."

"Also, Mrs. Tyler prefers the windows closed. All windows."

The house felt quite warm. But then I remembered the guards at the gate and said, "Of course."

Louise's room was lovely, with windows overlooking a garden of carnations and snapdragons on the right side of the house. As I unpacked, I heard singing. Something about the tune was familiar; I could recall hearing it as a child. It brought up memories of women sitting on front steps, soothing fretful infants. *Fa la ninna, fa la nanna . . .*

Going to the window, I saw Sofia walking in her white dress, Frederick content in her arms as she sang. They made a pretty picture, her dark head bent, her cheek gently nuzzling his hair, as she made her way slowly toward the woods that surrounded the property.

"Sofia." At the sound of her name, the girl stopped. I watched as Alva Tyler came into view. "Where are you taking Freddy?"

"I . . . I am not *taking* . . ." Her voice was fearful, but with a thin note of defiance.

"I told you the children should be inside."

"Yes, I know, but—"

"And so they should be inside."

Waving at the clear sky, Sofia said, "It's nice, it's . . . fine . . ."

"It is not nice." Alva Tyler advanced on the younger woman. "It is not fine. It is not safe. As I have told you many times and yet you do not listen. I wonder why you do not listen. Why do you not listen, Sofia?"

Unnerved by her employer's anger, Sofia opened her mouth, but made no answer.

"Take the baby inside," said Alva Tyler. Then she turned and went back to the house. For a moment, Sofia stood where she was. Distressed, she put her hand to her forehead and breathed deeply the way one does when trying not to cry. She glanced once at the woods, as if still yearning to walk. Silently, I urged her back.

Rubbing the baby's back, she seemed to collect herself. She began to walk.

Toward the house.

★ ★ ★

Louise was quiet that night when she came to bed. When I asked how dinner had gone, she said, "Awful."

"Mr. Tyler talked a lot about crime and he was very funny. But

Alva Tyler asked him to stop. She was a bit sharp with him, I guess she didn't think it suitable. Only, she didn't have much to say and neither did the rest of us. Then Mother started talking about the fund for the *Titanic* memorial and I could see William's mother didn't like it. So I started babbling about orange blossom and then Alva Tyler said her head hurt . . ."

Oh, dear, I thought. Between Mrs. Benchley's fund and Louise's talk of orange blossom, Alva Tyler's head must have ached.

"Then William's mother said she was planning to go to Paris and Mrs. Tyler said she must see the Gardner-Smiths. Then they all talked about places I haven't been and things I haven't done and people I can barely remember."

She fell into a chair and turned unhappy eyes on me. "Jane, I'm worried. I just don't see how I can ever be . . . Mrs. William Tyler."

I understood her fear. As Mrs. William Tyler, Louise would be expected to take her place in society, joining charity boards, entertaining the right people in the right way, serving as a sterling example of the moral rectitude of her class. Louise was fine on moral rectitude. It was the rest of the job that posed a problem. Anyone who knew Louise liked her. But when she became Mrs. William Tyler, people would not so much get to know her as get to know *of* her, and she had yet to develop the qualities of a successful public wife.

But they would come with time and effort, and so I said, "You will be an excellent Mrs. William Tyler, because William Tyler loves you and you love him. The rest is not important. Go to sleep. You have mothers and wedding plans to battle in the morning."

That got a small smile and I felt reassured. Then the smile faded and she said, "William told me that he has to go back to the city at the weekend, the *same* weekend his sisters are coming to visit."

"We'd better start reading Plato, then. Emily's studying philosophy at Vassar."

Louise groaned and fell back on the pillow.

Mrs. Briggs had warned me I might get lost, and sure enough, I turned the wrong way as I left Louise's room and found myself at the end of the hall near the master bedroom. I recognized my mistake when I heard raised voices. A more civilized person would not have stopped at the sound of tears. But my step slowed when I heard a tear-choked voice say, "Don't treat me like a child, Charles . . ."

Then Mr. Tyler's voice, placating, "I'm only suggesting that you might have misunderstood . . ."

"I have not misunderstood. I understand perfectly well. We cannot trust her—"

"Please lower your voice."

"She is a liar and . . . a thief . . . and all you can offer me is 'lower your voice.'" She strangled on this last word and for a few moments, she seemed overcome. Then she managed, "You never believe me . . ."

"Dearest, I do . . ."

The situation had become too painful for me to listen to with any pretense to decency, and I walked quickly and quietly up the stairs.

But it was hard to forget what I had heard. The ugly words kept sounding in my head like a fragment of song. The accusation of theft was common. Neglected wives used it as a way to engage their husband's attention, extravagant wives who pawned jewelry to pay bills they'd rather not show their spouses, or angry women looking for scapegoats. I had known too many girls fired unfairly to put faith in Alva Tyler's claim. But I was very sorry to hear her make it. Clearly, she and the nanny did not get along, but to accuse the poor girl of theft was unworthy of the brave, laughing woman I remembered. Did marriage make all women so small and suspicious? No wonder Louise was anxious about married life.

Falling asleep in a strange bed is part of the job as a ladies' maid; you go where your mistress does. I hadn't slept in a bed that didn't feel borrowed since I was thirteen. I had tricks to take my mind off strangeness. Usually they involved planning outfits or sewing, but I had no sewing tonight and I had planned Louise's ensembles when packing. Kneeling down, I pulled my suitcase out from under the bed and rummaged in an inside pocket. When I found what I was looking for, I sat on the bed, legs tucked up, and looked at the small package on my lap.

I hadn't meant to bring them; while packing, I repeatedly dismissed the impulse to throw them in the suitcase. But I also knew that it was a pastime among hired girls to search the rooms of absent staff. I could remember with shame being fourteen and shrieking with laughter over a photograph of an ugly farm boy another maid kept hidden in a Bible at Mrs. Armslow's. And I didn't want Elsie or Bernadette laughing over these.

They were in a small bundle tied with a ribbon I'd carefully chosen to be plain and serviceable. There was nothing to indicate that these letters were in any way special—except that they were the only letters I'd ever received. And they were all from one person.

The first letter arrived a few months after I had last seen Michael Behan. I remember the childish excitement of seeing my name—Miss Jane Prescott—written on the front of the envelope, which I opened very carefully. Inside was a folded newspaper clipping; I saw the headline as it fluttered open: MAN FOUND IN BARREL WITHOUT HEAD.

And there was a letter.

> *My dear Miss Prescott,*
> *I seem to remember making a promise to write you.*
> *Also to keep you apprised of my literary efforts, of*
> *which I think the enclosed is a fine example. As your*
> *employers are no longer in the newspapers—or*
> *presumably killing people—I worry that you might*
> *not be up to date with the city's latest doings. This*
> *particular incident involves a recent attempt by our*
> *Italian American brethren to thin the economic*
> *competition by slitting its throat and placing the*
> *head in a nearby sewer (although the head's discov-*
> *ery is not official, and you should not mention it to*
> *the Benchley ladies or other polite company). As you*
> *can see, I am no longer chasing down badly*
> *behaved debutantes, but on to the real squalids and*
> *grotesques.*
>
> *Should you wish to give your opinion of my*
> *humble endeavors, you can write me at <u>The New</u>*
> *<u>York Herald,</u> at the address below.*
>
> *Yours,*
> *Michael Behan*

I had had to search out a piece of paper and pen, finally bor-
rowing them from a new maid who wrote regularly to her family
in Manchester. Sitting down before I had time to think too much,
I wrote,

> *Dear Mr. Behan,*
> *How do you know the head in the sewer belonged to*
> *the body in the barrel? It could have been someone*

else's head. This is just the kind of sloppy, inaccurate reporting that distresses the conscientious reader and has no doubt led to a decline in subscribers.

Yours,
Conscientious Reader

A week later, I received a second letter.

Dear Conscientious Reader,
I've always said you can't beat a girl educated by Presbyterians for lurid imaginings. Something about that stripped-down, joyless faith spurs the brain to conjure visions beyond the reach of saner minds. Still, you raise a good point. No doubt there are many in this city wandering around without heads.
    Enclosed, please find my latest scribble.

Yours,
MB

And it went from there. Every week or two, there was another letter. Dear Conscientious Reader became Dear Conscientious or Dear Lacking in Taste or Dear Can You Not Read? But I stayed with Mr. Behan.

Dear Mr. Behan,
Regarding your last article on the so-called Murder Stables of Harlem, I think you do Miss Lenere a grave injustice. If she insists that Frank "Chick" Monaco met with an accident in her apartment, why shouldn't we believe her? Can a man not be stabbed twenty-five times by accident? Perhaps Miss Lenere is very clumsy. Perhaps she tripped. So her clothes were

clean when she arrived at the police station, too
clean for someone involved in such a dreadful
"accident." This does not mean she is shielding the
actual guilty party. I think you place too much faith
in the word of Zopo the Gimp. Someone named
Zopo can hardly be accounted a credible witness.

Then one day, his letter read,

Dear Will-Not-Be-Pleased,
Since you've nothing good to say about my efforts,
you might as well insult me to my face. In this free
and just land of ours, all men have a right to face
their detractors and demand satisfaction when they
have been maligned—as I have been. Please write
back and tell me when and where I can expect
redress.

Yours,
MB

I did not write back. I meant to. In my head, I wrote many
times.

Dear Mr. Behan,
As enticing as the chance to insult you to your face
is, I must decline . . .
Dear Mr. Behan,
I think it is better if we restrict our encounters to the
purely epistolary . . .
Dear Mr. Behan,
When would you like to meet? My days off are as
follows . . .

You can consider your words too carefully. In this case, I chewed on mine until they had the consistency and character of mush. A few times, I managed to set the truth straight in my head—*Dear Mr. Behan, I want to see you, but I have no compelling reason to see you beyond the desire to do so. That desire, if you did not have a wife, would be in no way controversial. But you do have a wife.*

Even so, please do not stop writing to me—

I didn't even have to put these words on paper to know they were impossible.

I did not want to say yes. I did not want to say no. I ended up not saying anything. I never wrote back.

And neither did he.

Extinguishing the light, I lay down on the bed. It was a warm night and the room was low ceilinged and close. The stale air weighed on me, making me uncomfortably aware of my own skin. I felt damp under my arms, at the crevices of my knees. My nightgown clung to my belly, to my back when I rolled over.

From outside, I heard the wind blow through the leaves of the trees. Mrs. Briggs had said all windows were to be closed, but would it truly make a difference if I cracked the small window in my room just a little? Even an inch or two would let the fresh air in. In the dark, you wouldn't be able to see that the window wasn't firmly shut. Anyway, this room looked out onto the back lawn of the house, a dark, deserted place at nighttime, ringed with tall trees.

I got up and raised it a thumb's height. A welcome gust of air blew in. I sat down on the edge of the bed, putting myself right in the wind's path. I put my elbows on the sill and let the breeze air out the thin cotton of my nightgown. I breathed deep, nudged the window farther open still.

At first I thought it was a leaf, blowing through the night sky. Then I registered a young tree waving in the wind. But no, the form was moving rather than swaying, making slow, careful progress across the lawn. Once it stopped, seemed to turn. And that's when I realized I was looking at a person.

More than that was impossible to see in the darkness. The distance made it hard to judge height. Still I leaned out, forgetting the need to be invisible. As I did, the figure seemed suddenly aware it was being watched and hurried out of sight. One of the guards, I told myself. But . . . far too skittish for a professional watchdog. Nor was I sure that the shape had moved like a man. And Mrs. Briggs had said doors were locked at ten.

I brought the window to its lowest point and lay back down. The room was fresher now, but my mind was wide-awake. I heard the faint chime of a clock from a distant floor. I counted twelve bells.

The chimes at midnight.

4

The following day was given over to the pressing and complex issue of Louise's grand entrance. The ceremony was to take place in the garden, which was accessible from the house through two wide French doors. Louise and her father would proceed through them, down the aisle, and to William's side under a beautiful oak tree.

It seemed simple. Should have been simple. But then Mrs. Benchley noticed the staircase.

The staircase wound down from the upper floors to a large entry foyer, which was full of light. Wouldn't it be lovely, argued Mrs. Benchley, if Louise, her father, and the bridesmaids could come down the stairs, and *then* come out to the garden?

"But the guests will be seated outside," said William's mother, who had devised the original plan. "No one will see them, no matter how lovely they are."

"Well, perhaps we could move the wedding inside," said Mrs. Benchley.

There was a long and ominous pause. During which Mrs. Benchley encouraged Louise to walk down the stairs, so everyone could "see the possibilities." Louise had just made her first tentative step when Mrs. Tyler unclenched her jaw long enough to say, "We are not moving inside."

"Louise, keep moving." Louise took another step. "Now, Florence, just watch . . ."

But William's mother called, "Louise, stop." Louise stopped. "Caroline, there isn't enough room."

"Oh, but there is. Keep going, darling."

Louise took a step down, then, sensing what was coming, stepped back up again.

"Perhaps," I said, "we could ask the opinion of the lady of the house."

That lady had chosen wisely to remain in her room through the discussion. There was a suspension of hostilities as the mothers sought out Alva Tyler's views. While they were gone, I said, "What do *you* want, Miss Louise?" She shrugged in despair.

Alva Tyler decided the issue in favor of outside, awarding Mrs. Benchley the consolation prize of having the photographer take pictures of Louise and the bridesmaids on the stairs afterward. The discussion moved on to the question of whether Roquefort should be included in the cheese course, given its effects on the breath. Roquefort was struck from the offerings. Then Mrs. Benchley expressed concern over the string quartet—was it sufficient for the occasion? Should it not be a quintet or sextet? William's mother wondered aloud if Mrs. Benchley would like a full orchestra? Well, bridled Mrs. Benchley, perhaps she would. Then again, said Florence Tyler, given the Benchleys' Scarsdale origins, the bridal march could also be played on the kazoo with paper-and-comb accompaniment.

This flippancy escalated the argument to a dangerous level.

Spotting William and his uncle on the lawn with the chauffeur, I decided it was best Louise step outside; no one cared what she wanted and if blood were shed, she could truthfully claim to have seen nothing. We left by way of the gallery, which boasted a vivid if unorthodox collection of fine paintings and animal heads. Alva Tyler was gazing at one of the portraits. It was not, I saw as we approached, Sargent's painting of her, but a lovely vision of a woman sewing while a child leaned on her lap.

Seeing us, she said, "We brought it back from Paris. It's painted by a woman. Critics complain that she shows women separate from men, but I think it's marvelous." She smiled at Louise. "Lovely to think, isn't it? This might be you in a few years."

Louise went pale; clearly the prospect of a tranquil domestic life seemed remote at the moment. Then as we made our way onto the rolling front lawn, she gave a short shriek.

Mr. Tyler was holding a large gun. Next to him stood William and Mr. Grimaldi.

"Not yet on the market," he announced. "It's the new Winchester. Internal hammer. Pump action. Holds up to three or four shells at a time and fires as fast as you pump, which can be pretty fast, believe me."

I wasn't sure William understood a word of what his uncle was saying, but he nodded nonetheless. The moment he saw Louise, he stepped away and took her by the hand. She smiled, but tears threatened.

"An argument about the entrance," I explained.

"Mamas battling it out over their chicks," said Mr. Tyler. "Not to worry. You two go off and let them settle it. Alva and I left it all to her mother and showed up an hour beforehand. Aldo, bring round one of the cars, let these two take a drive."

Aldo started off to the garage. As he did, the nanny approached with the baby carriage, Mabel skipping along behind. At the sight of Sofia, Aldo slowed his step. She ignored him—pointedly, I thought—but brightened when William called out, "Hello!"

At the sight of Mr. Tyler's gun, she hesitated. "I don't know if I should bring the children near that."

Mr. Tyler laughed. "Quite right. Aldo! Take this back and lock it up, will you?" Then to Louise, he said, "I assure you, Miss Bench-ley, all my guns are kept under lock and key—except for the one I sleep with under my pillow at night." He grinned, and I could not tell if he was joking or not.

William reached into the carriage and lifted what he called the "third in line" up in the air. Roused, the baby began to fuss.

"Ah," said William to the nanny. "He only wants you."

He handed the baby back to Sofia with a smile that was perhaps too warm for Louise's agitated spirits, and when the car came, I pointedly noted its arrival. As Louise got in, she called out, "Jane, would you like to come?"

Surprised, I groped for excuses. "I think I will stay here, thank you, Miss Louise."

"They'll be all right," said Mr. Tyler approvingly as they drove off. "Yes, they'll be just fine."

Having dispatched the couple out of harm's way, Mr. Tyler retired to his study, leaving Mabel to formally introduce me to the nanny as "Sofia who takes care of us and sings," and "Jane who looks after Miss Benchley and I don't know what else she does."

Then she reached for her brother. "This is Freddy. He's enormous."

Sofia swung him gently out of her reach. "Your brother is very handsome, Miss Mabel." Her English was good, but she had a strong accent. "Brother" was "brudder" and the *h* sound eluded her entirely. But there was something charming about the way she strung the words together, making "very" and "handsome" into a single superlative *veryandsome*.

Then our eyes met over the baby's head. Sofia said, "Mabel, Mrs. Sherwood will be here soon for your music lesson. Why don't you go wait for her?"

Mabel twisted resentfully. "Can't I stay out here till Mother calls?"

Sofia put a firm hand on her back. "You practice until she comes. You need practice."

I watched as they walked back to the house, Mabel protesting with every step. When Sofia returned, she said, "I'm going to take the baby for a walk. You want to come?"

I glanced toward the library, where the first sullen plinks were sounding. "You don't have to stay?"

She smiled and whispered, "Mabel play very badly. Better to be outside. Come, we get away from the house."

And so we walked, accompanied only by the sound of the carriage wheels squeaking along the grass and a view of the ocean in the distance. A gentle wind blew Sofia's hair off her forehead and she tilted her head back in pleasure. At the start, I felt the walk had a purpose. Now I wondered if perhaps the goal was simply a brief escape, the sort of benign rebellion those of us who work in others' homes resort to when we feel too closely watched.

As if she guessed what I was thinking, Sofia said, "It's good for the baby, fresh air. Good for me, too. I get tired of being—"

"Cooped up?" I guessed.

She nodded, eyebrow raised to signal we were now being candid.

I looked out at the water. "It's beautiful, but quiet. Do you mind being away from the city?"

For a moment, I thought she had not heard me. But then she answered, "No, I don't like the city. I'm better here." She glanced up from the carriage. "You know the Tylers a long time? Mr. and Mrs. Charles?"

"I used to work for Mr. Tyler's aunt. I saw them when they came to visit her. I thought Alva Tyler was wonderful."

I had the sense I hadn't given her exactly the answer she wanted, so I asked, "Have you worked for them for very long?"

She shook her head. "They're nice, the Benchleys? Good to work for?"

Her inquiry was hasty, cutting off other questions. I wondered if that was her insecure English or something else. "Better than most."

Sofia looked down at the sleepy baby. "You are verygood to work for, too. You are a nice and pleasant boss. Even if you make me work terrible hours."

We were now on the outskirts of the property; the ground was less even and Sofia carefully navigated the carriage around tree roots and rocks. We felt far from the house, and so it was a surprise to spot one of the guards walking slowly at the edge of the trees in the distance.

Seeing that Sofia had noticed him, too, I wondered how it felt to her, as an Italian, to see the house guarded against her people. Gesturing to the man, I said, "Feels a little silly, doesn't it?"

"I don't think it's silly. There are . . . bad people." She hesitated, as if unsure whether to trust me. Then she seemed to make her mind up, because she added, "But some people, afraid all the time of *everybody*. That's . . ." She waved a hand to indicate madness, and I nodded in agreement.

I asked, "What was the song you were singing yesterday? You have a lovely voice."

She smiled at the compliment. "*Fa la ninna, fa la nanna* . . . it's an old lullaby. It's a terrible song, though. All about the baby won't sleep, mother is tired. If he don't sleep, she's going to give him to the dark one. Poor baby!"

We settled under a large tree. Sofia stretched out her legs, her arms reaching high over her head. From where we sat, I could see a small cluster of markers in the distance. There were two short stones—property markers, I thought at first. But then I took in a crooked cross made of sticks and realized I was looking at a grave site.

I was about to ask who was buried there when Sofia said, "Miss Benchley—she killed a man, no?"

It took me a moment to understand. "No. Her sister's fiancé, the man she was going to marry, *he* was killed. But by someone else."

"Some men, they need killing." She was joking and I laughed. "Mr. William, he's very nice. I do not want him having a killer in his family." She stared at the branches overhead. "People, it's hard to know."

Here it was again, the invitation.

"What's it like working for Alva Tyler?" I asked.

She shrugged. "I don't know. The nursery, she never comes there."

Her tone was bored, and I took it as a young girl's apathy about an older woman who nagged. "Well, the less she comes to the nursery, perhaps the less she complains."

"Complain!" Sitting up, Sofia burst out with what had been on her mind from the start. "Always she find fault with me. Over nothing. She gets so"—she wrestled with the word—"*nervous.* Worry all the time. Always 'Why is baby awake, he should be asleep.' 'Why is he asleep, should be awake.' What he eat, what he do, what his diapers look like. She never let me open the window, baby might get cold." She tugged at her blouse. "I am dying in that house, so hot I can't sleep. But no open windows. No air. I tell her it's not good for the children. Mabel, she's so—" She jogged her hand in the air to indicate Mabel's eagerness. "But because she needs outdoors. Not this." Now she froze, a grimace on her face. "Everything like this."

I thought her unfair. Italians were freer with their emotions than other people; Sofia was not yet used to the manners of a well-born American family. But then I remembered what I had overheard in the hallway last night—Mrs. Tyler tearfully accusing Sofia, her nerves so on edge. She had moved the family out of the city, but clearly she wasn't sure they were out of harm's way. Charles Tyler had said he liked the Italians as a people; did his wife feel the same? She seemed quite mistrustful of the young woman in her home.

"It may not be the easiest time for her," I said carefully. "Her husband's car blown up. The Moretti trial. *And* a wedding," I added, trying to make light of it.

"I know. I tell myself that. She has . . . pain. Fears. But I have fears, and I am not some rich woman with a husband. I am also scared, but you can't live like that. It makes you . . ."

I waited for her next word, but her mood changed and the subject with it.

"Mr. Tyler, he's wonderful, but he is the other way." She saw I didn't understand and tried to explain. "Men like that, who are good, sometimes, they're *too* good. Too trusting. They decide, 'Oh, he is one of my people, I trust him, he's a good man. Good woman.' But they don't see . . ."

She found a blade of grass, worried it between thumb and forefinger. "Once, I try to tell him, I say, Mr. Tyler, you want to trust this person, but—" She rolled the grass to paste. "But he was very angry with me. After that, I don't say nothing."

As if sensing her frustration, the baby began to fuss. Instantly, she was on her feet, clucking and cooing as she lifted the youngest Tyler from his carriage. She stroked his head, murmuring in Italian. Snuggling him close, she said to me, "You want to hold him? He's wonderful."

It does me no credit, but I was not overly fond of babies. It seemed an insult to refuse, though, so I took him—and decided that if one had to hold a baby one could do much worse than Frederick Tyler. The silky hair that covered his broad skull was reddish brown like his mother's. He was very satisfying, sweet and heavy and if I didn't know quite how to make him comfortable, he did, dropping his head against my chest and blowing a bubble of spit. His little fingers crawled along my blouse until he found a button and pulled.

Sofia laughed and said, "Men." Taking him back, she lifted him high in the air. "I want one just like you." She lowered him to kiss each plump cheek. "I want *twelve*."

Then she joked, "But maybe I have to find a man first. That helps."

"So I hear."

Lifting herself off the ground, she said, "Come. Mabel is done with her 'torture.'" Whether Mabel was the victim or made others the victim of her playing was unclear.

We were faster on our way back, partly from necessity and partly because Sofia seemed less burdened. My shoes were not ideal for country walking, and I struggled to keep up. At one point, I gestured that she shouldn't lag for me; Mabel would be waiting. And so Aldo didn't see me when he appeared from the garage.

Spotting Sofia, he began making his way toward her. She tried to dodge him, but he stepped in front of her. He was smiling and when he spoke in Italian, it was in a tone I knew well. Pleasant, but warm to the point of insinuation. Sofia's answers, in contrast, were short and ill-tempered. I knew a little Italian; not enough to understand the exchange—but well enough to know he was offering her something she didn't want.

The conversation grew heated. Aldo's tone became accusatory.

Sofia gestured angrily to the carriage. Then she threw a hand up in denial and turned to go past him. As she went, he called after her in English, "I know! I know what you're doing—"

I hurried forward and in a neutral voice, said, "Mr. Grimaldi."

Caught short, he offered his sour smile. "Miss Prescott." Then he went back to the garage.

Catching up to Sofia, I said, "What was that?"

"Nothing. He's a man. He has the ideas all men have."

"You should tell Mrs. Tyler." She made a face of eloquent derision the Italians are so skilled at. "Then Mr. Tyler."

"He don't want to hear anything against that one, believe me."

"Whether he wants to or not—"

"No," she said, interrupting me. "*You* know. You work in someone's house, you live there, you take care of their children—it feels like family, yes? You think these people, they care about you."

"Yes." Because they did, I thought, the Benchleys did care. Louise did . . .

She shook her head. "They don't. You are not family. Just worker. They decide they don't like you? Gone. Yes, now you are here, but you don't . . . belong. You are in between. Not here, not there. Nobody."

I watched her go, a knot in my stomach. I recalled at my first employer's house, there had been a butler that every young woman knew to steer clear of when he was drunk. And once or twice, we had trouble with guests. I could still remember the time a Mr. Bradley, a gentleman famous for his manners and sailing prowess, came up behind me one early morning when I was sweeping the ash out of the library fireplace. Without a word, he put one hand around my waist and the other on my breast. I had screamed more out of shock than outrage and he immediately stepped back with a smile as if nothing had happened and left the room.

Mechanically, I had gone back to sweeping; surely nothing had happened, he would have apologized if he'd really done . . . what he had done. It had taken a few minutes before I realized I was crying and dropped the brush on the ground. But the Bradleys left the next day and I never told anyone.

What had happened between Sofia and Aldo felt more dangerous than a squeeze. The chauffeur had to know he was not the kind of man to attract a young, pretty girl—and yet he was furious that she rejected his advances. That kind of rage, I knew, easily turned violent. And yet I also knew Sofia was right. No one wanted to hear that kind of thing. Especially not from young women paid to sweep ashes or change diapers.

Later that afternoon, I ran short on beige darning thread. I was on my way to beg from Mrs. Briggs when I heard raised voices from the front parlor. Tea was long over; and from the tone, this was not a friendly chat over toast, but a heated argument between two people. One of whom was Mrs. Florence Tyler.

"You *will* do this, William."

There was a brief pause, which I guessed was William's attempt to speak. Then his mother's voice came back, full force.

"Well, I'm very sorry, but as your grandmother once said to me, your personal sentiments are of no concern. Unless you have other means of guaranteeing your security, of which I'm unaware."

There was silence.

"No," said his mother. "I didn't think so."

I walked on, feeling downcast. I knew Mrs. Tyler's interest in the marriage was purely financial. But I had thought William was fond of Louise. Small wonder she was beset with anxiety. William played the role of enamored suitor well enough, but clearly she sensed reluctance.

Why did marriage have to be such an economic concern? Or,

I thought rebelliously, why did it have to be at all? Why could women and men not just come together for the pleasure of each other's company? Wasn't that what the free-love advocates said?

But Mrs. Tyler was right: free love was not an option for William and Louise. They would simply have to make the best of it.

* * *

If I hoped that matters would improve over dinner, I was disappointed. Or so Louise's drooping shoulders and spirits told me when she came up to her room that night. Sinking into a chair so I could brush her hair, she sighed deeply and closed her eyes. I let her sit for a long while, pulling the brush through more to soothe than smooth. Then I whispered, "And how was your evening, Miss Louise?"

A despairing hand rose and fell. "Mabel asked when we were going to have babies."

"What did you say?"

She stood and let me pull her nightgown over her head. Voice muffled, she said, "I didn't. William did." She appeared again, adding, "He said soon, he hopes. He wants a big family."

Given the conversation I had overheard, I was heartened to hear William enthusiastic about any aspect of matrimony. "That's nice—isn't it?"

"Oh, of course." As I started to gather her discarded clothes, she said, "Jane?"

"Yes, Miss Louise?"

"Do you know what happens?"

I echoed, "Happens."

"Not when babies come, but . . . before." She sat awkwardly on the bed. "You know."

Suddenly, I did know. And could only say, "Oh."

"I asked Mother. She said I'd know when it happened."

Which was true, but hardly instructive. That could be for the best, I reasoned. Mrs. Benchley could become incoherent on a matter as simple as toast. The mind boggled at what she would make of sexual hygiene.

Growing up in a home for working women of a very old and very particular profession had been educational; one of the women at the refuge had told me the basic facts when I was nine. It sounded so improbable, I thought she must be making it up. But when I got up the nerve to ask the cook if that was really what men and women did, she said, "It is—and don't you let none of them do it to you."

Privacy being scarce on the Lower East Side, I learned to look away if the noises in an alley were such that I could guess the sight would be two people, pants down, skirts up. Once or twice, I didn't look away, curious as to what could be so urgent. As for personal experience, I could claim a single conquest: Peter Beckwith, a hall boy at Mrs. Armslow's. Months of flirtation had culminated in a few pleasant, fumbling minutes in the pantry on New Year's Eve. The next day, the other maids were planning a wedding and the housekeeper informed me that if I did it again, I would be thrown out. I had no desire to be fired or Mrs. Peter Beckwith, so I refused to speak to him ever again. I had hopes of breaking his heart, but he moved on to a kitchen maid named Tess, who did become Mrs. Peter Beckwith in a year's time.

Louise's lack of knowledge was surprising, but not unheard-of. I was aware of couples who remained in ignorance of their spouse's exact anatomy for their entire married lives, conducting all re-productive efforts in the dark as swiftly as possible. But lack of knowledge was never a good thing. More than a few of the women at the refuge were of the opinion that, in the words of one, "if the wives weren't so ignorant, the husbands wouldn't be so itchy." I didn't want William to be itchy.

I was debating whether or not to begin with menses, when there was a knock at the door. From the other side, we heard, "It's Mabel. Are you sleeping?"

I went to the door prepared to tell Mabel she must come back another time, but Louise said, "Not at all. Please come in, Mabel."

The door immediately opened and Mabel came in, a large scrapbook under her arm. Settling herself in a deep, soft armchair near Louise, she said, "I wanted to show you my album. It's a sort of history of my family." To me, she said, "You can look, too."

Mabel opened the bulky volume on her lap and angled it toward Louise. Pointing to the first photograph, she said, "There's Mother and Father getting married."

I saw the Alva Tyler of my memory, handsome and vital, her brazen hair gathered under a veil. Beside her, Charles Tyler, slimmer, mustache more modest.

Mabel turned the page. "And here's my brother Charlie, and there's my brother Arthur." Two small Tylers stared solemnly from adjoining pages. "This is when they were little. They're at school now. I don't have a picture of Freddy yet. Oh—here's our dog, Bunkum. He's dead."

There was no picture of the child who had died, I noticed. Nor did Mabel refer to him. I wondered what she remembered of him.

After a few pages, the family photos gave way to newspaper clippings. All of which prominently featured Charles Tyler striking a heroic, ebullient pose. "Here's Father shaking hands with President Taft. Here's Father after he arrested Ludo . . . vico"—she peered at the tiny caption—"Albini. Oh, and here he is at the trial of Johnny Spanish—that's a different one than the one that's going to happen next month. See, this is him with that little boy who got kidnapped . . ."

It was a triumphant photograph taken just after the boy had been found, all the policemen responsible and the many weapons seized from the gang—guns, clubs, and knives. At the center, Charles Tyler with a wide-eyed child on his lap. The picture showed Mr. Tyler making a present of one of the more gruesome knives to little Emilio Forti. Smiling, the boy brandished the knife, while Tyler grinned as if he were six years old himself.

"You're quite the chronicler, Miss Mabel," I said. She looked puzzled at the word. "You keep an admirable record of your parents' lives." As if they were celebrities to be gazed at, I thought.

"Thank you. Mother doesn't like me to read newspapers, she says they'll frighten me and that I don't understand the words, but I do."

"Perhaps you'll be a reporter when you grow up," said Louise.

Mabel sat up eagerly. "I know—I'll interview you about the wedding." Putting on an adult voice, she said, "Tell me all the details, Miss Benchley."

"Yes, tell her, Miss Louise," I said.

"Oh, well . . ." Louise began, prefacing every statement with, "Mother decided" or "Mrs. Tyler thought." Within a few minutes, we heard a snore. Snuggled into the velvet recesses of the chair, Mabel was fast asleep.

"I can take her back to the nursery," I said.

She smiled. "No, leave her. Charlotte and I used to share a room. I miss it sometimes. And if I'm going to have so many children, I ought to practice."

I was not even aware of passing from consciousness to dreams when I was broken out of sleep by a frantic knocking on the door. Disoriented, my first thought was fire. Pulling on my robe, making a mental list of what must be saved, I opened the door to see Louise and Mabel wide-eyed and out of breath. Louise held a candle, which made me realize there was no smell of smoke. No roar of flame . . .

Mabel grabbed my hand. "You have to come . . ."

I looked at Louise who said, "It is strange."

I allowed Mabel to pull me down the hall and to the stairway. There was no light except for the flickering illumination of Louise's lone, thin candle, and I wondered if I were still dreaming or if this was one of Mabel's games.

"Mabel, what is this?"

"Can't you hear it?"

"Hear—"

But now I could hear it, muffled by distance, but unmistakable: the alarm of a baby crying.

Relieved and irritated, I said, "Sofia is there, Miss Mabel. She'll take care of Frederick."

"But that's just it. He's been crying for forever."

"Maybe he doesn't feel well. Maybe he's teething."

"No, something's wrong, I know it. Come see, just come see."

I looked at Louise, who said apologetically, "I told her we could check on him."

As we made our way up the stairs, I listened for the sound of Sofia's voice, a snatch of humming or song. But all I heard were Frederick's cries. I felt the prickle of foreboding down my neck and spine.

When we reached the nursery wing and there was only silence except for Frederick's frantic howls, my stomach twisted. Staving off panic, I knocked at Sofia's door and called her name.

There was no answer. I wrenched the door open, saw that the little bedroom was empty. I turned toward the nursery itself, called, "Sofia? It's me, Jane."

There was no answer.

"We have to go in," said Mabel. "Freddy's hurt, I know it."

She was right. But I also had the uneasy sense that what lay beyond that door might not be something a child should see. I knew Mabel would argue if I told Louise to take her downstairs; she must be made to feel she was helping her brother.

I knelt. "Miss Mabel, will you do something for me?" She nodded, eyes darting to the closed door. "Take Miss Louise to your father. Tell him he must wake up and he must come here." I looked briefly to Louise. "Tell him to bring the gun he keeps by the bed. Can you do that?"

". . . Yes. But you'll help Freddy?"

"I will, I promise."

Mabel grabbed Louise's hand and began pulling her down the hall. Louise glanced back at me, worried, but I raised a hand as if to say I had everything well under control.

Which I didn't. Knocking on the door, I called, "Sofia?"

The wailing increased in intensity.

"Sofia, are you in there?"

The baby's screams were coming in compulsive gasps now. On instinct, I twisted the doorknob and leaned against the door, which opened easily.

For some reason, the first thing I understood was the open window, the curtains blowing wildly into the room. A lamp lay overturned on the floor, a little china dog in pieces nearby. The baby was on his stomach near the rocking chair, his little arms stiffly outstretched. His head was raised and there was . . . mess on his pajamas. The billowing curtains obscured and restored the moonlight, making it hard to judge. Crossing to him, I put a hand on his back and felt no injury. Gently, I picked him up and felt a wave of relief that he seemed to be whole. Just hysterical and exhausted.

But there was something damp on his romper. Sticky. Placing my fingers around the back of his head, crooning tunelessly, I became aware of the smell of copper. The floor felt wrong. The quiet whisper of carpet had given way to something ominously different: heavier, wetter. I forced my gaze around and down. And saw what I had, on some level, knew I would find when I opened that door.

Half hidden behind the crib, Sofia on her side, arms akimbo, eyes staring. Her throat had been cut. Some of the blood had sprayed, spattering the walls and the white rails of the crib. The front of her nightgown was a slick of gore. The rest had soaked the rug where she fell, the blood pumping from her artery, weaker and weaker until it would have dribbled and stopped. One hand, I realized, had been stretched toward the baby, a last, pathetic attempt to reach him.

5

"*You must call the* police, Charles."

"I agree, Uncle."

William's mother also agreed. As did Louise. Only Mrs. Benchley differed in her priorities, loudly insisting that "Mr. Benchley must be informed."

I agreed the police should be called, but no one had asked me. Which was probably just as well; my mind wasn't working very well. I had a dim memory of Mr. Tyler's sudden arrival in the nursery, his bellows to me to stand back, touch nothing, then the sense of Frederick being taken from my arms. Murmuring, "Dear God, dear God . . ." Mr. Tyler had guided me out of the room, down the long hallway, and into his study. I had been placed in a large, comfortable chair by the fire and been given a brandy. For some time, I listened to the crack of the logs, the rush of flames, and the argument taking place around me. And thought about Sofia, that hand desperately reaching . . .

Then I heard Mr. Tyler say, "I'm not calling the local hawk-shaws, they're only good for missing livestock."

"Then your people in the city," insisted his sister-in-law. "Call them."

"They may not have jurisdiction," William said.

"Hang jurisdiction," shouted Mr. Tyler. "I want good men on this. Reliable men. *Honest* men." He sat at his desk, elbows planted on the edge, his large hands held aloft as if he would shape that honest man. I sensed an exchange of looks in the silence that followed, but no one had the courage to point out that his "good men" had been on duty tonight and yet here we all were.

"Charles."

Up to this moment, Alva Tyler had chosen to remain silent. She had sat gazing at the darkness beyond the window as she waited out the fretful, quarrelsome chatter. Now with a word, she commanded her husband's attention.

"We must send the children to my mother's. It's not safe for them here." Her voice was thin with exhaustion; she stroked her throat as if to ease it. But her fingers tightened around her windpipe, and I had the sense she was choking off feelings far less measured.

"Not safe?" Mrs. Benchley asked. "Are we in danger?"

"No," barked Mr. Tyler. "We are not."

The mood in the room remained tense. Finally, William said, "I'm afraid I agree with Aunt Alva. After all—there's no reason to think the kidnappers won't try again."

"Kidnappers?" gasped Mrs. Benchley.

"The window was open," William explained. At this information, Alva Tyler closed her eyes. "The doors were all locked, so it's the only way he could have gotten in. He would have been hiding in the woods. Probably he's been watching the house for some time, learning the routes of the perimeter guards."

I had a sudden jagged vision of Sofia walking toward the woods as she sang.

William continued, "Once he was on the grounds, it wouldn't be difficult to climb up to the nursery if you used the window ledges and drainpipes for footing. And it would explain why poor Freddy was on the floor."

"And who opened that window?" Alva Tyler demanded. "Who . . . opened it, Charles?" Her eyes were sharp with strange emotion; her entire aspect was that of a woman who has been dismissed as foolish, and had been proven right in her fears—too late.

Mrs. Benchley broke in, saying, "I must call my husband. I must call him right now."

Charles Tyler rose from his seat. "I'm afraid I must insist you not call anyone, Mrs. Benchley, until we have decided on a course of action. It's essential that we keep one step ahead of the kidnappers . . ."

Kidnappers. The word struck me as odd. In fact, this entire conversation struck me as odd. They were all so focused on the danger to themselves that they had forgotten the poor girl lying dead upstairs.

"Killer," I said.

Louise laid a hand on my shoulder. "What, Jane?"

I was barely aware I had spoken out loud and it was hard to put my thoughts together. "Surely the man you're looking for is a killer." I took in the puzzled expressions around me. "Someone *killed* Sofia. Doesn't that matter?"

Mr. Tyler got no further than "My dear young woman" before Alva Tyler said, "Jane is right." She looked at her relatives. "They are all . . . right. We must call the police. No, *don't* argue with me, Charles. For once, *listen.* Someone got into the house. A woman has died. It's time we stopped pretending that we are safe." She turned her gaze to him. "It is time you stopped pretending that you alone can keep us safe."

I thought I saw Charles Tyler shake his head, rejecting the very idea. "Alva . . ."

"We almost lost Freddy!" she cried. "We almost . . ." She covered her mouth, turned tear-bright eyes to the window again.

A painful silence followed. Feeling partly responsible for it, I asked, "Has the rest of the staff been told? Mrs. Briggs?"

Mr. Tyler answered. "We gathered the staff in the kitchen and made the announcement. With strict instructions to say nothing to anyone, of course."

The injunction to silence was strong enough to quiet everyone in the room. Until Mrs. Benchley yelped, "The wedding!"

Louise looked horrified. "Mother, we can't think about that at a time like this."

"No, no, no." Mrs. Benchley waved an agitated hand. "No, we must think about it. It's only weeks away. How on earth will the guests feel, being invited to a house where . . . well . . . it's bound to dampen the mood," she finished forlornly.

I could see both William and Louise were embarrassed, but Charles Tyler seemed to take Mrs. Benchley seriously. "Dear lady, I am also anxious that we keep this as quiet as possible. We must proceed as though nothing has happened. Sofia's killers must not be allowed to throw us off course. The only answer to intimidation is defiance."

"It might be difficult to keep it out of the papers," said William.

"I'll handle the papers," said Mr. Tyler grimly.

"What about Sofia's family?" I asked. "Don't they have to be told?"

There were glances around the room; once again, I sensed a sullenness around the subject of Sofia. Finally, Mrs. Tyler said, "I'm not aware that she had family."

Mr. Tyler pulled a face to indicate an appropriately masculine ignorance of matters domestic. I was about to suggest the agency might have that information when Mrs. Benchley announced that she was worn out and must retire.

"Louise, would you come up with me? And stay? To think that a murderer was here at Pleasant Meadows, and all of us in the house with him!"

And might still be, I thought. Or close by. I remembered Aldo, the way he fixed his tongue in his cheek when he spoke to Sofia. I also remembered Sofia's words, "He don't want to hear anything against that one, believe me." Stronger souls than mine had trembled at the thought of telling Charles Tyler he was wrong. But someone had to ask.

I said tentatively, "Mr. Tyler?"

"Yes, Jane?"

I began badly. "Of course you know best, but I wonder if maybe we aren't deciding things too quickly."

The Tylers exchanged looks. William said, "What do you mean, Jane?"

"Yesterday, Sofia had an argument with the chauffeur. I had the impression that he was attracted to her, but she did not return his affections."

Mr. Tyler took this in. "That's absurd."

Startled that he wouldn't hear me out, I stammered, "It's not unheard-of—"

"What are you saying?" he roared.

"Charles . . ." Alva Tyler raised a weary hand, rubbed her eyes.

Coming around the desk to stand in front of me, he said, "No, Alva, I want to understand quite clearly what this young woman is saying."

I saw no choice but to be frank. "She told me he wanted what all men want, those were her words. Some men can turn violent when rejected."

"And you think that's what happened."

"I think you should consider it."

Mr. Tyler's eyes widened at the novelty of being questioned. "And is there a particular reason you suspect him rather than, say, my gardener, whose name is Wilson?"

Somehow to be accused of prejudice felt nearly as shaming as being caught in prejudice; perhaps we always feel undeservedly accused of such things. For a few seconds, I could not remember a single thing Aldo had done that would make me suspect him.

Then I gathered myself. "Sofia said he was bothering her. I witnessed it myself. They spoke mostly in Italian—"

"Which you speak, do you?"

"His interest was clear from his tone. As was her lack of it."

"And being a violent, impulsive Italian, he butchered her."

"I didn't say that."

"Uncle, you needn't badger her," said William.

Tyler shouted, "I will not accuse a man who's worked for me for years . . ."

"You don't have to accuse him," said Alva Tyler, her voice loud and unsteady as she strove to be heard. "But we can't ignore what Jane's told us."

Charles Tyler turned on his wife. "You know what he's been through, Alva. You know it wouldn't be the first time someone's accused him without cause."

But Alva Tyler was not afraid of her husband and she met his eye, saying, "Nonetheless. You should insist he speak with the police. For his own good."

And search his rooms, I thought. No weapon had been found in the nursery. Unspoken was the message that Alva Tyler was no longer willing to indulge her husband's optimism—either about his staff or his own abilities. I felt sorry for encouraging her mistrust. But to see the way her hands trembled, the bone-deep weariness, the slackness and pallor of a once healthy complexion, I knew that his optimism had already cost her a great deal.

Finally, Mr. Tyler said almost petulantly, "Very well. For his sake."

After that, it was suggested that we all follow Mrs. Benchley's example and retire. I left the study and headed toward the servants' stairs. As I did, William said, "Jane, will you be all right?"

He approached, hands in the pockets of his night-robe, hair falling into his eyes. "I mean, you found her. That must have been . . ."

I said, "Yes," to spare him the trouble of producing a word that could only be inadequate. "I'll be fine, Mr. William, thank you. You take care of Miss Louise."

He looked up the stairs. "I think she'll be busy taking care of her mother."

"Then she'll need you even more."

He smiled. "Good night, Jane."

★ ★ ★

Perhaps I was exhausted or still unused to the house, but instead of my room, I found myself in the kitchen, where I found Mrs. Briggs ironing in her night-robe. Her jaw was rigid with the effort of pressing down as she worked the iron over a sheet.

"You are very dedicated, Mrs. Briggs."

"I'm unable to sleep is what I am."

I suspected I would be, too, so I sat down at the kitchen table and watched as she expertly folded the ironed section over and began on a new part.

Finally, I said, "It's terrible."

I wouldn't have thought this a controversial statement, but Mrs. Briggs simply raised her eyebrows and kept ironing. Perhaps she was annoyed by my company or my statement of the obvious. But I felt the chill of differing opinion.

"Mrs. Tyler wants to send the children to her mother's."

"Quite right." A wrinkle caught her eye and she went after it, arm bent, lips compressed.

"Then you think it was a kidnapping attempt."

"Oh, I know it was, Miss Prescott."

Recalling the shadow figure I had seen the first night, I asked, "Did you see anyone strange on the grounds tonight?"

She sighed, set down the iron. "Who says it has to be a stranger?"

Did she also suspect Aldo? "You're thinking of the open window . . ."

"Yes, that open window. What good luck for kidnappers, eh?"

"What do you mean?"

She looked at me for a long moment. Then said, "Nothing. As I said, I'm not a nice woman after ten. It's been an awful night. Time it came to an end."

And she took herself and the half-ironed sheet up the back stairs.

6

The next morning, the village police arrived and Sofia's body was taken to a nearby hospital, where it would stay until it was claimed. I watched from a window as the ambulance drove off, wanting in some useless way to mark the moment. It was an incongruously beautiful spring day, just the sort of day Sofia would have liked. It seemed impossible that only yesterday she had been wheeling Frederick's carriage across the lawn. One of the guards at the front gate removed his hat as the ambulance passed. The rest of the family and staff stayed indoors.

Charles Tyler's low opinion of the local police was not unfounded, but they were quietly and politely mediocre. They treated the great man with deference, allowing him to give his version of events he had not actually witnessed. When I was called into the study to say what I had seen and heard, Mr. Tyler stayed. I saw with disappointment that Sheriff Peterson was a young man with the awkward officiousness of the inexperienced. Beyond the city, it was left to rural towns to organize their own police force and

apparently in Oyster Bay, many men had decided there were better jobs than corralling drunken joyriders and tracing lost spaniels.
The sheriff had big hands, a big forehead, and looked one genera-
tion off the farm. Sitting opposite me, hands clasped between
his knees, he said, "Now, you first became alarmed when you
heard the baby crying."

"Miss Mabel heard him crying. She had fallen asleep in the
second-floor guest room and came to get me."

"And you went to the nursery to see what was happening?" I
nodded. "Did you hear anything other than the baby?"

"I did not."

"And when you got there?"

"Miss Bernardi was not in her room and the door to the
nursery was shut. When I called to Miss Bernardi, she did not
answer me."

"What did you do then?"

"I sent Miss Louise and Miss Mabel to find her father."

"Why did you do that?"

"Because I was going to open the door and I did not want Mabel present when I did."

"Because you knew it would be pretty bad."

"I suspected it might be."

"And it was . . . pretty bad, right?"

I told myself he was a nice man and I should resist the urge to
echo "pretty bad" in a way that would make him feel foolish. "Yes."

"Now, how did you know that?"

"Because Miss Bernardi wasn't deaf," I said. "She would have
answered me if she had been able to. She wasn't able to because
she was dead."

Mildly alarmed, Sheriff Peterson looked to Charles Tyler, who,
with a little gesture of his fingers, indicated that he wasn't to take
offense.

Gathering himself, the sheriff said, "And the window was open, right?"

"Yes, the window was open."

"And the baby was on the floor, as if he'd been dropped."

"Yes."

"Was he lying near the . . . was he lying near Miss Bernardi?"

It was the first interesting question he had asked. "No, he wasn't."

"So, someone else dropped him on the floor."

"Possibly. Or she dropped him, then staggered."

"Any idea why she didn't put him back in the crib?"

"She may not have been able to reach the crib, but needed her hands to fight. Who knows what happens in a struggle?"

"Still. Someone took him out of the crib."

Sheriff Peterson had been told it was a kidnapping attempt; therefore, he was interested in only the facts that supported that version of events. I could feel Mr. Tyler watching me through narrowed eyes.

I said, "Miss Bernardi, I assume. If the baby were crying, she would have gone to comfort him." I met Mr. Tyler's gaze. "She loved him very much."

"She told you that?" asked Sheriff Peterson.

"Not in so many words, but I could see it."

He glanced back at Mr. Tyler, then said to me, "You were friendly with Miss Bernardi? You talked?"

"Only once, but she was an open person . . ."

"Open."

He pounced on the word in a way that made me self-conscious. "Not reserved. She showed her feelings, her affections."

"So you knew her pretty well."

He was talking faster now; I felt pressured. "I know she was a good person. I know she cared for the children."

The men exchanged looks. Then the sheriff said, "Did Miss Bernardi talk about her family at all? Where she came from?"

I looked at Mr. Tyler, who said, "As you suggested, we're trying to find the poor girl's relatives."

"No, she didn't."

"What she did before she came to work for Mr. Tyler? People she might have known?"

I shook my head.

"Did she talk about letters from home, anyone she might still be in touch with?"

"No, nothing like that. She seemed . . . alone to me."

Sheriff Peterson offered a suitably sad expression. Then said, "And no romantic attachments?"

Wary at the sudden shift, I said, "Not that she mentioned. She did say something about wanting to be a mother, but . . . lacking a father." My face felt very warm and I wished I had a glass of water.

"Are you sure, Miss Prescott? I know girls like to talk about that kind of thing. Confide."

I suspected that everything Sheriff Peterson knew about girls' confidential talks could be written on a postage stamp. "She confided nothing in me."

The men consulted each other through a look. Frustrated that there was clearly a conversation taking place to which I was not privy, I said, "May I ask why you want to know?"

Confronted, the sheriff puffed, "A young lady leaves a window open . . . we want to know who she was expecting. She was pretty, the kind to attract attention. Even visitors."

I stared at this young man, who no doubt prided himself on his manners. "You don't know that she left the window open. Even if she did, the only thing she was expecting was fresh air."

Chastened, the policeman said, "Of course. My apologies."

I smiled, teeth clenched. Then said, "Of course, you'll talk to the rest of the staff. They would know Miss Bernardi much better than I would."

Putting his notebook away, Sheriff Peterson said, "Already done that. But thank you, Miss Prescott."

I was free to go. As I wandered out to the hallway, I heard the sheriff say, "Forgive me for asking, sir, but how well do you know the people you employ?"

"I trust each and every one of them with my life," said Charles Tyler stoutly, not answering the question.

"Miss Bernardi was Italian. As is Mr. Grimaldi."

"Yes, I'm sure he's aware of it."

Failing to catch the sarcasm, Sheriff Peterson persisted. "In view of the threats, don't you think it would be best to have only trustworthy people around the house?"

A slam as a fist came down on the desk. "I do trust them. And it is important that people see that I do. In my position, it is vital that the public has faith in my integrity. That they understand that I fight the Black Hand not out of animosity or prejudice, but from an unwavering commitment to fairness and the rule of law. More than anyone, the Italian people suffer from the predations of these villains. How, then, shall I turn away from a deserving individual in need of a job?"

I could disagree with Mr. Tyler's defense of Mr. Grimaldi. But it was hard not to admire the sentiment behind it.

The clock chimed twelve; luncheon would soon be served by the ever-capable Mrs. Briggs. I went outside in search of Louise and found William alone on the lawn, staring up at the nursery tower.

"It's funny," he said. "I can't stand to be inside and I can't stay out for long either. Did you talk to the police?"

"Yes. They seemed more interested in whether Sofia had a lover than anything else." William winced. "Honestly—does no one consider the possibility that the window was open because the killer climbed out of it to get away?"

"How did he get in, Jane?" William's voice was low. "That's the question."

And not one I wanted to answer in my present mood. I could see happy fluttering sails out on the bay, hear the thud of hooves and shouts of excitement as carefree hunters set out across the fields, the toot of a car horn. The sky had no right to be so blue. Not today.

Glaring at the garage, I said, "I don't expect they asked Aldo Grimaldi about his past."

"Aldo Grimaldi has told us everything he remembers from last night. And one of the things he told them was that he saw the window open at eleven. The police believe Sofia died sometime after midnight. The blood was still . . . she was . . ." Unable to articulate the more grisly details, William shrugged unhappily.

Eleven o'clock—before she was killed, but well past the time she should have been in her own bed, given the erratic schedule of babies. It was disobedient, without doubt. And stupid. Still, we only had Aldo Grimaldi's word that it was open before the murder.

"Did they ask him *why* he was staring at the nursery late at night?"

"He doesn't have to stare. He can see it from his room."

"Did the fact that he argued with Sofia earlier in the day come up?"

"No, it didn't, because we don't know what they said and we don't even know that they argued. They might have been discussing the weather."

"You might find out if you asked him."

This, I knew as I spoke, was too far. William might accept being bullied by his mother and sisters, but not from me. "Jane, I know you don't like Aldo. And maybe he was . . . forward with Sofia, I don't know. Italians are different in those things. But I was there when they told him Sofia was dead. He was distraught."

He wanted me to feel sympathy for the ugly little man. But all I felt was impatience; there were too many questions. Where had Aldo been when Sofia was killed? What had their argument been about? Had Charles Tyler even told Sheriff Peterson about the argument? Why had William introduced Aldo as his uncle's new chauffeur when Mr. Tyler said he'd worked with him for ten years? And perhaps most important, Mr. Tyler had said Aldo had been accused in the past. Of what and by whom?

One look at William's wary expression told me I wouldn't get answers from him. His uncle trusted Aldo. He was, as Sofia had said, "one of his people." Anyone taken up by Charles Tyler would be protected by William as well.

Stymied, I wandered to the spot that lay under the nursery. The window was closed now. I gazed up the side of the house as if it could tell me something.

"Does that window open from the outside?" I asked William.

"No," he said pointedly.

I took in the four stories. "It seems a long way to climb without help."

"Actually, it's easy," said William. Happy to be off controversial subjects, he pointed to a first-floor window. "You use the window ledge to get the first foothold, struggle up the drainpipe until you get a rest"—he swung his arm to point to a Juliet balcony that led off Mr. Tyler's private study on the third floor—"and from there, you've got a good purchase on the nursery window."

"You're making that up."

"Not at all," he said. "I used to do it all the time as a boy. That was my room when I stayed here. When I went exploring, I had to leave it open a crack and put a book as a stopper in case it slipped down. Part of me wanted Uncle Charles to catch me so I could impress him with my adventurousness."

I smiled, but my mind was still on Sofia. I looked back at the woods that surrounded the back of the property and thought back to the first night we arrived. The dense forest would make for excellent cover, but could you reasonably carry a baby, who would no doubt be crying, through it undetected? Unless there was a way to make sure the baby didn't cry. Someone to soothe them. My mind caught again on the memory of Sofia singing to Frederick as she walked him along the grass.

Discarding that memory, I looked at the ground. Around this side of the house, there was a border of tiger lilies and azaleas. It was nicely tended, an excellent balance struck between wildness and order. Fixing my eye on the nursery, I took several steps until I could almost touch the wall of the house. Then I looked down. Tiger lilies and azaleas in a lovely unbroken row.

Except when you looked under the blooms and at the dirt. Then you saw one small spot where the soil was trampled, the edge of the lawn broken.

"Mr. William, look at this."

William frowned. "Could have been the gardener."

"Would a gardener have trampled these azaleas?" I pointed to the bruised petals and broken stems. I knelt down to look more closely. And saw a footprint.

Stepping well out of the way, I said, "Look. Don't step."

William did, his eyebrows telling me he saw what I did.

"We should tell my uncle." Then as an afterthought, "And Sheriff Peterson."

"We will." Carefully, I raised my own foot and let it hover above the print. Not much bigger than mine. Small for a man's foot.

Digging in my pocket, I pulled out a tape measure—always in my possession, as any fluctuation in Louise's waist span necessitated frantic communication with the dressmaker.

I didn't want to touch the print itself, but I judged the length to be about seven inches. How much did soft earth spread when you stepped on it?

"Mr. William, could you step there, please?" I pointed to a turned-over patch of ground near the fence at the side of the house.

Uncertain, he moved toward the spot. "Step?"

"As if you meant to climb over the fence." One foot would have borne the full weight of the body as the man made his way up the house.

William did as he was asked, although climbing was a little more difficult for him as a grown man. Puffing he said, "Now what?"

I went and looked. "What size shoe do you wear?"

"Eleven. Do you need my collar size as well?"

"I could guess that. You're about a fourteen."

I measured the print he had made—almost a foot. Which equaled an 11 shoe with a man who weighed—I would guess—150 pounds. As carefully as possible, I measured the depth of the prints as well. They were roughly equal, which meant the killer was just as heavy if not more so than William. But William was a slender man. It could also simply mean the dirt in this spot was looser than the patch I'd used for William's print.

But seven inches. That was still a small shoe. You might send a small man to break into a house if it meant climbing. Aldo was barely my height. But was he fit enough to manage the climb? And even so, would Sofia have let him in? Perhaps if he knocked loudly, threatened to wake the baby . . .

Almost to myself, I said, "I just can't imagine why Sofia opened it."

William sighed unhappily. "Neither can I. But other people have stronger imaginations."

That brought to mind Mrs. Briggs's strange comment about the kidnappers' luck. "Did people dislike Sofia?"

He sighed. "I know my mother thought she was unqualified."

"She was wonderful with the children."

"Yes. But most women want their nannies to have worked for at least a minor member of royalty before they'll let them near their children. If Sofia had any prior experience, I didn't know about it."

"How did Mrs. Tyler find her then?"

William shrugged. "I assumed Mrs. Briggs took care of hiring staff."

If Mrs. Briggs had had a hand in bringing Sofia into the house, she probably regretted it now. She took pride in working for the Tylers; ties to anyone who brought trouble to the house would be threatening to her. Perhaps that explained her strange mood last night.

From inside the house, we heard Mrs. Tyler instructing Mrs. Briggs to have the children's things packed and ready by evening.

"She's sending them today?" I asked.

"Tomorrow. Doesn't want to give the kidnappers another chance."

At that moment, a car drove up and several men with rifles got out and headed toward the back of the house. "Who are they?" I asked.

"More of Uncle Charles's men. He must have called them this morning."

Armed policemen at the wedding—that would throw the mothers-in-law into fresh panic. "Can't you talk your mother into a simpler ceremony in light of what's happened?"

William shook his head. "It's not just my mother. Uncle Charles is adamant everything go on as planned. He thinks once you show fear of any kind, you've as good as lost the battle."

In the distance, I heard the creak of metal—a breeze had caught the weather vane and swung it suddenly north. It called to mind the sound of the carriage wheels on the grass, that walk with Sofia when we had talked about the quiet life in the country and the things that men want.

What had Aldo said again? *I know what you're doing!* Many a jealous man had said those words. And many a jealous man had committed murder.

William broke into my thoughts, saying, "You can't dwell on it. If you do, the Black Hand wins. That's what Uncle Charles says."

I nodded as if I agreed, then said, "Why don't you go find Miss Louise? I did her hair a new way and it looks exceptionally pretty. Perhaps you could tell her so."

And then I went up the servants' stairs to the nursery.

7

When I first came to Mrs. Armslow's, there had been another new girl who shared a room with me. She was homesick, often ill—at least she didn't leave her bed—and was generally thought lazy and unsuited for the job. Everyone had expected her to leave or be dismissed when her trial was up. But instead she had taken a spoonful of rat poison. I remember standing in the hallway of the servants' quarters as they carried her out, the sense of irritation and disgust that filled the house. That girl—I can't even remember her name now—was never mentioned again. A few days later, a Polish girl arrived, I had a new roommate, and that was that.

I remembered that girl as I climbed the stairs to Sofia's room, or what used to be her room. Servants came and went; traces of them were quickly erased. So what I expected to find, I wasn't sure. The police would have taken anything of interest, a family photo, letters, keepsakes. Then I remembered pink-faced Sheriff Peterson and thought perhaps I gave them too much credit. I hoped so anyway.

I listened carefully as I climbed the stairs to the tower; the children had been moved to their parents' room, but I didn't want to run into Mrs. Briggs or a policeman. Just as I stepped onto the landing, I heard the creak of hinges, the gentle click of a latch. And saw Mabel standing outside the door of Sofia's bedroom.

"Miss Mabel."

"Hello."

For a long moment, we gazed at each other warily.

"You shouldn't be in Sofia's room."

"I know. I just wanted to think about her a little."

"I see."

Sensing I was not going to punish her, Mabel drifted a few steps toward Frederick's room. "No, don't," I told her. "It's not the way you want to remember her."

That she seemed to understand because she came back. "I would like to have something of hers. Do you think they'd let me? Just a keepsake."

"Maybe when the investigation is over and her family have been contacted."

"She didn't have family."

"How do you know that?"

"Because I asked her once. I was showing her my scrapbook and I asked if she had any pictures of her mother or father and could I look at them? She said they were dead. She didn't have brothers or sisters either. All she had was us."

There was no doubt in my mind that Mabel was telling the truth, yet it sounded strange to me. It was rare, in my experience, to find an Italian who would say they had *no* family. My friend Anna had no parents, but she had aunts, uncles, cousins, brothers—family.

Mabel said, "That's why I want something to remember her by. Otherwise we'll all forget. And anyway, Aldo went in there."

"When?"

"Last night." She looked slightly guilty. "After they took us to Mother and Father's room, I came back. Please don't tell. I'd left my scrapbook in my room and I was worried the Black Hand might steal it. So, I snuck back and that's when I saw him coming out of Sofia's room."

How had the chauffeur gotten inside? I wondered. Then I remembered: the staff had been gathered in the house to be informed of Sofia's death. Aldo must have slipped upstairs, unnoticed by people in shock and distress. And by Mrs. Briggs—which was surprising. I wouldn't have thought that sharp-eyed woman missed anything.

"Mabel, did you notice his clothes at all?"

"He wasn't wearing any. I mean, he was wearing a robe. They must have got him out of bed. Why?"

A robe. Outer clothes hastily torn off, shoved someplace safe, robe pulled on to cover any remaining bloodstains. It wasn't inconceivable.

"May I ask you a strange question, Miss Mabel?"

She nodded.

"Do you like Aldo Grimaldi?"

It was an odd and improper question. But the child immediately said, "No."

"Why is that?"

"Because Sofia didn't."

"I see. Thank you, Miss Mabel. I'll talk to Mrs. Briggs."

★ ★ ★

As it happened, I ran into that very efficient lady as I was going down the servants' stairs to the kitchen. She carried several burlap sacks and a duster. Seeing me, she slowed her step, as if aware an argument was coming. The stairs were not wide enough to pass someone unless they stood to one side.

I did not stand to one side.

"Miss Prescott."

"Am I right that those bags are for Sofia's things?"

"Not that it's any of your business, but yes."

"What will you do with them?"

"What do you suggest I do, Miss Prescott?"

"Keep them. For a little while at least." She made to go around me, and I blocked her. "She was alive yesterday. You can't just throw away her things."

"I can if Mrs. Tyler says to and she does. She said, 'Clean it up.' That's what I'm doing."

It was on her list, I realized, and would stay there until she was able to wipe it away as done. "But not now, surely. When the police have finished . . ."

"The police have finished, Miss Prescott," said Mrs. Briggs wearily. I was committing that gravest of domestic sins: stopping someone from getting their work done.

"I'm only asking because Mabel said she wanted something."

At the mention of Mabel, her face softened. "Oh, dear."

"It's not surprising, is it? She was very fond of Sofia."

"Yes, well, she's a child."

"What does that have to do with it?"

There was clearly something Mrs. Briggs expected me to understand—and I was failing. Exasperation pinched her face as she said, "Look, she wasn't what you think."

It was a bizarre statement; how did Mrs. Briggs know what I thought? "I thought she was a nice young woman who loved the children."

She kneaded her forehead with the heel of her hand. "People

are different, Miss Prescott, their ways are different. And their ways may be fine for where they come from, but I don't want them here. Let them kill each other in their own country."

Struggling to stay civil, I said, "I can't agree with you. I didn't know Sofia Bernardi very well, but—"

"You didn't know her at all. If you did, you wouldn't be the least surprised at how she ended up. I'm only sorry it had to happen here instead of the gutter where she belonged."

★ ★ ★

There was only one person who might prevent Mrs. Briggs from completing her task, and that was the lady who had given it to her. Going to the front of the house, I hoped to find Alva Tyler. I found her on the front porch, gazing into the distance where Mabel swung halfheartedly from a swing suspended from the branches of a large beech tree.

Hearing me approach, she looked up. "Yes, Jane? Did you need something for Miss Louise?"

"No, but thank you. It was something for Miss Mabel."

"Mabel." She looked at her daughter.

"Something of Sofia's . . ." A shadow of irritation passed over Mrs. Tyler's face. "Mrs. Briggs is cleaning out her room, and I just wondered if perhaps it was too soon."

"Too soon? Not soon enough."

I must have shown my surprise, because she added, "I'm sorry, that sounds dreadful, but I can't have that poor girl's things in my home. I want it all—gone."

"Mabel would like something of hers."

Mrs. Tyler's lips tightened for a moment. Then she managed, "Yes, at some point, I'll . . . never mind, Jane, I'll take care of it."

"I would be happy to help her, if it feels too much for you."

She was silent a long time, her eyes dark with exhaustion. "Forgive me, I haven't been sleeping and all I can think is, they'll be back. At some point, they'll come back, just as they did last night, and I won't be able to stop it, and the children . . ."

Her mouth began to tremble and she worked her jaw until it was still, then hurriedly wiped her eyes.

"I'm sure they'll be safe with your mother," I offered weakly.

"No, they will be, of course. Please don't think me heartless. The only way I can manage is to see last night as something that's happened, that can't be changed, and now we must take action, we must do what we can. And . . . cleaning is one of the things I *can* do."

Then she smiled crookedly. "Truth be told, I was never that fond of Sofia. She was more Charles's concern . . ."

It was an odd choice of words, but she did not explain, instead patting my arm and saying, "But yes, of course, I'll help Mabel find something. Thank you for coming to me, Jane."

Dismissed, I left her. As I walked around the house to the servants' entrance, I realized all I had accomplished was the saving of one item for the sake of her child. The rest of Sofia's belongings would be consigned to the garbage.

At the back, I caught sight of Aldo outside the garage. He was rubbing down the hood of the car. Leaning over, arms extended, washing with wide, angry sweeps of the arm. The sight of him cleaning put me in mind of what Mabel had said. Why had he gone to the nursery floor last night? And was it once or twice?

As if aware he was being watched, he looked up. Caught, I nodded briefly and went inside.

Going upstairs, I wondered if William had followed my advice. But when I found Louise sitting on the window seat gazing out at the lawn, she did not look like a woman who had been recently praised.

"Are the police gone?" she asked.

"They are."

"I spoke with them, but I don't think I was much help. And I spoke with Mother. I wasn't much help there either."

"Spoke with her about what?"

She wobbled one shoulder. "Well . . . this poor girl has been killed and it seems like the only thing people are worried about is whether the news will get out and ruin the wedding. It's *awful.*"

There were times I was reminded how fortunate I was to work for Louise Benchley, and this was one of them. Of everyone in the house, she was the only person to speak of Sofia with kindness.

Still, I said, "I can see Mr. Tyler's point. If the Black Hand is trying to intimidate him, it wouldn't do to change plans."

"I'll feel as if I'm walking over her blood," said Louise, shuddering. "The only good thing to come out of it is William's mother has decided Beatrice and Emily aren't to come this weekend and she and Mother have stopped fighting about the music. But I'm sure they'll start up again tomorrow. And Beatrice will come eventually and say snide things and the newspapers will start up again and—honestly, sometimes I wish it were someone else getting married."

"I'm sure Miss Charlotte would be happy to change places. Other than that, I can't think of a candidate."

She smiled, then hugging her knees, asked, "Do you ever hear from your cousin Henry?"

I was puzzled: I had no cousins, much less one named Henry. Then I remembered. I had once told Louise that Michael Behan was my cousin Henry.

"No, I haven't."

"Do you know what's funny? I thought you were going to marry him."

No, darling, I'll be home soon. That fragment of overheard conversation that told me the reporter was married. Crossing to the bed in order to straighten the pillows, I said, "I am very sure that I will not be marrying Cousin Henry."

Just then we heard the crunch of tires on the gravel path. Louise pulled back the curtain. "Oh, dear."

"What is it?"

"It's Father," she said unhappily. "I knew Mother would tell him to come."

A car door slammed. Then another. And a third. Memory informed me this was odd. There should only be two slams. One for O'Hara and one for Mr. Benchley . . .

Louise drew back, startled.

"Isn't *that* your cousin Henry?"

I joined her at the window. And saw Michael Behan standing on the Tylers' lawn.

★ ★ ★

"I won't have it! No, sir! No grubby, ink-slinging hack on my property! I have my own press hounds, thank you. Ones that heel when you tell them to."

Michael Behan and I were standing outside on the lawn, listening to Mr. Tyler's tirade as it resounded through the open library window.

He had a new hat. When I last saw Michael Behan, his derby had seen better days. The felt was nubby and worn, the band frayed, and the ribbon around the brim had sprung loose in several spots. This one was sleek and crisply finished around the edge, the felt still handsome. He still wore it tilted back on his head, however. And the smile was the same.

There was a pause in the diatribe during which I guessed Mr. Benchley was making a point. This we could not hear. Mr. Benchley was not a man to shout; often he preferred not to speak at all. If you saw him on the street, you might guess he was a man of wealth from the cut and quality of his dress. But you might not have known that the quiet, tasteful shoes came from Alden, the coat was imported from Henry Poole, and his suit from Gieves and Hawkes. You might judge him well groomed without knowing that his appearance demanded a level of care few could afford. His nails had been tended to that morning, the clean lines of his thin and graying hair were trimmed neatly above his ears at precisely the same length every week, and he kept to a strict diet that allowed no sweets, minimal starch, and—for a man of his era and profession—remarkably little alcohol. In short, anyone seeing the family home or the Daimler would have understood that Mr. Benchley was a prosperous man. But they would not have guessed that he was one of the richest men in the country. And I think he preferred it that way.

"What are you doing here, Mr. Behan?"

"I was asked to come, Miss Prescott."

"By Mr. Benchley?" He nodded. Without discussion, we had reverted to the formality of surnames. I had never called him anything other than Mr. Behan. But I had at one time said he could call me Jane, and I was relieved that he had either forgotten it or decided it was unwise.

At that point, the front door opened and Mrs. Briggs presented herself. "Mr. Benchley would like to see Miss Prescott upstairs."

To Michael Behan, she said, "You wait here."

"Outside with the dogs and fleas, yes, ma'am."

When I entered the study, Mr. Tyler was looking mutinous and Mr. Benchley was winding his watch. As I came in, he put the watch back in his pocket and said, "Mr. Tyler and I have agreed that it is inevitable that the newspapers will take an interest in the recent tragic event."

I could see from the expression on Mr. Tyler's face that "inevitable" was not a word he cared for.

"Therefore, it would be wise to trust the story to a reporter we know. Someone familiar with the Black Hand. And as you discovered the body and you knew the girl—"

"Not well."

"—Mr. Behan has asked for your assistance. And I feel it is better if he gets his facts from someone who is both sensible and sensitive to the families' interests."

"I see."

Mr. Benchley peered at me as if to make sure I did see. Then he indicated the door and followed me out. As we left, I looked back at Mr. Tyler, but he stood over his desk, head down, hands clenched. He had been beaten, and he did not like it.

Hurrying down the stairs after Mr. Benchley, I said, "I think Mr. Tyler would be happier with one of his own reporters."

Without turning, Mr. Benchley said, "It is Mr. Tyler's theory that given his line of work and his role in the Moretti trial that the criminal underworld has decided to target his family. He thinks that is why this poor young woman is dead."

He stopped. "One way or another, that is something I would like to know before my daughter marries his nephew."

"I understand." And I did. But I had one more concern. "I don't see why Mr. Behan feels he needs . . ."

"But he does. Or says he does. And says he will not do it without you. So."

He continued down the stairs. When he reached the bottom,

he adjusted his cuff, and said, "Did you know Mr. William's father, Jane?"

"No."

"I did. Many years ago, I made his acquaintance through a business matter. His end came as no surprise whatsoever."

His cuff adjusted, he went into the parlor to greet his wife and daughter.

8

Once, in circumstances too complicated to relate here, Michael Behan had lent me his coat and I had been glad to have it. As we walked down the hill that led from the house to the bay, all I could think of was that coat, the rough wool at my chin, the smell of tobacco, the round black button, tightly sewn—by his wife as it turned out, but I hadn't known that at the time.

Still, I felt I should apologize for never responding to his last letter. I waited for him to reproach me or tease me, so I could offer up a dignified "Yes, I'm very sorry. But I think you understand why I could not." But annoyingly he never gave me the chance. Instead we walked in silence, making our way farther and farther from the house, until I said, "Mr. Behan, you said you needed to talk to me. I think you can start."

He turned, hands in his pockets. "Who's designing the dress?"

"Dress?"

"The wedding dress. I say it's Worth, but a friend at the *Tribune* says Paquin. Loser pays the winner fifty dollars."

"How much would I get?"

". . . Ten?"

"Ten? I think I'll call your friend at the *Tribune*."

Close to the water, someone had placed a bench so one could gaze at the horizon; it was long enough for us both to sit and I took care that there was distance between us. Here, it was marshland, the water thick with reeds. Ducks glided along the surface, some flapping in agitation as a wide-winged heron leapt from sea to air. I could imagine Sofia bringing the children here. Shoes kicked off, skirts held high as they tossed bread to the ducks.

To Behan, I said, "So you're here to write about the latest Black Hand slaying."

Stretching his legs, Behan said, "I'm not sure what I'm here to write about. When your boss said he had a story on Charles Tyler that might interest me, I told him no, thank you. Only then Benchley calls my editor, who tells me I better get interested."

"Why?"

"My editor likes Tyler, he's good copy, especially since the Forti kidnapping. A lot of my friends like Tyler; he makes their job easy. Hands them big stories, all wrapped up with a sparkly headline that usually includes his name. You write down what he says, take a picture, you're in the saloon by lunchtime. I guess that's all right, but this time, there's a dead woman involved, so I'd like to get within spitting distance of the truth." He looked at me. "The Benchleys still pay your salary, not the Tylers—or has that changed?"

I knew what Mr. Benchley wanted me to do, and I knew it did not include investigating any member of the Tyler staff. Mr. Tyler's opinion on that issue had been made abundantly clear. But if anyone were going to look beyond the Black Hand, it would be Michael Behan, who lived and breathed for the story—and sometimes the truth.

I must have been quiet too long, because he said, "You don't have to say yes. I know you're busy with the wedding of the year. Or is it decade?"

"Oh, century at least." And I had always liked his sense of humor.

A swan stuck its head underwater in search of food, long neck arching as it reemerged. I thought of Sofia lifting Frederick high in the air, joyful as she imagined the children she would now never have.

Then I looked at Michael Behan. "Yes."

"Yes what?" But he was smiling.

"Yes, I'll talk to you."

The smile broadened into a grin and he bounced his feet on the grass, like a boy whose stone has just made six skips on the water.

"So," he said, "according to your boss, the Morettis tried to kidnap the Tyler baby. That's ambitious, but not a surprise; they've been threatening Tyler for weeks. Only the nanny woke up, rushed into the nursery, and got her throat cut. True?"

"Could be true," I said, not wanting to prejudice him.

He waited.

"I don't particularly care for Mr. Tyler's chauffeur."

"Tell me why."

In as neutral a tone as possible, I recounted Aldo Grimaldi's argument with Sofia, her statement about what men want, and the fact that Mabel had seen him coming out of Sofia's room that night.

"What's the name again?" he asked.

"Grimaldi."

"Italian."

"Yes, but that's not why I . . ."

"Did the police talk to him?"

"Yes. He told them he had seen the window open at eleven."

"And what was he doing looking in the window?" I nodded. "But Tyler doesn't suspect him."

"Mr. Tyler thinks well of his people. Anyone who works for him is wonderful . . . splendid." I remembered how he had found me behind the charabanc the day we arrived, the fond stories he told about my time at Mrs. Armslow's. Foolish, maybe. But sincere. "That's just the kind of man he is. It's admirable, but . . ."

"You think he's protecting Grimaldi."

"It's more likely that he doesn't believe he could be guilty. He's strangely innocent. Also, since he makes a career out of fighting the Black Hand, he's anxious people see him as unprejudiced. And men like him don't believe that men harm women—unless they're criminals."

Behan took that in, then asked, "What did the room look like?"

"Look like?"

"Did it look like there'd been a struggle?"

I thought. The overturned lamp, the broken china dog. "Yes."

"Can I see the room?"

"I don't see why not."

As we walked back up to the house, I wanted to ask Michael Behan if he believed me, if he thought that a man could both love a woman—or think he did—and be capable of killing her. But it seemed an awkward question, and I decided to let the room speak for itself.

★ ★ ★

The bright light of day made the chaotic, bloodstained scene all the more horrible. The crib had been moved to another room, but the rocking horse, the stuffed rabbit, a pile of freshly laundered diapers were all there. On the rocking chair, a bright shawl of red, yellow, and green. It had to be Sofia's; no doubt it would be thrown away by the end of the day.

A little blue smock hung on a peg; seeing it, I thought of Frederick's heavy, trusting head and swallowed. If only he could talk, the mystery would be solved. Although I would never wish the memory of that night on any child.

Pointing to the darkest pool of blood on the rug, Behan said, "She was here?"

I nodded. There was a spray of blood nearby, quite different from the dark, damp patch. Also, I noticed, small dark spatters on the white wood of the changing table, which stood a few feet from where the body had fallen. I pointed them out to Behan.

"He cut her throat from behind," he said. "Blood went—" He popped his fingers in the air to replicate the spray.

"Well, that's what the Black Hand does, isn't it? In your articles, you're always writing about stilettos and slit throats." Remembering how it had all seemed so entertaining, I felt vaguely ashamed.

"Sometimes. Guns are also popular."

"You wouldn't bring a gun to a kidnapping, though. You'd want to be as quiet as possible." I looked to the window; it was closed now. I could see the remains of the powder the police had used to look for prints.

"The baby was on the floor?" Behan asked.

"Over there." I pointed to a spot between the window and where the crib had stood. "It seemed like someone had dropped him in the struggle."

"And the window was open . . ."

"Yes. It shouldn't have been. The house is tightly locked up at night, and the windows are always shut."

"Keep out the kidnappers and cutthroats?"

"Yes, but Mrs. Tyler was also concerned with drafts. She lost a child last year and she was very specific with Sofia about the windows staying closed."

"And did Sofia always listen?"

". . . Not always."

"Why's that?"

I took a deep breath. "If she left it open, I think she did it for the baby. She said it was too warm for him. Also for her. She must have thought four floors would be too challenging for a kidnapper, so it would be safe to break the rules."

Behan leaned out the window and looked down. I joined him.

"It would be challenging," he concluded.

"William—young Mr. Tyler—says it's possible. You step there, and there, and then pull yourself up."

I waited for Behan to accuse Sofia of something worse than negligence. But stepping back inside the room, he said, "So, kidnapper comes in through the open window, grabs baby . . ."

I pointed to the door that connected the nursery and Sofia's room. "Sofia would have heard the baby cry, come rushing in . . ."

"They fight, baby lands on the floor, her throat gets cut . . ." He looked at me. "Then what?"

I thought. "We come. The kidnapper hears our feet on the stairs, he hears Mabel's voice."

"Now he can't take the baby out one of the doors, in case he runs into you . . ."

"And he can't carry him down."

"So, he decides to save his own skin and run." He tilted his head this way and that as if sifting the story. "Nothing wrong with it on the surface."

"No."

He paced around the room, then said suddenly, "Can I talk to the little girl?"

Surprised, I said, "Mabel? She's just a child."

"She's the first person in the house to know something was wrong. I want to know what she heard and when she heard it."

I couldn't argue with that. The Tylers would likely not approve, but Mabel would adore talking to a reporter.

"All right. But I have to be there when you speak with her."

We found Mabel in her room, sitting on her bed, gazing sadly at a half-packed trunk on the floor. Knocking, I opened the door a little wider and said, "Mabel? A friend of mine would like to talk to you." I glanced back at Mr. Behan, who was straining to get a look. "He's a reporter. But he's a *kind and polite* gentleman, I promise you." I stepped hard on his foot to emphasize the point.

Her little face lit up. "Oh, yes."

Michael Behan stepped into the room, moving carefully among the child's toys on the floor. "Hello, Mabel. My name is Michael Behan. I work for *The New York Herald*."

"I've seen that newspaper," said Mabel.

"You have? Well, you're a well-informed young lady." He sat on a chair near the bed. "I'm very sorry about your nanny."

"We have to go away because of it. In case they come back." She struggled a little. "She saved Freddy. You should put that in the newspaper. Sofia saved him. She's a heroine."

"I know she is. But you saved him, too, didn't you? Miss Prescott tells me you were the one who heard Freddy crying."

"I always hear him."

"Sure, because you love him." Not for the first time, I was struck by Michael Behan's ease with children. "So, you were here, across the hall, when you heard it?"

She shook her head. "I was in the guest room with Miss Benchley."

"Miss Louise," I supplied. "Mabel fell asleep in her room that night."

"Where is that room?"

"On the second floor." He nodded, then turned back to Mabel. "So you heard Freddy crying, then what did you do?"

"I woke up Miss Benchley and she said Jane would know what to do so we went and got Jane."

"Not your parents?"

"They sleep all the way on the other side of the house. Jane was closer, and I wanted to get to Freddy. Also, Miss Benchley thought they wouldn't like to be woken just because Freddy was crying."

"Right. So you woke Miss Prescott and told her to come. Mabel, did you hear any voices apart from Freddy's?"

"I heard Sofia."

I felt a rip in my heart as I thought of Sofia screaming for help. "What did you hear, Mabel?"

"Just screaming. Maybe I heard *No*. But I was still sleepy, so I'm not really sure."

Behan asked, "Do you remember anything else, Mabel?"

She shook her head. "Jane told us to go get Father and tell him to get his gun, but by the time we got there—"

Her face twisted and her eyes filled with tears. Sitting down next to her, I put an arm around her shoulder. "You were very brave, Mabel. And Mr. Behan's right. You saved Freddy by waking us all up. That's why the kidnapper had to leave him behind."

"But Sofia's the one—"

"Mabel . . ." To distract her, Behan dug a card out of his coat pocket and handed it to her. "Miss Prescott tells me you like newspapers."

She nodded.

"Well, that's my office, right there. The next time you're in the city, you come by and see me and I'll show you the presses. My father worked on the presses. He was a typesetter. Do you know what type is?"

"It's the blocks with letters that they use to make words."

"Smart girl."

As she took the card, Mabel shifted slightly on the bed and I heard the rustle of paper. Looking down, I saw the corner of a newspaper sticking out from the coverlet. Mabel instinctively put her hand over it.

"What is that, Miss Mabel?"

"Nothing."

"Then you can show it to me."

She hesitated. "You won't tell, will you?"

"That depends," I said, holding out my hand.

Pulling the newspaper from behind her, she handed it to me. "Please don't take it away. There's a story about the Moretti trial and I need it for my scrapbook."

There was indeed a story about the Moretti trial. An ugly headline screamed, MORETTI THREATENS DEPUTY COMMISSIONER. Dear God, I thought, poor child. No wonder her mother didn't want her to have newspapers.

"Where did you get this?" I asked her.

She hung her head. "Sofia's room."

Sofia's room? That made no sense. Sofia showed no interest in politics. I gazed at the pages, trying to see what would draw her. An advertisement or—

Then I noticed something was circled in dark, heavy ink. Folding it carefully, I said, "I'm going to take this, Miss Mabel. When Mr. Moretti is convicted, you can put that article in your scrapbook. This one isn't worth including in your history."

She accepted this, but her gaze didn't leave the paper. Remembering that she wanted something of Sofia's, I went quickly down the hall to the nursery and took the shawl from the rocking chair. The little girl recognized it the moment I came back, saying excitedly, "That's—"

"Yes, it is," I said, folding it carefully and tucking it into the bottom shelf of her bureau. "I think she'd want you to have it. But we'll keep it here, a secret, for now. Yes?"

"Yes," said Mabel, probably as thrilled by the secret as she was by the shawl.

I indicated to Michael Behan that we should leave. He extended his hand, saying, "I hope to see you at the *Herald* soon, Miss Tyler."

Only when we were two floors down and well out of earshot did he say, "What?"

Opening the paper, I showed him the circled advertisement. It was not for employment—not specifically, at any rate. Men and women looking for companionship or even mates sometimes placed personal ads for people they had seen on the street or on trains, asking for a meeting. It was a habit with some men to become fascinated with young ladies they saw on public transport. Certain newspapers—such as the *Herald*—printed these ads: "Will lady leaving elevated car, 42nd street, Monday evening communicate with gentleman opposite who tapped her shoe?" Women also advertised. "Refined miss, 18, plump, pretty face, good form, desires acquaintance gentleman of means; object matrimony. Girlish." Or: "Woman finds paddling her own canoe dreary task. Seeks manly pilot."

Recently, there had been an outcry against such ads on the grounds that they were being used for the purposes of prostitution. But the ads still ran. And Sofia had circled one of them.

It read,

> Hoping to see the dark-eyed miss at noon Wednesday the
> 20th on uptown 9th Ave elevated. Third car. For your
> price is far above rubies.

"I take it Sofia had dark eyes?" Behan guessed.

"Yes. But she never said anything about going into the city. In fact, she said she was . . . better here."

"Well, sure. You don't want to go around boasting of meeting strange men on trains."

I shook my head. Yes, Sofia had noted that you needed a man to have children, but this sort of flagrant flirtation seemed unlike the girl I knew. It was dangerous, for one thing. Girls had gone hoping for romance and found something quite different.

"I can't believe she meant to go."

"And yet she circled the ad. Maybe"—he caught my eye—"you didn't know her as well as you thought."

"I never claimed to know her that well," I said sharply. "She did want children and made jokes about needing a father. . . . Anyway, it's the twentieth tomorrow. We should be on that train."

"*We* should."

"I knew her, you didn't."

And, I thought, Behan wouldn't recognize any of the Tyler staff. Just in case one of them happened to show up.

Or . . . someone else from the Tyler household.

★ ★ ★

That night, I found Mr. Benchley alone on the porch after dinner and told him what we had found and what we meant to do. He made no objection, simply reminding me that I should call the house and let Bernadette and the cook know I would be returning for the evening.

"Or do you think it will be longer than that?" he asked.

"I don't know. We probably won't even recognize the man Sofia was meeting on the train, so it may all be for nothing." I thought of the chauffeur. "But if we do . . ."

Mr. Benchley disliked idle talk, rumination, or even pleasantries. Now he waved a hand to indicate he did not want to hear out any sentence containing the word "if."

"You'll keep me informed," he said.

It was a point of departure. Preparing my pleasant leave-taking smile, I was about to turn when Mr. Benchley said, "I have promised Mr. Tyler that Mr. Behan will not be making up stories that do not match the facts. You will of course tell me if it looks like he is breaking our agreement."

"Of course. Will Miss Louise be all right when I'm away?"

"Mrs. Briggs seems very capable. I'm sure she'll manage for a day."

I nodded. But the mention of Michael Behan brought to mind a question that had been nagging me.

"Mr. Benchley?"

"Yes?"

"How did you know Michael Behan wrote about the Black Hand?" There was no answer. "The articles aren't signed. How did you know they were his?"

Mr. Benchley brought his fingertips together and seemed to examine the neat symmetry of his hands. "Given my business, I have an obligation to know everything that occurs under my roof."

He had read my letters. The reality and the improbability of it struck me at the same time. For a few moments, I struggled. He was my employer. His business was sensitive. What I did reflected on him. Employers had rights, employers had . . .

I had rights. That alien idea came screaming into my brain. *I* had . . . my letters, my words, my . . . feelings. He had looked at those, he had read them. I looked at his hands on the desk, imagined them plucking the letter from its envelope, then refolding and sliding it slowly back inside, precise fingers moving over the paper like a spider. I tried to think: What had I said? How shaming was it? What must he think of me?

He said, "You're a very intelligent young woman, Jane. I'm sure you understand."

Praise, distracting and emollient. The lowered voice suggesting a confidence, even intimacy. Mrs. Benchley, his daughters—they would not understand. They were not sensible and intelligent. But I was. To me, he could admit freely that he had . . .

Read my private letters. I tried to get the anger back, grope my way back to righteousness and rage. But the flame had been doused—by praise. And the lack of knowledge as to how to express such feelings.

"Yes, Mr. Benchley."

★ ★ ★

That night, as I fixed a dragging hem before Louise went into dinner, I apologized for leaving her for a few days.

"Especially," I said, "since Mr. William is going back to the city as well."

"Oh, didn't I tell you?" I looked up to see her smiling. "He's not going after all. He said he didn't feel right leaving me alone, what with everything that's happened."

"I'm very glad to hear it."

9

Mr. Tyler did not question Mr. Benchley's assertion that I had to return to the city to fetch some things for Louise. He was the sort of man who accepted that women were strange, changeable creatures who felt sudden passionate needs for random objects. If Mr. Benchley said his daughter was inconsolable without her garnet hair comb, then clearly it must be brought to her.

O'Hara drove us to the train station. He and Behan immediately struck up that jovial rapport the Irish pride themselves on—saying absolutely nothing as if they were speaking with great wit and insight, simply because they said it loudly. I was on the verge of pointing out that laughing at your own joke for a prolonged period of time does not make the joke funny, even if you do your very best impression of a braying ass, when we came to the station.

The station was a squat brick building best known for its famous commuter, Theodore Roosevelt. The stucco on the exterior was said to contain actual oyster shells and inside, there was a large fireplace, which was left cold on this spring day. Mr. Behan went straight to the newsstand and bought several newspapers. Joining me on a bench in the waiting area, he examined each of the front pages. And then, almost as an afterthought, asked, "Want one?"

I was not a regular reader of any newspaper; whatever turned up in the kitchen did just fine. Not wanting to seem less well read than a six-year-old, I said, "Yes, thank you. I'll have the *Times.*"

He handed it over. "An excellent sedative for the trip."

We boarded the train. Mindful of my humiliation over Mr. Benchley reading my letters, I kept some distance from the reporter. Behan didn't seem to notice as he switched from paper to paper; he was either comparing or searching for a particular story. The *Titanic* still dominated most of the front pages. When he held up the *Herald*, I saw MANY DIED NEEDLESSLY; LIFEBOATS LAUNCHED ONLY HALF FULL.

As the train lurched into motion, I dedicated myself to the front page of the *Times*. There was election news and I decided I should be better informed. Not that I was going to march for suffrage, but it seemed . . . unethical to entertain the idea of voting and not have any notion whom to vote for.

I read:

ROOSEVELT WINS TWO MORE STATES

Defeats Taft and La Follette in Nebraska and Oregon Primaries.

Omaha, Neb., April 19—Theodore Roosevelt has carried Nebraska by anywhere from three to ten to one. Taft where from three to ten to one. The race between La Follette and Taft for second place is close.

Champ Clark will, in all probability, receive the
Democratic preferential vote. Harmon is a close second,
and Wilson far in the rear, according to received returns.

I read the paragraph three times and still failed to understand it.

Not wanting to show ignorance even as I tried to remedy it, I
asked Michael Behan, "Do you have a chosen candidate?"

"What?" Reluctantly, he looked up from his paper.

"The election. Do you like any of the candidates?"

He shrugged. "All the same, aren't they?"

There was an echo of Bernadette here; maybe I wasn't the only
one who found electoral politics confusing. "What do you think
of Mr. Roosevelt's challenge to Mr. Taft?"

"I think it's two blowhards bellowing at each other and Roosevelt makes better copy than Taft."

"So, you're voting for Mr. Roosevelt."

"Fine." His eyes were back on the newspaper. Stymied, I decided to forget the election and give myself over to the latest about
the *Titanic*. Taking up another newspaper, I saw a photograph of
an elderly, well-dressed couple.

MR. AND MRS. STRAUS GO DOWN WITH
ARMS ENTWINED

A vision of Mr. and Mrs. Isidor Straus clinging to each
other after the last boat was gone was revealed by Mrs.
Schabert of Dary, Conn., who, with her brother was
rescued, Mrs. Schabert had stateroom twenty-eight on the
starboard side amidships.

"Mrs. Straus had a chance to be saved, but she refused to leave her husband. As our boat moved away

from the ship, the last boat of all, we could plainly see
Mr. and Mrs. Straus standing near the rail with their
arms around each other."

I gazed at the photograph. She sat in a chair, he stood behind
her, his hand on the chair near her arm. They inclined toward each
other, in defiance of formality. She leaned sideways, he slouched
slightly. There was humor in his eyes behind a pince-nez, a small,
patient smile. She did not smile, but looked wryly at the photographer, eyebrow raised. She's impatient, I thought, he knows it
and without speaking, has reassured her it will be over in a moment.
They know each other well. They are happy. They are . . . together.
No wonder she had refused to leave him.

I heard Behan say sarcastically, "Let me know if you need a
handkerchief."

Suddenly aware that my throat was tight, I recovered myself
enough to say, "No, thank you," and distracted myself reading
about a doctor who had performed a special surgery on a lamed
Austrian boy to allow him to do something called a goose step. The
chance to join his friends marching on the schoolyard had improved the child's spirits to no end.

Behan went through the *Herald*, passing pages from one fist to
the other. "Ah, Moretti Sr. has another message for Charles Tyler."
He showed me the headline: MY BOY HAS A WEAK CHEST: *Sirrino
Moretti Worries over Son's Fate in Prison.*

Behan read aloud, "'I appeal to him as a father. He has sons.
Can he not treat my son with the same compassion he would want
for his own?' Says Tyler will have blood on his hands if junior per-
ishes from the damp."

"Is that a threat?"

"Sounds like one, doesn't it? They're operatic people, dagoes."

That word again. Why was it so difficult to object when something objectionable was said?

Scanning the article, Behan said, "He sounds like a man who wouldn't say no if someone showed up on his doorstep with the Tyler baby." He raised an eyebrow. "Maybe some low-level bimbo got it into his head to try and curry favor with Moretti by snatching the kid . . ."

"How is it you're suddenly an expert on Italians? I thought you were more interested in society scandals."

If he heard the rebuke, he didn't show it, saying cheerfully, "A neighbor of mine is a police officer. He's got a girl stashed in Woodside and occasionally finds himself hard up for cash. So he gives me a call when something good comes in."

"That's why you're not writing about the *Titanic* like every other reporter."

"That story'll be dead in a few months. I'll stick to my lovely murderous wops, thank you."

This time, I let silence speak. After a moment, he glanced up. "What?"

"I'm just wondering if that's your headline for Sofia. 'Lovely Wop Murdered.'"

"'A Pure and Blameless Girl of the Italian Persuasion . . .'"

"Why does she have to be of any *persuasion*?"

He peered at me. "You think the fact that she was Italian had nothing to do with her death?"

"Why should it?"

I waited for him to explain what he meant, but the conductor came through and announced we were arriving in Pennsylvania Station.

It was just after eleven, almost an hour before we were supposed to be in the third car of the Ninth Avenue elevated. There was a stop near Pennsylvania Station, and Behan had suggested we get on and ride until "our fellow," as he called him, arrived.

"Of course," he said as we walked to the station, "we may not know our fellow when we see him. 'Excuse me, sir, are you of Italian extraction?' 'Were you hoping to meet a young lady with dark eyes? I'm afraid we have some bad news . . .'"

"We don't know that he's Italian."

"Oh, now, that's true. Maybe Sofia found herself a nice home-spun American boy."

As we climbed the stairs to the platform, Behan asked, "Any idea what we do if you do recognize the man?"

"It depends on whether he's holding flowers or a bloody knife."

Behan paused. "You think we might be meeting up with her killer?"

"It's possible."

"Why would he show up? Presumably he knows she's not coming."

"This might be his normal route. Maybe he's a salesman. Or an engineer. I don't know, Mr. Behan. But whoever he is, he knows more about Sofia Bernardi than we do, so let's go meet him."

Behan did have a point. It wouldn't be easy to spot Sofia's suitor—or killer or both—on a train full of strangers. I could only hope he was obvious in his search for the dark-eyed girl whose price was above rubies. My hopes were not bolstered when I saw the third car was extremely crowded. The man could get on and off the car without me ever seeing him in the press of people. Behan and I had to stand for several stops, lurching and swaying with every turn of the train. I strained my arm to stabilize myself, focused my eyes on the front pages held aloft by men who preferred not to see me so they wouldn't have to give up their seat. Although, I thought, craning to see past my fellow passengers' shoulders and hats, sitting would not help me see better.

I grew more and more anxious as the meeting time approached. People got on the train, people got off. Anytime the crowd grew thick, I moved from foot to foot, trying to get the best view of the doors and cursing the fact that I was not taller. Behan was also watching the doors, but he stayed still, shifting his gaze from entry to entry anytime there was a stop.

The train pulled to a halt, followed by the now-familiar rhythm as the car emptied and refilled. There was a brief moment between ebb and flow when you had a clear view of everyone coming in, and I was aware of straining my eyes wide as if that would help me see more.

And then I saw him. Aldo Grimaldi. Dressed in street clothes—a nice suit, just what you'd wear if you wanted to impress a girl—he came onto the train, clearly looking for someone.

I looked pointedly at Behan and nodded to the chauffeur. I heard him mutter something profane as he realized I had been right and started moving toward Grimaldi.

But as he made his way through the crowd, bodies shifted and I was able to see a dark young man I had missed earlier. He looked panicked and was also moving hastily toward an exit.

I knew him.

The recognition came in a flash, an instinct with no information attached. Without thinking, I shouted something—*You!* Or *Stop!* Or some other single syllable of accusation. The young man froze, began looking to the doors. But the train was still moving and there was no way out. At the same time, Behan had reached Grimaldi.

The train slowed, stopped. The doors opened. Both men pushed toward the exits, Grimaldi shouldering his way through,

murmuring apologies. The young man was not as polite. He shoved
bystanders aside, leaping in a panic. Behan was close on Grimaldi,
who was moving faster as he neared the exit. I started pushing to
block the young man from leaving.

Grimaldi slipped through the door and began running down
the platform. Behan ran after him. There was a ripple of unease
in the crowd; what was going on? The young man made good use
of their distraction to shove past me—a cry of approbation went
up as people were jostled—and ran out the door. Calling, "Sorry!"
to the passengers, I made it through the doors just as they closed
and hurried after him. But he had too much of a head start and
my skirts made it hard to run. I continued to chase, but the distance
between us grew steadily until he made it to the staircase, knocking people aside and leaping four steps at a time. Frustrated, I
gazed down from the railing. As he landed on the street, I shouted,
"I know you!"

My voice reached him and for a brief moment, he turned in
my direction, then kept running.

"I know you," I said again to myself, furious that I could not
think how.

The differences in their employment made it easy for Behan
to catch the chauffeur: Behan was used to sprinting, while
Grimaldi, used to driving, was soon out of breath. Triumphant, Behan hauled him over to me, a broad smile inviting praise and
admiration.

"It isn't him," I said. "There was another man. He ran, but I
couldn't catch him."

Panting from his chase, Behan looked annoyed. He gave the
chauffeur a shake and said, "Come on, you. You made me run,
you must have something to tell us."

Grimaldi stood very still. Then in a sudden move, he threw his
arm up in an attempt to dislodge Behan, but the reporter held on.

"Why were you on that train?" I asked.

"I drive"—he waved a dismissive hand in the air—"the nephew. I drive him in."

No "Mr. William" in private, I noticed. "William Tyler is on Long Island. He canceled his plans."

Grimaldi recovered, saying, "He tell me to run errand for him. Because he cannot come. He tell me to buy something," he said vaguely. "A present for Miss—"

"That train was going uptown. There's nowhere on the Upper West Side to buy the sort of thing William Tyler would buy for his fiancée."

He smiled thinly, barely bothering to lie. "Private. Surprise."

"And you thought you might run into the fair Sofia on the way," said Behan, wrenching the man's collar. "Except of course, she's dead, so—"

"Don't talk about her."

"Anyway, it's not likely she'd be meeting a toad like you, is it?"

"I said you don't talk about her."

Shaking his head, Behan said, "I sympathize, friend, it's hard when a woman doesn't return your affections and you look like the back end of a baboon. . . ."

If Behan's intentions had been to inflame Grimaldi's temper to the point of violence, he succeeded. Taking advantage of the fact that the reporter was effectively single-handed—the other hand holding tight to his jacket—Grimaldi swung wildly, managing to land his fist in the reporter's ribs. Behan responded by swinging the Italian toward the brick wall. Shoulder first. Then head for good measure.

I had seen too many fights growing up to be panicked by violence. But I stood wary in case the fight was not entirely out of Grimaldi. He slumped to the pavement, cradling his head in his hand, the picture of defeat.

"Did you place that ad?" I asked him.

He grunted in bitter amusement. "Why would I do that?"

"Those ads are blind for a reason. Maybe you thought if you got her away from the house, she'd see you differently."

He stood, wearily brushing his pants. "No. I have no hope of that. Young girls . . ." A tired wave toward the pavement.

"Young girls what?"

"They are foolish."

Behan seemed ready to shove him into the wall again, but I made a motion to leave him be. "Why do you say that?"

Grimaldi straightened, pulling at his coat. He took some pride in his appearance, I noticed. "How about I ask you a question? Why are *you* here?"

"Sofia was coming here today. We wanted to know why."

He nodded. "Yes. And it is not the first time. Three times in the past few months, Sofia comes to the city. She says she is seeing her family. But when I ask, 'How's your mother?' she doesn't have answers for me. Just 'Fine. Good.'"

Simple answers meant to discourage conversation. From a girl who said she had no family.

"What did you argue about?"

"This foolishness. I tell her, I know what you're doing. I know you are meeting someone. She says I am crazy, there is nobody. After she died . . ." His face twisted and I felt a pang of sympathy with the ugly little man. "I think I know who it is who has done this. That man. So that night, I go to her room. I find newspaper, I see I am right." He made a circle in the air with his finger to indicate the ad.

"Who?"

"I don't know."

Behan said, "But you have an idea."

"I have no ideas." He gave the last word a sarcastic twist. "I come today to see if the *stronzo* comes . . ."

"Or maybe you don't really think he killed her," said Behan. "You just wanted to kick his head in now that she's dead and won't hold it against you. After all, he was the only thing standing between you and the girl of your dreams. Aside from your good looks and charm."

Grimaldi sneered, no longer intimidated by the reporter. I picked through the tangle of maybes, trying to find a truth. It was possible he had killed Sofia in a jealous rage, his suspicions confirmed by the newspaper advertisement, and now meant to kill his supposed rival as well. I glanced at his feet. They were small for a man. But the little man's face was running sweat and he was still out of breath from the chase. A four-story window would be difficult for him.

While the young man who had run, he had been quite fast.

I asked Grimaldi, "Do you have any idea who this man might have been?"

He was quiet a long time. "I don't want to say. I don't like to think."

His reluctance surprised me. "You don't think the man she was meeting had anything to do with the kidnapping, do you?"

"Evil gets in many different ways," he said cryptically. "As I said, young girls are foolish." He adjusted his tie. "I have to go. Mr. Tyler expects me back."

Anxious to keep him talking, I said, "Does he know why you came here today?"

"Mr. Tyler doesn't need to be bothered with these things." Before leaving he took a sudden step toward Behan, who instinctively backed up. This restored some of the chauffeur's pride and he walked away head high.

When he was gone, Behan said, "You believe him?"

"He seemed resigned to the fact that she didn't care for him. And he sounded genuinely worried about her, almost protective."

Actually, now that I thought of it, I only had Sofia's word for it that Aldo was making a nuisance of himself because he was attracted to her. Yes, he had seemed overly familiar as he approached her, but perhaps he had been nervous? And perhaps she had been foolish? The vision of Sofia wandering idly toward the woods, crooning with Frederick in her arms came to my mind. Alva Tyler demanding, "Why do you not listen, Sofia?"

Why hadn't she?

Behan interrupted, saying, "So, Grimaldi's not our killer—but he wanted to kill our killer. That is the general idea with them, you can never kill enough people. Big believers in eye for an eye."

I decided to ignore the anthropological analysis. "What do you think he meant by 'young girls are foolish'?"

"Fair observation—they're only marginally smarter than young men. Speaking of which, what about your man who ran off the train?"

"He must have been meeting Sofia. Why else would he run?"

"Some of them do, when their business is dirty. First sign of trouble that might bring the police, they figure it's better to be elsewhere."

"But he looked familiar. I feel like I've seen him before."

"They do tend to look alike."

I thought of what my friend Anna would say to that, regretting I didn't have her words or temper. I imagined her taking Behan by the arm and pointing to a passing Italian and saying, "Oh, yes, do I look like him? True, he is elderly and wears a mustache. How about her? Maybe you confuse me with that six-year-old girl across the street—we all look so much alike. Or my brothers, they have dark hair, just as I do . . ."

Brothers. Brothers. The word stuck in my head.

Then I knew where I had seen the young man before.

And he had, in fact, been attacking a woman.

I started walking. After a moment, Behan followed.

"Excuse me, where is it we're going?"

"Home," I told him.

10

About a year ago, I asked my uncle why I had never gone to school like other children. He answered, "You did. For one day."

I had no memory of this day. "What happened?"

"The children called you a whore." He began to clean his glasses. "They said you lived in a whorehouse. At the end of the day, the teacher told me it was best if you did not come back. She seemed to think it would be impossible to persuade the children they were wrong. Perhaps she agreed with them, I don't know. She didn't strike me as a woman who had much to teach anyone."

And placing his glasses back on his nose, he went back to his book.

I didn't have to ask my uncle why he hadn't just explained to the teacher that he did not in fact run a whorehouse, but a refuge where women would be protected from former employers while they learned the less dangerous trades of sewing and secretarial work. I didn't ask if that was why, whenever I stood on the steps, waiting for an invitation to play, other children gave me strange looks or giggled before running off.

Nonetheless, during the long summer days, the boredom of chores and the drone of adult voices drove me outside, where I would lean on the iron banister of the steps, idly swinging my foot, trying to look disinterested in company, which I understood to be the best way to get it. It was also the best way to look as if I didn't hear what children said when they ran by.

But one day, when I was about eight, a boy had marched up to the steps and offered a greeting. I noticed several things that served as warnings: he was a boy, a little older, and there was something in his smile I didn't like.

But maybe this was how play started, so I nodded.

In a bright voice, he asked, "How much?"

That was when I saw two other boys waiting at a distance, their eyes bright with anticipation; rather than being asked to play, I was somehow the game.

Still, wanting to be wrong, I said, "How much is what?"

The waiting boys squealed and jiggled in excitement that they had gotten me to speak.

The other boy rolled his tongue inside his cheek. "I got a nickel."

I still didn't understand the joke, but I knew this was not a game I was going to win. I started inside.

"Aw, come on," he called. "It's a whole nickel."

"But for all three!" called one of his friends.

There is something about mockery that renders you helpless. I knew I ought to defend myself, hurt them back. But I also felt worthless and foolish for being in this situation to begin with. All I could think of was how I might have spared myself this, what I shouldn't have done. I shouldn't have come outside, I shouldn't have answered their questions, shouldn't have shown any interest. . . .

The boy placed his foot on the stoop. His friends crowed, fairly hugging each other in excitement. He took another step and the space between us diminished very fast, along with the chance for escape. I was horrifyingly close to tears, which somehow I dreaded more than anything else, and when he grabbed my wrist, I screamed, "Get off!"

Just then the door to the refuge slammed open and there stood Berthe Froehlich, who had come to the refuge a few months ago. A tall woman with broad shoulders, big hands, and a pugnacious face, Berthe had plied her wares at McGurk's Suicide Hall, a saloon so violent and degraded that a number of its patrons were inspired to end their existence—the record was six in a single year, with seven unsuccessful attempts. Berthe was one of the unsuccessful ones. Having purchased carbolic acid with intent to swallow, she had bolstered her courage with several shots of gin. Unsteady on her feet, her aim poor, she ended up pouring the acid on her face. Part of her upper lip was eaten away, giving her a permanent snarl, and her chest and arms were mottled with scar tissue. From one side, she looked almost normal; the other half of her face was a purpled slab of flesh with one wild eye glaring out at the world.

The waiters at McGurk's were trained to eject suicides onto the street before they could expire, and that was where my uncle found her. He took her to the hospital, visited while she recovered, then brought her to the refuge. The other women steered well clear of someone so desperate and unfortunate, so Berthe spent most of her time in the kitchen.

Coming out onto the stoop, she held a broomstick, which she promptly slammed into the boy's head, knocking him backward.

Then she pointed it at all three and demanded, "Anyone else want a taste? I won't take your nickel. This, I give for free."

She advanced down the steps, swinging. The two other boys hesitated for the briefest moment, then ran off. The one with the nickel was bleeding from the nose. Clumsily, he wiped it, smearing blood across his mouth and chin. He looked dazed, unsure what had happened. Berthe told him, "I see you around here again, I jam this up your arse." That seemed to wake him up and he raced down the street after his friends.

Before I knew it, Berthe had pulled me back inside. Then she slapped me.

"Did that hurt?" she demanded.

My jaw and neck ached and I could taste blood. But tears were somehow beside the point. I nodded.

"Good." She crouched down and put gentle hands on my shoulders. "You remember that hurt. The next time you want to go out there and talk to boys, you remember that pain, how fast it came, too fast for you to stop it. You remember how hard I hit you because they would have hit you even harder and it wouldn't have been only once. You remember how unfair it felt, how mad you are. And you remember there isn't always going to be me or somebody else behind that door."

Confused, I stared at her until I understood.

"Can I have a broom?"

She laughed and said, "Later. Later, I get you a broom." Some of the other women were coming down the stairs for lunch. Seeing Berthe out of the kitchen, they paused in wary surprise. "Every girl needs to know how to use a broom, right, ladies?" There was general agreement, followed by a raucous discussion—most of which went well over my head at the time. But I remember that afternoon sitting at the table surrounded by laughing women and feeling that outside was not the only place to find friendship. The following day, Berthe took me into the backyard. Setting an old bucket on a stool, she handed me a broom and said, "For practice." I swung—tentatively at first. Then with more energy and determination, finally smacking the bucket off the chair so hard it hit the fence.

Of course, I did go outside again, but I never approached children in the street or expected an open smile. Which was fortunate, because it was not an open smile that I saw in Anna. It was rage.

The year I turned twelve, I had been pouring water over the steps of the refuge to wash away the stink of urine that in the summer months rose straight into the open windows of the front parlor. I heard a scream from a nearby alley; in an instant, the old, half-buried memory of a boy, his hand gripping my wrist, a smile that was all teeth, became immediately vivid. As did the fierce pleasure of that broom handle landing with a crack. My fingers tightened on the bucket and I ran down the steps and toward the screaming.

In the alley, I saw a skinny girl kicking her way free of two young men. I hesitated—should I rush at them, swinging the bucket, or simply hurl it at them? While I debated, she flung dirt into one's eyes and kicked the other solidly in the guts. Beaten, the men retreated. As I watched them go, I saw one was much bigger than the other; the second man was really a boy, with large ears and a soft child's face, wrists sticking out of a shirt that had grown too short in the arms. Aware that he was being watched, he glanced back, then continued on his shambling way.

The girl looked at me as if I were crazy when I suggested telling the police. The young men, she explained, were her brothers; they didn't want to work, but they didn't want her to work either. At least, not in a factory.

And then she ran off.

But she came back. All that summer, she came to the refuge on her way home. I was careful to let her in the back door, so she wouldn't be seen going into what many still saw as a house of shame, and we sat in the kitchen and talked as Berthe peeled, chopped, and cooked. Anna was the first person I had known to look Berthe in the eye and show no squeamishness.

I never took her farther inside the refuge, out of some odd notion that if the aunts who cared for her ever objected, we could say she had only been in the kitchen, as if that would shield her from corruption. But once we heard a burst of chatter as the women made their way out of a classroom, and she said curiously, "So all the women here are—"

"Were," I said, before she chose a word we didn't say at the refuge. Then the words I had never had a chance to say to anyone else came tumbling out. "And it's not what they *were*, but what they did, and not the only things they did. Some of them were wives or mothers or even had their own business. We don't say they were . . ." I trailed off, thinking this had sounded better when my uncle had explained the distinction to me.

When she left, I worried that would be the last I saw of her, that the reality of my life was too ugly, too strange. But a few days later, Anna presented herself at the door. Arms stiff at her sides, she said, "My aunts want you to come to dinner."

I stared at her. These were words I had never heard before; she might as well have spoken in Italian.

"Tonight," she added. "Now."

"I should ask my uncle."

My uncle did not say no, did not say yes. He simply said, "Do you want to?" and when I said, "Yes," waited for me to go.

Anna's aunts, Theresa and Maria, both lived on Bayard Street. They not only lived on the same block, they lived in the same building, albeit on separate floors. The two women hated this because meals were a shared endeavor and it meant one of the two walking up or down stairs with heavy pots and platters of hot food. There was a family story that once, Theresa's husband had had a notion of moving three blocks north so he might be nearer his restaurant. Maria had wept. Theresa had prayed. They both shouted. The move was never mentioned again. Maria's husband had died some years ago; she sighed, changed her clothes to black, and went on with her life.

Describing them once, Anna had said, "You know when two babies are born and they don't separate?"

"Siamese twins," I said.

"Theresa and Maria. Two people, but they share one heart, one brain. One dies, we're going to the other one's funeral the next day."

All blocks had good buildings and bad buildings—places owned by landlords who skimped on repairs; rented to tenants who were drunken, insane, or both; and let the structure rot around the people who lived there and paid money for the privilege. Some of the buildings did not have bathrooms, only one communal sink where all the tenants got their water. Anna and her family lived in one of these buildings. The front stoop had a chunk missing, the door lock no longer worked, and the first floor smelled sour. Apprehensive, I followed her up the dark stairs.

But then I smelled the food and heard the language as women called to each other, apartment to apartment. I had never smelled anything so rich, so generous. Anna took me past an open door on the second floor. Peeking, I saw a woman busy at a skillet and macaroni drying over a cupboard door. Then up to the third floor, where Anna held her arm out to another open door.

Once we were inside, she called, "*Zia Theresa, ho portato la mia amica.*"

Out of the kitchen came a woman, wiping her hands on an apron. She wore dark, heavy shoes and her hair in a bun. She had a strong face, with a long, Roman nose that ran between her heavy-lidded eyes and a smiling mouth of crooked teeth. She took my face in her large hands, patting and smoothing my hair as if I had been lost for a very long time and was now, thank God, home. In a low voice, she made observations to Anna I didn't understand. Then she pulled me into the parlor, sat me down, and returned to the kitchen.

"What did she say?" I asked Anna.

She rolled her eyes. "She's glad you're here, that's all."

Zia Maria came upstairs, shorter and rounder than her sister. Everyone was called to the table. Anna's brothers slid in, were introduced by Anna as "Carlo and Alessandro." I put my napkin on my lap to avoid meeting their eyes. Food was put on my plate and we ate.

And *ate*.

The meals at the refuge were filling, but bland, cooked quickly, and lukewarm when they came to the table. Meat, vegetables, and starch made hot and so digestible; salt and onion were the only flavor. This food had been . . . *created*. Not that the cuts of meat or the vegetables were of the best quality, but you wouldn't know it from the tenderness and flavor. There was macaroni in a sauce of red peppers, chicken cutlet fried in bread crumbs, and a dark green leaf limp and shining with olive oil. Carlo ate his food mechanically with his head down. If he remembered me, he didn't show it. Alessandro, whom the family called Sandro, tried to follow his brother's example. But every once in a while, his eyes would dart my way, meet mine, and drop again. The three women spoke in Italian; the boys didn't speak at all. I didn't understand the words, but I felt the emotions: humor, irritation, uncertainty, enthusiasm, sharp dislike. Carlo cleared his plate and left—for work, he claimed. Not looking at him, Maria made an inquiry. I heard doubt in her voice, but Carlo ignored it, slamming the door as he left. There was a short pause, then Theresa gestured that we should all go back to eating.

At one point, Theresa caught me staring, and asked Anna something. Anna shook her head.

In explanation, Theresa said, "You." Then she touched her ear and widened her eyes; I was being imitated.

"She asked if you speak Italian," Anna added. "If you understand."

I shook my head. "But I would like to learn." Anna translated.

"Me, too," enunciated Theresa. Then she pointed to Anna and began, "How—"

But that was as far as her English went and she said the rest in Italian.

"She wants to know how we met each other," said Anna. Sandro looked up, eyes darting. He suddenly seemed very small to me, with his plump cheeks and anxious expression. His ears really were ridiculous.

"Some boys were bothering me," I told Anna. "You scared them away."

She rolled her eyes at me, but she must have repeated what I said, because her aunt smiled and patted her arm approvingly. Sandro glanced over, but it was my turn to stay focused on my plate.

When the meal was over, I wanted to help clear. But as I reached for a plate, the women looked panicked and Anna said, "Nobody touches the dishes except Maria. They're from her mother and she loves them more than God."

Maria didn't understand the words but clearly knew her

niece was being rude. Tutting, she pushed my hand away and gathered the plates with such care they might have been baby chicks.

I visited often after that. They never let me touch a dish. But I didn't feel I could keep eating their food—and such food—with no contribution. So, I watched for my chance and after one meal, I quietly collected the knives and forks and brought them to Maria, who was starting her work at the buckets that served as their sink. I laid them carefully one by one on a cloth on the counter. She didn't say anything, but from the quick raise of her eyebrows, I knew I hadn't failed.

The next time, I was allowed to bring the cutlery and the glasses. The next, I was allowed to dry them. Finally, I was permitted to hold and dry the plates themselves, copying Maria's gentle, unbroken circles. When I said, *"Belle,"* she smiled in conspiracy: we knew what beautiful things were.

Anna complained good humoredly, "You never let me near the sink." Without turning around or breaking the rhythm of her strokes, her aunt explained why this was so. At the end, she said in English, "Jane . . . is . . . careful. She *cares.*"

I never knew if Maria and Theresa understood their niece's politics. They had never worked outside the home and neither of their husbands had ever been involved with labor disputes, as they often hired the latest cousin or friend's nephew to arrive in this country. When Anna had first started organizing, she had gone door-to-door in apartment buildings, knocking on doors and handing out leaflets. One time, she had come back with a blackened eye and a chipped tooth. After that, the aunts took turns accompanying her; while she spoke, an aunt stood behind her with a rolling pin.

But when I went to work for Mrs. Armslow, I saw Anna and her family less. Sometimes, when I did see her, we argued. She often talked about the one great strike that would happen when all the workers were organized. It would, she imagined, bring the city to its knees. I sometimes wondered which was more important to Anna: organization—the community and collaboration that implied—or bringing the world to its knees. Anna could be ruthless. If an effort did not contribute to the desired end, she had no interest. If it did, she pursued it with a ferocity of devotion that no lover would ever command. She seemed to have been born knowing what the world was and what it ought to be. At least until a year ago.

A year ago, Josef Pawlicec, an associate of hers, had pleaded guilty to the murder of Norrie Newsome, claiming that the young Newsome had been executed for his industrialist father's crimes. In the months that followed, Anna had had high hopes that the American working classes would be inspired by this act to rise up. But the working classes had given no sign that they were aware of Mr. Pawlicec's brave example, much less inspired by it.

This had led to a melancholy period of reflection; Anna was not used to doubting herself, and she liked it no better than any of us do. But she saw the necessity of it and dedicated herself to the task with her usual unflinching resolve. Over dinner one night, she confessed that perhaps she had misjudged the usefulness of violence.

"In some countries—Russia, say—when you kill a wealthy man, it means something. The people understand you have struck that blow for them, they see that the rich are not all-powerful, they can be fought. They understand that they are in a war and that there are sides. But in America, everyone—everyone, even the man who cleans garbage in the streets—thinks one day they'll be rich. They don't see Frick or Carnegie as the enemy, they see them as something they want to be." She threw up her hands. "So if you attack them, they see it as an attack on their fantasies of 'someday.' 'I'm poor now but someday, I'll be an Astor.' Insanity."

I decided not to point out that Carnegie had started as a telegraph messenger boy. "What will you do?"

She brooded, chin on her hand. "We have to find a different way to make them see." She glanced at me. "Don't smile."

"I'm not smiling."

In her search for a different way, she had left the International Ladies Garment Workers Union and joined the Italian Socialist Federation and the IWW. (I had suggested the AFL, but she snorted, "The American Assassination of Labor? No.") I had not seen much of her this year. Her body had been in New York, but her heart and mind had taken up residence in Lawrence, Massachusetts.

In January, textile workers in Massachusetts had opened their pay envelopes to find themselves thirty-two cents poorer. Since their weekly salary was usually less than nine dollars, and their working conditions such that one out of three workers died before the age of twenty-five, they felt the reduction keenly. By the next day, more than ten thousand workers—Italians, Poles, Slavs, Syrians—were marching through frozen streets chanting, "Low Pay! All Out!" What would become known as the Bread and Roses strike had grown increasingly violent, and hard-hit families had sent their children to families in other states to care for them. One of the few times I had seen Anna that year was when the first group of children arrived in New York and marched down Fifth Avenue. It was a powerful sight, these solemn little people, many of them gaunt from hunger and wearing red sashes over their ragged coats, and carrying signs that read SUFFER THE LITTLE CHILDREN and THEY ASKED FOR BREAD, THEY RECEIVED BAYONETS. I had wondered if Anna would take one of the children, even though she was unmarried. But she was not one for traditional bonds; she loved her aunts and uncle, so she saw her aunts and uncle. Her brothers she did not particularly love and she saw no reason to see them. And so I had not seen them either.

Until today.

11

I couldn't say for sure that the man who ran was that brother who glanced over his shoulder in the alley all those years ago. Anna was rail thin, he was round. But he had her eyes—dark, almost too large for his face. And the ears, I remembered those ears, the comical way they stuck out. And if I was right, only Anna would be able to help me find him. But first I had to find Anna—and that was not easy these days; ideological wandering meant physical wandering. I hoped to find her at the offices of the Social Labor Party, but she might just as easily be at the headquarters of the Italian Socialist Federation, or at a desk in Il Proletario—which was in Brooklyn—or simply out, organizing at a factory or arguing around a kitchen table.

I told Michael Behan he didn't have to come. In fact, I told him I did not want him to come. Everything I knew about both parties told me they would dislike each other, and if Sandro was connected to Sofia's death in any way, I wanted to hear about it without a reporter listening in. Anna's brother Carlo had been sent to prison two years ago. The oldest of the three, he had never liked America, often talking of going home. Even when he lived with his uncle and aunt, his name was seldom mentioned in their home. Now, on the rare occasion it was, a sadness came over the room. Her aunts went quiet, her uncle thin-lipped with anger. A store owner had been badly beaten and robbed. One evening at his restaurant, Anna's uncle had brooded, saying, "That's Carlo, always wanting to be the big boss." And Anna had said sharply, "The big boss made him do it."

I did not want Michael Behan putting his smudgy fingers on the Arditos' pain. But when I suggested I go alone, he looked suspicious and said, "We travel together, Miss Prescott."

Now as we climbed the stairs of the Socialist Labor Hall, he took in the banners of raised fists and signs demanding justice for Ettor and Giovannitti, and his eyebrows nearly reached the brim of his derby.

"I told you not to come," I reminded him.

"And miss the chance to hear the gospel of revolution? Not on your life."

Labor they were called, and labor they did. The hall was a busy, crowded space with each desk occupied by several people, one it seemed to do the work, and three more to argue over it. There was no receptionist, so I went from desk to desk asking if Anna Ardito was there. I was ignored several times, waved off three times, answered in German twice, Russian once—I think it was Russian—and finally pointed toward a back room, where I found Anna attacking a typewriter. I waited until she had struck a particularly emphatic period, then said, "Anna?"

She took in the sight of me. "Were we meeting today? I forgot?"

"No," I said as she came from behind the desk to hug me. "No, I have a question—"

Glancing over my shoulder, she said, "Who's this?"

He touched the brim of his derby. "Michael Behan."

"Are you a policeman?"

"I'm a reporter for the—"

"You look like a policeman." She turned back to me. "What's your question?"

"It's a family matter."

Before I could go further, she held up a finger and asked Behan, "What paper?"

"The *Herald*."

"Why don't you work for a real newspaper like Jack Reed or Waldo Frank?"

Behan massaged his jaw as he considered his response. "Well, you know, I might do if Mama's people had made a fortune in pig iron—as Mother Reed's did—allowing me to go on to Hahvahd. Or if Papa had been a shill for Wall Street, like Frank senior, I might have had the depth of soul to lick Villa's backside. But I'm afraid since my old dad was a typesetting tool of the capitalist machine, I'm just a reporter for the *Herald*."

I was about to tell Michael Behan to go interview the Russian when I heard a burst of laughter from Anna.

"Yes," said Anna, suddenly and shockingly agreeable. "You're right, they're frauds."

She stood, hands on her hips. "So, this family matter."

I realized Anna was expecting me to talk about *my* family. She had very little patience with anything Benchley-related, so I had to talk quickly as I told her how I had come to Pleasant Meadows and gotten to know Sofia.

It wasn't quick enough because she interrupted, "Why are you telling me about Charles Tyler's nanny?"

"Because she's dead," I said.

"Someone cut her throat," added Behan.

Anna looked annoyed that he was still present. To me, she said, "I'm very sorry the poor girl is dead, but what does this have to do with family?"

This was not at all how I wanted the talk to go, but there was no changing it. "Have you seen your brother Sandro recently?"

"I haven't seen anybody recently."

"How long since you've seen him, Anna?" She shrugged irritably. "How long?"

"A long time. We don't talk."

"What about your aunts? Do they talk to him?"

". . . Sometimes."

"And you never ask them how he's doing?"

"They tell me anyway. Why?"

"We know Sofia meant to come to the city today to meet someone on the train. I saw him at the meeting spot. Once he saw us, he ran."

Anna put up a hand. "Wait—"

Unfortunately, Behan chose this time to jump in. "Is your brother involved with the Black Hand, Miss Ardito?"

"Oh—" Anna snapped her hands in the air. "I'm not listening to this."

"So he *does* work for the Black Hand."

She glared at him. "Stop using that name, you sound like a child." She let her jaw go slack and said in a voice meant for ghost stories, "'The Black Hand.' *'Mano nera—'* It's an invention of the newspapers. Why not say 'boogeyman' and be done with it? Or is boogeyman not Italian-sounding enough for you?"

Giving Behan a warning look, I said, "How *does* Sandro make a living these days, Anna? Who does he work for?"

"I don't know." Her tone was bland; she was lying and wanted me to know it.

"Has he been short of cash recently?" Behan asked. "In need of money?"

"Are you?" she snapped. "Well, then you must be a murderer."

"You once told me he had a job working for a man on Mulberry. Driving a wagon . . ."

"Yes, it's a very criminal act. The horse is in on it, too."

"Who was the man?" I asked.

"I don't remember."

"You do."

Anna was a fighter; pretense went against her grain. Finally, she said, "I think the man was called Morello, Morelli, I don't remember. He sells vegetables on Mulberry, enough eggplant to buy a store. Sandro does deliveries for him, that's all."

"Might this be Sirrino *Moretti?*" Behan asked.

Anna ignored him, saying to me, "You think this young woman, because she's Italian, she was killed by gangs? Jane."

"Well, the baby didn't cut her throat," said Behan.

Turning on him, I said, "Mr. Behan, would you wait in the other room?" He looked mulish, but I gritted my teeth at him and he went.

I took Anna over to the window, let her gaze at the street below for a while. She looked defeated. She was too thin and I wondered when she had last slept.

"I don't see you anymore," I said. "I miss you."

"I miss you, too." She rubbed her forehead. "Let me guess, your friend writes about the Black Hand."

". . . Sometimes."

"Do you have any idea what those stories do to people? What kind of hatred they stir up? The Irish have gangs, Jews. But no, it can't be that people in a new land work together to make a living and protect themselves. It's dark, bloodthirsty men with knives in their boots. Mysterious symbols and funny names. Because just being poor doesn't sell newspapers and Standard Oil isn't a criminal enterprise." She sighed. "My brother is a fool. He isn't going to know anything."

"He'll know why he was on that train this morning."

"So, he was on a train, it's not a crime."

"To meet a murdered woman, that doesn't strike you as strange?"

"You don't know that's why he was there."

"Why did he run when he saw me?"

"Maybe he doesn't like you," she said flippantly.

I waited. Finally, she sighed, "I don't know why he was on the train. I don't know why he ran. I do know: Sandro's a nobody. Maybe he runs errands for this man and maybe not all of them are . . . what I would want for him. But murder? That's not Sandro."

Whom she had not spoken to in a long while, so how could she know? The thought came unbidden, and I did not give it voice. Instead I said, "But he may have heard something. That's the thing with nobodies. No one notices us and we end up hearing things we shouldn't."

"Even if that's the case, he won't be able to tell you anything." She hesitated, then said, "With bosses like his, you keep your mouth shut. That—he can probably do." Then before I could press her, she raised her hand. "And I'm doing the same and not saying anything more about it. Tell me, how are your Benchleys? The wedding. You're happy she's getting married to William Tyler?"

"Yes. Why? You're saying something."

"I just said his name." I waited. "I don't even know why I remember that name. Maybe because you used to say it a lot."

"I'm sure I didn't."

"He's tall?" I nodded. "With brown hair? How do I know all this if you didn't tell me?"

I had a sudden, scalding memory of earnestly informing Anna

that not all wealthy people were insensitive to the lives of working people.

"That was years ago, and I was very young."

Anna, who could be a generous friend, chose not to say it had only been two years. To change the subject, I said, "Louise is very needful right now. Nervous. I don't think her mother has prepared her very well for . . . married life."

"Oh." For the first time, Anna smiled. "I see. Wait a minute, I may have something for—which Benchley is it?"

"*Louise.*"

"That's right." Anna went to a filing cabinet, rummaged in the top drawer. "I think it's here. Yes." She held out a pamphlet. "*What Every Mother Should Know.* By Margaret Sanger. It will explain."

"What, that?"

"*That.* You weren't able to explain it to her?"

"It was difficult to translate the subject for that audience."

"But you understand the subject yourself," teased Anna.

"As well as you do," I said. Then wondered.

But before I could ask Anna if she subscribed to the theory of free love, she said, "Please. For me. Leave Sandro alone."

"I just want to ask him some questions."

"Sure. That's what the police say, 'We just want to ask you some questions.' That's what they said to Carlo two years ago. He's still in jail."

Tired to be arguing again, I said, "Your brothers were never good to you. I don't know why you protect them."

"He's family. All right? He doesn't know anything. But if you ask him questions, you might get him in trouble with the people he works for."

"Then he should work for different people."

"And that's so easy."

"Maybe I could ask the Tylers—"

But she cut me off with an abrupt wave of her hand. "Tylers. You have always been stupid about that family."

I went still as if I had been slapped. In the silence, I felt we were sharing an ugly moment of doubt as to our genuine liking for each other.

Then, taking my arm in a gesture of conciliation, Anna said, "Come, I walk you downstairs."

On the stairs, I asked her if the ISF would be at the suffrage march. Anna shrugged. "Voting. It's like some sort of exciting shop everyone wants to get into. Crowds of people, everyone talking about what they'll get—the riches! Then they get inside and it's three shriveled turnips and a dead mouse."

We were at the door. I was about to ask if she considered Eugene Debs an old root or deceased rodent when she said, "Don't listen to the reporter. He's just happy when he has dead Italians to write about." She tapped my forehead. "This is who you listen to."

Then giving me a quick kiss on the forehead, she hurried back up the stairs, leaving me to wonder when I would next see her.

★ ★ ★

I was still holding *What Every Mother Should Know* when I met Michael Behan on the corner. He glanced at it, and I stuffed it into my coat pocket.

"Let me guess," he said. "Karl Marx's latest. With color pictures."

"Karl Marx has been dead for nearly thirty years."

"What is it then?"

Angry—and wanting to be off the subject of the pamphlet—I said, "Do you know that was my oldest friend you were just rude to?"

"Do you know you have some very unusual oldest friends?"

"Do you know that's none of your concern?" I walked ahead,

saying over my shoulder. "She's the one person who might tell us where Sandro Ardito is."

"Not that she actually told us."

"She told us enough. If you were listening."

"Fine, where are we going?"

"You're not coming."

"Hold on now . . ."

He took hold of my arm. Furious, I wrenched free.

"Do you honestly think he'll admit anything to a man who earns his living making up horror stories about Italians?"

"Those stories are not made up, Miss Prescott."

"Oh, yes, you get them from your source . . ."

"Would you lower your voice, please?"

"*You get them from your source!*" I shouted, surprising myself. For a long moment we glared at each other as people stepped around and in between us. I felt foolish first, I think.

"Anna's probably right," I said. "Even if he does drive a wagon for Moretti, he doesn't sound smart enough to be trusted with more than deliveries."

"Smart's not what they look for. You ever heard the expression 'wild dogs'? Young fellows, just starting out, join a gang, do the dirty work until they show they can be trusted. You fetch the boss his coffee. Drive the missus to her mother's. You talk to local businessmen, offer up your insurance plans, lay out the premiums. If they say your services aren't needed, you break a window or two to show them what kind of disaster might befall them should they fail to sign. Or you blow up the shop.

"A year or so goes by and if the coffee's been hot and the missus speaks well of you and the insurance plans are piling up, you might get a promotion. You might be allowed to do some knocking in of heads. Or cut the occasional throat."

I thought of Sandro. He had been small as a child. I couldn't imagine him knocking in heads. Although it wasn't hard to imagine him being quick and light enough to climb up to the fourth floor . . .

"And we still want to know why he was on that train," said Behan, uttering my next thought. "But he's not someone you should be talking to on your own."

"I've known Sandro Ardito from childhood. . . ."

"What was he like then?"

Beating up his sister, I thought. Or trying to. It was true, that growing up, I had seen that Italian men were quite violent. So were the Irish, Jews, Germans, Finns, Turks, and Swedes.

"Come on, Miss Prescott," said Behan. "We're what you might call partners in this. Partners work together. They share. Besides, I asked for your help. Without me, you'd be sewing seed pearls instead of looking for Sofia's killer."

"The dressmaker is sewing the seed pearls," I told him.

"And . . . who is it, doing the dress?" His fingers came to rest on the pocket where he kept his notebook.

"You'll know after the wedding. Come along, Mr. Behan."

12

Finding any one man on Mulberry Street was not going to be easy. Doing anything on Mulberry Street was not easy, as it was not so much a street as a throng of humanity, horses, and wagons. To make your way through, you were often obliged to step from pavement to cobblestone and back again when the path was blocked by café dwellers, vegetable stalls, barrels of wine, or a fistfight. Some might have called it Little Italy, but they would have been wrong. Mulberry Street was Neapolitans. Sicilians resided on Elizabeth Street, Calabrians and Puglians on Mott. Nearby was the Church of the Most Precious Blood, which held the statue of San Gennaro, which was paraded through the street during the festival. It was also the place Anna had almost not been confirmed in the Catholic faith, losing her battle only when Maria refused to eat for three days.

Ducking his head under a row of dresses hanging from an awning, Behan muttered, "Sweet Christ. Are we still in America?"

Then, planting his feet, he said, "All right, Miss Prescott. You go ask one of these nice fellows where you can find Signor Moretti."

I could have been mistaken, but I thought I saw at least two men frown at the mention of the name. Or possibly because they heard a voice that was not Italian, something that aroused suspicion on these streets.

"Mr. Behan, would you do me a favor and stay where you are?"

"While you go where?"

". . . Shopping."

With more confidence than I felt, I made my way over to the wooden bins of vegetables that lined the street. If the man Sandro worked for made his wealth in vegetables, this seemed one place to start. There was little storage space in these apartments and shopping was a daily job. Women with shawls on their shoulders and baskets on their arms picked expertly through the produce, examining onions, peppers, potatoes—and eggplants. A few of them glanced at me as I approached, raising eyebrows at one another. I had no basket. They spoke rapidly—and exclusively—in Italian. When I reached for an onion, they subtly shifted to close ranks, protecting their right to first choice. I stepped back in a show of respect. And because I had to.

I had learned a little Italian from those dinners at Anna's. I knew at least how to be polite to older women. And so I tried, "*Scusatemi, signore.*"

One woman in a vivid yellow shawl pulled an amused face at her friend who picked up, then rejected a pepper. Me, she didn't bother to inspect.

How to say I was looking for someone? What was the word for looking? Maria was always losing things. Theresa would snap, "*Guarda!*" as she pointed to drawers and tables. To which Maria would answer, "*Guardando, guardando . . .*"

"*Guardando per* Sandro Ardito."

This got a swift shake of the head, either "I don't know" or "I don't understand." I repeated, "Sandro Ardito." Then looked pathetic. *"Per favore . . ."*

The first woman was growing bored and the second woman would not be distracted from her peppers. I would have to tell them more about Sandro—or the man he worked for. The word for work I knew from listening to Anna. Snatching up a long, slender eggplant, I held it up and said, "Sandro Ardito, *lavora per un uomo . . ."*

There was a burst of laughter from both women. Puzzled, I said, *"Guardando per un uomo . . ."*

The women just laughed harder, loudly enough to attract the attention of the vegetable seller, who inquired in Italian. The second woman gasped, *"Sta cercando un uomo . . ."*

She fingered the eggplant and I saw my mistake. My blush was immediate. The grocer clucked something—probably a comment about the size—and the women started laughing again.

Then, taking pity, he said to me, *"Che uomo?"*

"Si, che uomo?" echoed the woman in the yellow shawl. I had her goodwill now. I had made a fool of myself and livened her day.

"Sandro Ardito?"

I did my best to look lovelorn, clutching my hand to my breast in the universal sign of supplication. The two women looked meaningfully at each other. Finally, the grocer nodded down the block and said, "Banca Stabile."

"Grazie," I said. *"Grazie . . ."*

He nodded genially, another silly girl in love. As I stepped back into the street, the yellow-shawled woman held up a thick, purple eggplant half the length of her arm and crowed, "Sandro Ardito!"

I laughed, then put my hand on my heart in a sudden surge of gratitude for things that went beyond eggplant or a nod down the street. Things such as welcome, humor, generosity. And yes, eggplant and peppers, too.

As I passed by Michael Behan, he started to move toward me, but I shook my head. A woman whose ardor has become the day's street comedy did not need another man's company. I kept moving and prayed he wouldn't follow. The story of the eggplant seemed to be making its way down the block. As I wandered, craning to see above shoulders, dodging children, stepping over manure, and evading the animals who left it, I could sense smiles and nudges in the crowd.

There were many banks on Mulberry Street, so many that it was sometimes called the Italian Wall Street. People in the neighborhood often kept their jewelry, papers, and other precious items in their vaults. The *banche* held other things precious to the community—telegraphs to wire home, money exchanges, even wine—and people often gathered there to gossip, making it an informal employment and real-estate agency. Who needed a job done? Who was moving out? Who needed a piano? Who was selling a piano?

I was almost at the corner when I saw him, the man I had seen on the train.

Sandro Ardito.

He was standing on the street, relaxed, foot set on a crate, elbow resting on his knee. He was chatting with another young man in Italian, so immersed in that conversation I was able to get quite close. His friend noticed me first, nodding to indicate they weren't alone. Sandro looked up.

And ran.

Or rather he tried to run. The crowd that had followed my progress from eggplant to inamorato had gleefully anticipated this reaction and blocked his path. Sandro found himself confounded by a solid wall of people who wanted to see how it all turned out. I was pushed forward by a stout-armed woman. Tripping slightly on my skirts, I took his arm and led him away from our audience, holding his arm tight to make sure he didn't run.

"I just want to talk to you," I said.

"You're Anna's friend," he said.

"Yes. We met on the train this morning."

"So? Anybody can be on a train."

"But you ran," I said. "Why?"

"I guess I was in a big, big hurry," he said sarcastically. We were away from the watching crowd now and he worked himself free of my grasp. A year younger than Anna, his speech was more "American" than hers. He wasn't much taller than I was, although his thick black hair made him seem a bit taller. His face was still moonlike, but the baby fat had gone with regular work, and he was now stocky rather than fat. He stood, hands in his pockets, knee jiggling; the motor was still running.

"I was a friend of Sofia Bernardi's."

"I don't know a Sofia Bernardi." He looked relieved, as if he genuinely didn't recognize the name.

"She was supposed to be on that train this morning."

"Sure. Like a thousand other people. I gotta go."

He started walking back to the wagon.

"Don't you want to know why she wasn't on the train?"

"Why should I be curious about a woman I never met?"

"Then you won't care if she's dead."

Sandro stopped. Then turned, his face drawn and tight, his jaw set. "What?"

"The woman you were going to meet. Someone killed her. They cut her throat."

He went pale, the word "*Dio*" escaped his lips.

"You wouldn't be frightened if you really didn't know anything about it."

He was so still that for a moment, I thought he had forgotten I was even there. Then in a burst of panic, he leapt past me and started running down the block—smart enough, this time, to run in the opposite direction of the crowd. I was so startled, I did nothing for a crucial few seconds. Then I gathered up my skirts and followed, shouting, "Sandro, wait!"

Skirts, skirts, skirts . . . I cursed skirts as I ran down the street. Every stride forward, the heavy cloth swung back between my legs and threatened to trip me. Sandro was increasing the distance between us. I thought to call for help, claim that he had stolen from me, or even committed an indecency. But that could end very badly in this neighborhood, and I didn't want Sandro beaten senseless.

Stopping, I took fistfuls of my skirts and growled in frustration. A few men smiled in amusement. An elderly gentleman patted me on the shoulder and said something consoling in Italian. I didn't understand the exact meaning, but the implication was that it was a large ocean with plenty of fish.

That reminded me that there was a fish waiting, an Irish one who was unhappy in foreign waters. I made my way back to the spot where I had left Michael Behan.

Only to find that I had lost not one but two men. The reporter was nowhere to be found.

★ ★ ★

It was a long ride back to the Benchley house. The train was crowded with people headed home, all of whom seemed to have had a very bad day. Weary, I clung to the strap. A seat was out of the question; chivalry was quite dead underground. One self-described middle-aged man had written to the papers complaining of "skylarking, gum-chewing girls . . . who could better afford to stand" than he. "I harden my heart against femininity in general," he said, "and 'fresh girls' in particular." Right now, I was not feeling remotely fresh.

Questions swirled around and around in my head, occasionally catching on a detail or brief insight, only to spin off into further confusion. Had Sofia come to the city to meet Sandro Ardito? Certainly the chauffeur thought so, and a girl hoping to be a mother, stuck in the country far from her own people, might answer a newspaper ad. But the ad—and Sandro's reaction to the news of her death—implied that they had met before. Was he the reason she had come to the city over the past few months? It seemed likely. But a lover would have wept at the news of her death, begged to know details. Sandro had simply run. His shock at hearing she was dead probably meant he hadn't killed her. But his terror indicated he knew who had.

How would he know that? None of the answers I came to were comforting.

It was dusk when I got off the train at Fiftieth Street, the air warm and pleasant as the sun went down. I could hear the bells of St. Patrick's calling the faithful to evening prayer. As I neared the Benchley house, my stomach reminded me I hadn't eaten since breakfast. But food was not what called to me. Bed seemed a marvelous, wondrous thing. I would go straight upstairs and fall upon it. Possibly I would not even remove my shoes. First I would hide the pamphlet Anna had given me. I didn't want—was it *What Every Girl Should Know? Every Wife? The Well-Kept Woman?* No, that had to be wrong. Whatever it was, I didn't want it falling out of my coat pocket.

I opened the back door to raised voices. For a moment, I stood, taking in the sight of Elsie on one side of the kitchen table, Bernadette on the other side, while Mrs. Mueller peeled potatoes into the sink.

"The sheets are your job!" Bernadette shouted.

"*Ironing* them is my job," returned Elsie. "Washing them is yours."

"That's not what Mrs. Benchley said—"

"It is so!"

Probably, I thought, they were both right. Mrs. Benchley could well have said one thing to Bernadette and another to Elsie.

"Good evening," I said, and shut the door.

"What are you doing here?" Bernadette demanded, ready for a fresh assault.

"I work here," I said tiredly. "Elsie, for today, could you manage the sheets? I'll take it up with Mrs. Benchley when I go back to Pleasant Meadows."

"Missus will tell you she's supposed to do washing and ironing," insisted Bernadette, jerking her head toward Elsie. Dear God, I thought, you've gotten your way, be gracious about it.

"She might," I said, heading toward the stairs. "And then forget she said it. This time, we'll have witnesses."

I could sense Bernadette and Elsie exchanging puzzled looks over the table. I went upstairs to my room. Taking off my coat, I remembered the pamphlet. I took it out of my pocket and sat on the bed.

The title, *What Every Mother Should Know: How Six Little Children Were Taught the Truth* and the author's name were clearly stamped on the front. Despite the gentle title, I felt apprehensive, as if I were holding something obscene. I turned to the front page. And read:

> Every parent knows that at one day their little boy or girl
> will have matured into the possessor of the powers of pro-
> creating yet they fail to teach the child how to care for,
> or how to regard these powers they possess.

Mrs. Benchley to a T, I thought, encouraged. From the intro-
duction, we progressed to flowers, not the botanical item, but a
family named Mr. and Mrs. Buttercup and their children. The
Buttercups resided in the petals of Butterfly House. When the
Buttercup children expressed interest in how they came to be,
their parents explained that the "pollen" of the father, which was
stored in the father's "stamen," must get into the mother's pistil in
order to reach her seeds. Unless Louise had done botany at school,
she was going to find this more bewildering than helpful.

We then moved on to frogs and the story of the Toad family.

> Like Mrs. Buttercup, Mrs. Toad has within her body a
> little nest where little seeds or eggs have been kept and
> have been growing, and now that the time has come
> when they need awakening to a new life, they need life
> from the Father Frog just as the buttercup needed pollen
> from the stamen. Mr. Toad (or Frog), too, is stirred by
> this new and wonderful life giving desire within him,
> and when Mrs. Toad (or Frog) feels the eggs are to be ex-
> pelled, he comes very close to her, and in order to fertilize
> every egg before it goes into the water, he holds her fast
> behind the arm, and as they are expelled he pours over
> them his life giving fluid, which enters every tiny egg and
> gives it life—a new life.

"Comes very close to her" and arm holding did not quite cap-
ture the experience as I understood it. By that measure, I might
well have been fertilized when Michael Behan grabbed my arm
this afternoon.

I turned a few pages, thinking perhaps in the next section, we
might move on to actual people. But no, the next section was birds.

We learned about the spiny anteater, the kangaroo, flying squir-
rels, and finally, Mrs. Pussy Cat. In the last chapter, human children
were taught about their own bodies.

> They were shown charts of the human figure (both sexes)
> and all parts of the body were named in the same way as
> parts of the flower were named. Parts of the organs of re-
> production were called by their names in telling of the
> works each part performed. No special stress was laid on
> the naming of these parts, but simply, casually, as one
> would speak of the various parts of the eye, or any other
> organ.

At no point did Mrs. Sanger name these parts, much less explain how they might be used in the process of reproduction. I had
to stop myself from strangling the papers in frustration. Why was
there so much timidity in discussing the act that had brought
every single person on the planet into being? I pushed the pamphlet into a drawer and wondered if this had been an elaborate
joke on Anna's part. Stamens and pistils! What on earth had stamens
and pistils to do with the urges that made men seek out women?
I thought of the people on Mulberry Street, the women laughing,
the grocer with his half smile, the woman who matter-of-factly
shoved me toward Sandro. They all seemed so . . . easy with this part
of life. They thought it natural, not something to be turned into a
lecture on the life cycle of the anteater.

Also, I fumed, folding my arms, there was no discussion whatsoever of the feminine side of things. Maybe women weren't
plagued by the animal instincts of men. But to say that they—*we*—
had no understanding or appreciation of those instincts or urges
or physical . . . feelings, well, that was also inaccurate.

A little while later, Elsie knocked on the door to tell me supper was ready. I said I wasn't hungry. A short time after that, there was a second, harder knock on the door.

"Honestly, I'm not hungry," I called.

The door opened. Bernadette put her head in. "It's that man for you."

I went downstairs, avoiding the gaze of the three women, and saw Michael Behan waiting in the back alley.

As I shut the door, he said, "I don't think Bernadette cares for you very much."

"She doesn't care for anyone very much. Where did you go?"

"I believe you left me, Miss Prescott. Walked right past me without so much as a 'Wait here, I'll be back in five minutes.' What was I supposed to think?"

It was true—but not the whole truth. I waited.

"Besides, I had an appointment."

"With whom?"

"You'll see." He looked me up and down. "Can you do something with your hair? It's—" He waved his hand uncertainly.

"Why?"

"Because we're having dinner."

"I'm not having dinner with you, Mr. Behan."

"Well, that's true, because I've got enough money for one meal and Officer Sullivan will be the one to enjoy it. Still, I thought you might like to hear what he has to say."

"Is this the man who gives you the Black Hand stories?"

"It is."

"Wait five minutes." I opened the door, then turned back to ask, "Where are we eating?"

"Keens Steakhouse. The gentleman is partial to their whiskey and mutton chops. And it's four minutes now."

I'm not sure whether I took three minutes or six, but as I raced back down the stairs, I admired my own speed; it wasn't every

woman who could refresh her hair and day-worn clothes to something presentable in the time I had been given. There had been a
recent trend away from an entire change of clothes from day to night;
instead the transformation was achieved with jewelry, hairstyle, or
other accessories. In my case, miracles had been worked with a
quick wash, a change to my navy suit jacket, which was nicely snug
at the waist, and my better hat, a trim little thing, shallow, gray
felt, with a light-blue band and a feather in the back. I confess, I
was half hoping for a compliment, but all I got was a brief look of
surprise before he said, "All right, let's go."

We had gone about a block when Behan said, "Oh, one thing.
I lied."

"How so?"

"You won't like what Sullivan has to say."

13

Had this meeting occurred a decade ago, I might not have been allowed in Keens Steakhouse. The establishment had opened in 1885, catering to men's appetites for meat, tobacco, and their own company. Women were not permitted. But the steakhouse was near the theater district and had become popular with the actors (and even less reputably, journalists). In 1905, the celebrated beauty and former mistress of Edward VII, Lillie Langtry, had been feeling carnivorous, but the restaurant refused to serve her. She sued—and won—and Keens wisely capitalized on the loss by serving a special dinner in her honor. Langtry arrived in full splendor, sporting a feather boa.

As we went through the oak doors of Keens that night, I was uncomfortably aware that I was neither famous nor a beauty nor owned a boa. Thankfully we were seated upstairs where the clientele was noticeably shabbier than those who might be seated in the Lincoln Room—which was said to hold the program the president had in his hand the night he was shot. The gas lighting was dim enough against the dark paneled walls that we didn't attract no-tice. As we were taken to an obscure table near the bar, Behan whispered, "Remember the limitations of the Behan family for-tune."

At the table, a genial man with blue eyes and just enough dark hair on his head to save him from baldness sat nursing a drink and stroking his high, stiff collar. Though he was out of uniform, I knew instinctively he was a policeman. There was something peremp-tory about the way he clicked his fingers at the waiter for another drink; he had a habit—even a taste—for authority. Some might call it bullying.

The two men shook hands, the policeman grasping Behan's hand and arm as he looked me over. His expression made me ques-tion the suitability of my dress; I felt suddenly . . . overt as Behan held out the chair for me and I sat. Then he sat down next to me. He was broad shouldered and long legged and the curved-back wooden chair seemed too fragile for him.

Mr. Sullivan sat as well. "Now, who's this then?"

"We'll get to that," said Behan. "You've ordered dinner?"

The officer had not, and the next stretch of time was taken up with finding a waiter, obtaining more alcohol, and debating the merits of various cuts of meat, then deliberating upon the neces-sity of oysters. While this went on, Michael Behan ignored me, but I sensed that was a ploy to keep Mr. Sullivan's attention on his own appetites, and I made myself as ignorable as possible.

They were just about done with the waiter when Mr. Sullivan said, "But we're forgetting the young lady. What will you have, my dear?"

"I'm not hungry," I lied.

"Bring the lady a mutton chop," Mr. Sullivan instructed the waiter, pretending not to see Behan swallow sharply. At that mo-ment, I understood Sullivan's gesture was not for my benefit, but a means of asserting power over the reporter. This was not a man to be trusted with secrets; I wasn't one, but he could make one out of me if he wanted to.

"No, thank you, truly," I told the waiter, feeling some embarrassment at showing myself a woman who spoke to waiters.

But Sullivan said firmly, "And a mutton chop for the lady."

I felt Behan sigh in the chair next to me. Then perhaps getting his own back, he inquired as to the health of Mrs. Sullivan. The policeman who kept a girl in Woodside replied that she was just fine.

Then he said, "And Maeve?" He smiled at me. "Or perhaps I shouldn't ask."

"Just fine," said Behan evenly.

"Still the most beautiful woman at St. John's?"

"Well, I think so."

There was a long silence, interrupted when the whiskeys arrived for the gentlemen. Then Officer Sullivan casually observed, "I'm not so fond of talking unless I know who's listening."

I decided to take the burden of explanation off Michael Behan. "I'm a friend of Sofia Bernardi's."

Sullivan looked at Behan, who said, "Yeah, same woman." I stared at him, but he refused my look.

Sullivan squinted at me through the gloom. "You don't look Italian."

"I wasn't aware that was a requirement."

"In her circle, it was."

The chops arrived. Attacking his chop with a knife and fork, Sullivan raised an eyebrow at Behan's empty plate. "Something wrong with your gut?"

"Ate earlier," said Behan. But he looked mournfully at my plate.

"What do you mean, same woman?" I asked.

Tucking his napkin into his collar, Sullivan said, "He means you might have known her as Sofia Bernardi, but most knew her as Rosalba Salvio." He scratched at his cheek. "Going to be a mess clearing that up with the morgue."

Startled, I said, "Then you know she's dead."

He nodded. "Got a call from the Oyster Bay constabulary this morning. Said they were having trouble locating a Sofia Bernardi in the records. I said, Not surprising, there's no such person."

"And who was Rosalba Salvio?"

"Let's put it this way, I'm surprised she lived as long as she did."

He then made it clear that he wished to focus on his chop, so we ate in silence. I cut into mine—it was excellent—and tried not to notice Behan averting his gaze. His expression was martyred and I had the distinct impression he was praying. Over his objections, Sullivan called for a second whiskey for him, and a third for himself. Then he announced that a trip to the necessaries was in order.

When he was gone, I handed a fork to Behan and said, "Eat."

"I'm not taking food off your plate."

"Then take it off yours." I shoved the plate in front of him. There was a second's hesitation before the reporter cut, chewed, and swallowed five pieces of mutton in a manner I can only describe as bestial. Seeing Sullivan emerge, he slid the plate neatly back to my place. Then he smiled. Clearly the blood of the lamb had been restorative.

When Mr. Sullivan was at the point of paring the bone, I said, "Who was Rosalba Salvio?"

Sullivan flicked a look at Behan. "Doesn't she read your newspaper, Michael?"

"She's a woman of taste, Joe."

The officer agreed to laugh at a joke at Behan's expense and said to me, "You're familiar with the Forti kidnapping."

"I am."

"Then you'll remember that the police had a tip on where they were keeping the boy."

"Yes."

"A Samaritan who chose to go unheralded for his bravery— excuse me, I should say, *her* bravery."

"Rosalba?"

Sullivan pointed a fork at me in acknowledgment of the correct answer.

"Tell her how she knew where the kid was," said Behan quietly.

The lieutenant puffed out his cheeks. "Well, that's not a pretty story."

"I'm not interested in pretty stories, Lieutenant."

He did not like being deprived of his moment of chivalry and let me know it by taking his time. At last, he said, "You know the Morettis were responsible for the kidnapping, although we could only grab the simp son, Dante. Well, Rosalba Salvio was an *associate* of Dante's. She kept the kid hidden in the cellar of her father's grocery and looked after him for the Morettis.

"Now, you'd think a young man would appreciate a woman like that. But Mr. Moretti was a thoughtless fellow, careless with his playthings—he had quite a few, you see." He smiled thinly and I understood I was to be insulted. "And while poor Miss Salvio was stuck keeping an eye on the Forti boy, he was in clubs, often in the company of one Cecillia Repoli. When Miss Salvio discovered that she was only one of a harem, she decided to pay Moretti back by blowing the whistle on the kidnapping scheme."

I looked at Behan. From the way he sipped his drink, I could see he believed the story.

"Did Miss Repoli explain all this to you? Or was it Dante Moretti?"

"How do you mean?"

"I mean, do you have any proof that Rosalba and Mr. Moretti were romantically involved? Her family may not have been given a choice about hiding the boy. The woman I knew was very fond of children. She wasn't the type to stand by while they were mistreated."

"She stood by quiet enough for a month," he returned.

"It might have taken her that long to get up the nerve to report it."

"Or she might have heard about Dante doing the foxtrot with Cecillia Repoli the night before she called."

"But you don't deny she told the police where the boy was being hidden."

"No, I don't."

The lieutenant calmly ate his chop for what seemed like ages. My fingers curled around my table knife. Then Behan nudged my hand with his finger; he was right, it was better to appear unaffected.

But I failed, saying, "Did the Morettis know who reported the boy's whereabouts?"

"Good chance."

"Then it sounds to me as if she was killed in revenge. They found out where she was and killed her."

I had caught him in the act of chewing. He took an inordinate time swallowing. "Maybe."

"Sounds not bad to me," said Behan.

Spotting the waiter, Sullivan raised his glass to indicate he'd like a refill. My hand found the knife again.

The officer took his time with his drink. Behan said, "You'll be wanting to get home soon, Joe. Or do you have business in Woodside tonight?"

It was a verbal shove, and the policeman's eyebrows raised

sharply. Taking up his knife and fork, he said, "Michael, you said something about a window being left open."

I stared at Behan; how could he give that kind of information to a man who obviously liked to misuse his authority? He knew he was in the wrong, too. I could see by the flush of red above his collar.

"Window's left open," murmured Sullivan. "You have to ask how it got that way."

"You're not saying Rosalba still worked for the Black Hand."

"He's not a bad-looking fellow, Dante. You step out on a girl, sometimes it makes her all the more eager when you come back."

"But she put him in jail."

"And as her reward, she became employed by the man who sent him there. Taking care of his infant son. Quite the opportunity."

Seeing the outrage on my face, he tried a gentler tone. "To be fair, Miss, they may not have given her much of a choice. Tyler thinks he's slick, but it wouldn't take a genius to figure out he was hiding her. Once they knew where she was, they had her back in their power. She's got a father, after all. Maybe she cooperated to keep him safe. Then after she'd gotten them inside the house, they decided they didn't need her anymore and paid back an old debt. That's often the way with these gangs. Slaughterhouses, too. Keep the animals calm before you cut their throat. They go easier that way."

"So this . . . animal, you won't be looking very hard for the man who killed her."

He pulled himself up, stretching his belly, and sighed. "Well, we know who killed her, Miss Prescott. They've killed lots of folks, but we can only get them on so many. Good news is we've got one of them behind bars already. We're hoping he gives us a few other names. Maybe one of them will be Rosalba's killer. But the likelihood is, we'll never know. And frankly, I'm not so sure it's such a loss."

I couldn't restrain myself. "It's your job, isn't it, to protect people?"

"It's my job to protect *citizens*. Voters. These Italians, all they want to do is make money here and go back to their village. They don't naturalize, they don't vote, they don't become American. So you tell me: why should Americans do a damn thing for them?"

He drained his glass and dabbed at his mouth with his napkin. "That's all for me, Michael." Getting up, he patted Behan's shoulder. "Be a good man and take care of it, will you?"

Behan gave a grim smile. "See you in church, Joe."

★ ★ ★

"Disgusting. Contemptible. Arrogant. Bullying."

We were nearing Fortieth Street. Upon leaving Keens, Behan had announced, "Say it now." Three blocks later, I hadn't run out of invective.

"Gluttonous. Mercenary . . ."

"Now he's got his friends at Tammany to answer to and it's no easy task, keeping two women."

"Adulterous. And . . . and . . . *liar*." I stopped and faced Behan. "You must see that. He's lying."

Behan dug his hands into his coat pockets. "I can't see that I do."

"About Sofia being involved in the kidnapping?"

"She *was* involved in the kidnapping. The Forti one anyway. How else does a girl like that get noticed by Charles Tyler? Why keep her out on Long Island unless he felt her life was in danger?"

"Yes—her life *was* in danger, for very honorable reasons."

"Then why would she come back to the city to meet with a man who works for Moretti, unless she knew damn well it wasn't? Because she was back working for them and giving them exactly what they wanted."

He had it all worked out in his head while I was still struggling to reconcile the girl who had sung to a baby on the lawn with an accomplice of the Black Hand. Miserable, I remembered the last words she had said to me: "Yes, now you are here, but you don't . . . belong. You are in between. Not here, not there. Nobody."

"Maybe she was involved with the Forti kidnapping in some way. But not Frederick Tyler's . . ."

"She left the window open, Miss Prescott. Either she was un-believably careless or she was in on it. My bet is your childhood sweetheart cut her throat himself."

"Sandro was shocked when he heard she was dead, he couldn't have killed her."

"You don't know that he was shocked to hear she was dead. He might have been shocked *you* knew she was dead—and that you'd tracked him down. Or maybe he was worried he'd been caught messing with the boss's girlfriend."

"She wasn't Moretti's girlfriend, that's a lie."

"Oh, I see. Sullivan's a liar when he says things you don't want to hear, but he's telling the truth when it makes your girl out to be a heroine."

"Charles Tyler would never have hired a woman like that."

"What was it you said to me about Charles Tyler? Doesn't believe bad of the people who work for him? Strangely innocent, those were your words, Miss Prescott. Going to be quite a story, Black Hand Infiltrates Home of New York's Hero Cop."

"You can't write that."

He strode ahead of me, saying, "Miss Prescott, you have always shown a shattering disregard for my need to make a living."

"I think I show enormous regard for your professional reputation." That got a bark of laughter. "What will people say if you print lies about a woman who was murdered because she saved a child?"

He swung around. "They're not lies, Miss Prescott. They're not fairy tales or stories about boogeymen or slurs upon the innocent. It is true, there are many fine, honorable people among the Italians. It is also true that a group of them make their living preying on those fine, honorable people, threatening them, terrifying them, extorting their hard-earned money, and butchering them when they don't get their way. And you don't help the first group by insisting the second one doesn't exist." His voice rose to a shout on this last point.

I was silent, blocked as much by his argument as by the ferocity of his emotion. Behan also looked at a loss. Finally, he said, "Are you going to the Benchleys'?"

I nodded.

"I'll walk you."

We made our way through Times Square, which in the previous century had been known as Longacre Square. At that time, its bustle and hustle had come in the form of transport; the carriage makers Brewster and Studebaker had their factories here, while the Vanderbilts' American Horse Exchange nurtured the businesses of blacksmiths, stables, and leather goods. Also, manure. So fertilized, the ground gave rise to vaudeville, music halls, and the theater.

Oscar Hammerstein had been the first to stake his claim, with the Olympia Music Hall. Others had followed. We walked under marquees that announced John Barrymore in *The Affairs of Anatol* and an exciting newcomer named Laurette Taylor in *The Bird of Paradise*. It was not until Mr. Adolph Ochs decided that if the *Herald* could have a square, so could the *Times* that the name changed. Mr. Ochs had celebrated the paper's arrival to its new home in 1905 with an enormous party in the square on New Year's

Eve. Not as disreputable as its neighbor, the Tenderloin, Times Square still had its share of brothels, opium dens, drunkards, and thieves, and despite our argument, Mr. Behan stayed close and we chose our streets carefully.

This took us past a row of restaurants that served theatergoers before and after. It was between services, and the waiters were eating their own dinners or smoking outside. As we passed one café, I heard the scratch of a phonograph, then the voice of Enrico Caruso floating through the air. I didn't know enough Italian to understand it, but it was more satisfying not to be distracted by the literal meaning of the words. Caruso's voice flowed like a torrent, carrying the listener with it, spinning and dizzy and transported.

I heard Behan say, "Now, there's a funny story about Signor Caruso."

Wary, I said, "What?"

"This was about six years ago. A Mrs. Hannah Graham decides to take her little boy to Central Park to visit the Monkey House. They're watching the chimps, baboons, and suchlike and she happens to notice standing next to her a little man with an impressive mustache. He's also very interested in the monkeys. Suddenly— Mrs. Graham feels a hand where she shouldn't, and it's not her tyke asking to go to the toilet. She turns to the man and says, 'See here, what are you up to you?' And he says, 'Wasn't me, it was the monkey!'"

I laughed. "Did he get away with it?"

"Oh, no, they arrested him. Thought he was just some foreigner with dirty ways. Everyone thought the scandal would destroy his career. Only, the next time he shows up at the Metropolitan Opera, he gets a standing ovation from the assembled great and good."

As we reached Fifth Avenue, he said, "So there you have it. Beware men with mustaches in monkey houses."

"Thank you for the warning."

The mood had shifted, and it seemed we were friends again. Still, I thought of the article he was no doubt already writing in his head, the pain it would cause the Tylers—and people like Anna and her family. There would be no room in those tight black-and-white lines for good intentions or human error. It would all be viciousness and stupidity . . . venal foreign hordes versus American goodwill and gullibility.

I asked, "Do you really think Sullivan was telling you the truth?"

"I think I put three whiskeys into him, that should be enough for candor. You really think it's not possible?"

"Why kill her if she was in on it?"

"Revenge and to stop her talking. The Black Hand's hard on the people who rat them out. She double-crossed them once, why trust her a second time? They get her to leave the window open. Use her to tell them the layout of the house. Then . . ." He waved a finger in front of his throat. "Revenge on her and Tyler both. Would have worked out fine if Mabel hadn't sounded the alarm."

"And you think Sandro Ardito was part of it?" He nodded. "But why make arrangements to meet a woman he knew would be dead?"

"Could be Sullivan's theory about keeping her quiet." He was tactful enough not to repeat the rest. "If the baby had been kidnapped, suspicion would have fallen on her right away. This way they make her think they're getting her out of the Tyler house, giving her refuge. Could also be his sister's right and he's an idiot and they don't tell him everything."

I was trying to think of a way to refute this when he said, "You ask your friend Caruso about the Black Hand. A few years ago, a gang sent him a *mano nera* letter, demanding two thousand dollars. And he paid it. Guess what happened then?"

"What?"

"He got more letters, a lot of letters. Famous singer's handing out cash, you put your hand out, right? One gang asked for fifteen thousand dollars. That's when the great tenor decides to go to the police. They arranged a drop-off, and when the two, er, business-men showed up to collect, the cops arrested them. But I'm sure it's just a coincidence that they happened to be Italian."

"There are Irish gangs, too." Although the only Irish name that came to mind was Paul Kelly—who was actually Paolo Antonio Vaccarelli.

"The Irish? We're amateurs. Like shining shoes, Italians shoved us out of that business long ago."

Nearing the Benchley house, we saw a small boy with a batch of newspapers under his arm, yawning where he stood, eyes half-closed. Seeing us, he said hopefully, "Evening paper, mister?"

"That paper's four hours old," said Behan. Nevertheless, he dug into his pocket and gave the boy some money. Then he took all the papers and said, "Go home."

As the boy ambled down the street, I said, "I've never asked. Are there smaller Behans?"

"We're not yet in a position to afford posterity." He held out one of the papers.

I took it. "What will you tell Mr. Benchley?"

"That Mr. Tyler's judgment on who he can trust isn't what he thinks it is. Why—what would you tell him?"

"Why tell him at all? If you're going to reveal to the world that Italians are violent criminals and Charles Tyler is a fool?"

"This wasn't a vacation, Miss Prescott. I owe my editor a story. It's going to be a long night as it is."

"You're printing tomorrow?"

"Or the next day. 'She was a Servant of the Black Hand. They Paid Her in Death.' No, you need Tyler in there . . ."

"*Please*, Mr. Behan."

He took my hand, either in apology or farewell. "Good night, Miss Prescott. I wish Louise Benchley every happiness."

14

I don't remember climbing the stairs. I half remember shucking off my clothes, the sound of the newspaper as it fell to the floor. I recall gazing down at its pages, OUR TRIBUTE TO TITANIC DEAD: *Men Who Sacrificed Life for Women Lauded as True Americans.* Thinking I shouldn't leave a mess. Deciding it could all wait until tomorrow.

I don't recall lying down or closing my eyes, but I do remember the dream. In darkness, I had the sense of being weightless, spinning in emptiness. My skirts billowed and clutched my legs, my hair lifted from my scalp, my arms were heavy when I moved them. I understood that I was underwater, and just as I understood, I felt I could not breathe.

I reached up, fingers stretching, hoping to break through, feel air. But I grasped only water. I flew—raising and lowering my arms, looking upward to where the light should be, but saw darkness. My lungs constricted, my arms grew tired, and I floated.

I did not see them, but I became aware that my mother and

sister were somewhere with me in the dark. In my mind, I called to them, but they had been dead when they went into the water and could not hear me. It occurred to me that I might be dead, but surely they would hear me in that case?

A dark shadow formed before me and my heart grew even more agitated—bad to drown, worse to be eaten. But it was no approaching leviathan, just a human form with floating hair like mine. A man. The water stirred the edge of his coat, roiled his pant legs, I knew the cloth to be rough, woolen. Once I had held it in my fist.

His arms were out and I reached. I kicked, tried to get closer. But the more I moved toward him, the more he moved away. I flailed, swinging arms, legs, twisting in the ocean to catch up, not be left, left alone to sink. Even as I struggled, the thought came, If I reach him, we are heavier together, we sink faster, there will be no reaching daylight. And it does not matter anyway because there is no more air and everything aches.

Dying hurts, your body swells, begins to burst, the bones crack, and you hear your heart pound its last beats . . .

There is a point, I suppose, when dreams become too dark. Death comes too close, and the body rebels. And so I flung myself up, covers falling back, hand on my heart, which was pounding against my ribs. I breathed in once, twice, several times, to reassure myself there was air. I was in my room in the Benchley house, and it was only the middle of the night. Not in fact the fathomless depths of the ocean.

There was even a knock at the door. Elsie's twanging voice saying my name. I called, "Yes?" and she peeked in the door.

"You were screaming."

Yes. In the dream, I had been screaming. I could remember the cold, salt seawater as it rushed into my mouth. I looked at the newspapers on the floor. "I should stop reading stories about the *Titanic*."

"I think so!" She sounded Midwestern and indignant, like a farmwoman who has caught the hired hand doing something he shouldn't. It was a comforting sound, an echo of a simpler world where the forthright expression of disapproval is enough to right wrongs.

"I'm sorry I woke you." I tugged at my hair and rubbed my eyes. It seemed we were both up. I could see the pink of dawn out the window.

Elsie perched on the edge of my chair. "That's all right. I keep dreaming something bad's happening back home and I'm not there."

"You miss your family?" She never spoke of them, and I had assumed otherwise.

"I guess. They wanted me to marry this old man down the road. He was a widower, smelled like one, if you don't mind my saying so. I told them no, I'm not doing it. First time in my life I'd ever told them that. They said, Well, you're earning one way or another, so I said, Fine, I'll get a job."

"And you came to New York."

"I was so mad at them, I thought, I'll get as far away as possible and then they'll be sorry." She wrinkled her nose. "You're stupid when you're young, you know?"

The younger self she referred to had existed just six months ago. But it was true, there was a big difference between the Elsie who had first arrived at the Benchleys' and the woman I was speaking to now.

Then she said, "You know how it is with parents."

"I don't."

"Oh, you're an orphan, I'm sorry."

"Orphan"—that was a title that had never occurred to me. "I don't know," I said truthfully. "My mother died a long time ago. But my father might still be alive." I smiled as if I found the memory funny. "He left me on a bench when I was three with a note pinned to my jacket."

Elsie's mouth dropped. "You ever think of looking for him?"

I thought of the personal ad in the paper, the one Sofia had circled. *If the gentleman who left a child at the docks many years ago sees fit to make the acquaintance of that child who is a child no longer . . .*

I shook my head. Changed the subject. "So, it was no to the widower." Elsie wrinkled her nose and stuck out her tongue. "Would it have been yes for someone else?"

She ducked her head. "There was one boy, he liked someone else, though. I think they got married."

"I'm sorry."

She shrugged, then asked, "Is it true someone got killed at the Tyler house? Bernadette overheard Mr. Benchley talking about it on the phone."

One day Mr. Benchley would open the door fast enough and Bernadette would be out of a job, I thought. But the news would come out sooner or later; Michael Behan was no doubt typing it up as we spoke.

"Yes. A young woman in the Tylers' employ was killed."

There are two questions that follow such a statement. Elsie chose, "How?" first. I told her.

Then she asked the second. "They know who did it?"

"Not yet. People have different ideas."

"What's your idea?" she asked.

"Well, there was another employee there who was in love with her."

"But she didn't love him?"

"She did not."

"That happened in my town," Elsie said. "Willa Turner. Sam Burdock liked her and she went with him for a while. But then she started up with Daniel Meecham, and I guess she forgot to tell Sam. He got real angry about it."

"And?"

"Well, he . . ."

She put a hand to her throat and squeezed.

"He *killed* her?"

She nodded. "It was so sad. I don't think he ever would have done it if she'd—"

"What?"

Elsie shrugged. "Well, you can't go with two boys and think it's going to be all right. That kind of thing would make anybody mad. Especially Sam. He was the type who feels things real deeply. Willa should have known better."

"What happened to Sam?"

"He left town. I think everyone thought that was for the best. Daniel took it hard, and it must have been strange for Sam, seeing Willa's family at church, and them feeling bad. It was all just a . . . mess, you know? I mean, three lives were ruined when you think about it."

Only one life ended, though. I thought to ask Elsie why Sam received her—and the town's—mercy when he had killed a woman and Willa received none because she should have known better. But did not. I had woken her up, that was enough.

"Didn't the police want to arrest him?" I asked.

"Why? It was a personal matter, you don't want the law getting involved in that. Wasn't like Sam was a danger. Just love gone wrong."

Love? Love. The word echoed peculiarly; had Elsie chosen the wrong word or was I just strangely preoccupied with the concept these days?

Elsie's day was about to start, so she went to wash and dress. Yawning, I decided I needed water, directly in the face. Going to a small table where there was a jug of water, a bowl, and cloth—the Benchleys gave the in-house staff their own rooms, but bathing facilities were shared and down the hall—I poured out some water, splashed it on my face, and opened and closed my eyes several times. Then I wondered what Michael Behan was doing. Had he gotten any sleep or had he stayed up all night writing his article?

I had just struggled into my clothes when Elsie called from downstairs, "Missus on the phone for you, Miss Prescott."

Hurrying down to the first floor, I took up the receiver. "Mrs. Benchley?"

"Oh, Jane! Jane, you must come back—"

"Yes, I'm coming on the afternoon train."

"No, now!" she wailed. "You must come *now.*"

"Why, what's wrong?"

"She's done it! The foolish girl has gone and done it. I don't know what to do with her—"

"Done what, Mrs. Benchley? Who has done what?"

"Louise! She's broken off the engagement. No wedding, she says, not now, not ever! She's packing her bags—packing her *own* bags, Jane!—right now. Says she's leaving this afternoon, even if she has to walk to the train station. You must come now, Jane. There's not a minute to lose!"

15

And so I returned to Pleasant Meadows. On the train, I tried to fathom what had inspired Louise to take such a drastic step. Had the mothers finally pushed her past the point of endurance? Had William's mother said something unforgiveable? Or William himself? Her nerves had been so taut, even gentle teasing might have struck her as unbearable cruelty.

Whatever the provocation, I couldn't help feeling that the cause of the break would be Louise's terror of marriage. I had only been away for two days, but that could have been enough time for her worst imaginings to run wild. I thought of *What Every Mother Should Know*, packed under several layers of clothes in my case. I doubted it had the answer to her problems.

I stepped off the train to see that the distress call had gone out to others. William's sister Beatrice was standing on the platform awaiting the Tylers' charabanc.

As fond as I was of Beatrice, her history with the Benchley family was byzantine in its complexity and malice. Beatrice had been Norrie Newsome's prospective bride for years. Tall and dark, she shared with Norrie a contempt for the proprieties of their world. She had been a poor relation for much of her life; some people in that position learn to grovel, but Beatrice's spine was too strong. But mourning had taken its toll and what had been a lively, if cutting, wit had turned bitter lately.

We had crossed paths for a decade, and now she approached, saying, "How bad is it, Jane?"

"I don't know. I was in the city. Mrs. Benchley telephoned and told me to come immediately."

"I got the same call from Mother. She expects me to talk Louise into going through with it. Emily, too. I don't know what Mother thinks either of us can do."

Mindful of Louise's terror of the Tyler sisters, I offered, "Perhaps if Miss Louise felt certain of her welcome . . ."

"I can't say I do welcome her. I know she's not so awful herself, although scintillating conversationalist is not how I'd describe her. Ma may be thrilled at the thought of spending the Benchleys' millions, but the thought of seeing that vicious little hussy, Charlotte—yes, I know you work for her—at every family gathering from here on in, it's enough to make me want to move to Kalamazoo and raise goats."

I tried a different tack. "Miss Louise makes your brother happy."

"Does she?" Beatrice gazed out at the road. "I can't say I'd noticed. Oh, he likes swanking around as the family savior, but do you think they really get along so well?"

Choosing my words carefully, I said, "I think they both know what it feels like to be belittled by those close to them."

"Maybe they're just little people," she said flippantly. "Oh, don't look at me like that. I'm sorry. I know you're very fond of her."

Not before time, Mr. Grimaldi pulled up in the charabanc. We avoided eye contact, each of us acting as if our meeting in the city had never occurred. I thought of Behan's article. What would happen to him when it was printed? Tyler would doubtless feel the pressure to fire everyone of Italian background on his staff. That I could feel no pleasure at the prospect of Tyler turning on Grimaldi told me how much my thinking had changed in the last twenty-four hours. Maybe I could persuade the Benchleys to take him on. He would be an improvement over O'Hara.

As we approached the house, Beatrice looked up at the top floor and asked, "Is that where the poor girl died?"

Aware of Mr. Grimaldi, I said, "Yes, it's sad. She was a lovely person."

"Weddings do seem to end in death with the Benchleys, don't they?"

Beatrice was met at the door by her mother, who took her inside. I went around the back of the charabanc, where Mr. Grimaldi was unloading the luggage, and said I would take Miss Beatrice's suitcase upstairs. He nodded curtly and I felt a flash of guilt that I had let Mr. Behan treat him so roughly.

But as he handed me the case, he said tentatively, "Miss Prescott?"

"Yes?"

He sidled closer. "Sofia. Did you find out anything?"

His eyes were anxious, his tone concerned. Still, I hesitated, not wanting to share a story I was not yet ready to believe.

I asked him, "Do you know how she came to be working for the Tylers?"

"No, but . . . I guessed. She was frightened when she came. Always—" He glanced nervously around in imitation. "She was smart then. But she forgot. So, *they* killed her?"

There was something odd in his voice, as if he were seeking

reassurance. Why would the news that Sofia had been killed by the Black Hand be comforting? Then I remembered his phantom rival.

"Yes. There was no other man." He didn't need to know about Sandro Ardito.

It is to Mr. Grimaldi's credit that this did not cheer him especially. Almost to himself, he said, "She was a good girl. Thank you for telling me, Miss Prescott."

"You're welcome, Mr. Grimaldi. I'm sorry"—the apology was complicated, and I stumbled. "I'm sorry for your loss. And I'm sorry for how my friend treated you."

He smiled briefly, then got back into the charabanc.

Going around to the servants' entrance, I found the inestimable Mrs. Briggs in the kitchen. She was taking stock of the pantry, but seeing me, she said, "Thank God. You're to report to Mrs. Benchley *immediately.*"

"Not Miss Louise?"

She paused a moment to count jars. Nothing, it seemed, stopped the lady in her task. "Miss Louise is out at the moment. She is spending much of her time 'out.'"

This was unusually crafty of Louise. I knew there was little hope of an answer, but I asked, "Do you know what happened?"

"I couldn't say. You'll have to ask the mother."

And with that ambiguous statement, I headed upstairs—first to unpack Beatrice's suitcase, then to face Mrs. Benchley.

I found Mrs. Benchley lying on her bed. As I came in, she managed to lift her head from the pillow and whimper, "Jane, you're here!" I fetched a fresh cloth, patted it with lavender water, pulled a chair close, and spoke the words few dared say: "Tell me everything, Mrs. Benchley."

"Well," she said, "it all started with the music. Or was it . . . no.

No, we were talking—Mrs. Tyler and myself, oh, and Louise. We were talking about that poor girl, the Italian, and I suggested we tell the staff not to mention it to anyone before the wedding, and Florence, Mrs. Tyler, said, 'I'm sure they understand without being told that the girl's tawdry scandal is not to be discussed.' Because you know, Jane, that's how she is, she *always* has to have the last word."

"Yes, Mrs. Benchley."

"Then I said that I had been thinking that perhaps during the reception, we might make a plea for contributions to the *Titanic* memorial. You know the committee I'm on with Mrs. Borcherling."

"Yes, Mrs. Benchley."

"But Mrs. Tyler said we could never ask for money and besides, weren't we just saying death was not a suitable subject at weddings? And I said, But this is quite different. I mean, no one's ever heard of the Italian girl. And that was when, for some reason, Louise went to pieces and said we were all being horrible."

She turned damp, anguished eyes on me. "Can you believe it, Jane? Mrs. Tyler said she had no idea it was such a sensitive matter. Louise shouted—*my Louise*—saying, Of course it's a sensitive matter, a woman has died. And I said, Well, we know that, dear, and we are trying to decide the best way to handle this very difficult situation. But she spoke right over me, saying it was a . . . a mistake and false and we were all pretending."

I frowned. "Pretending?"

"I've no idea what she meant. The poor girl was hysterical."

Mrs. Benchley smacked the coverlet with her handkerchief. "And *that's* when she said she wouldn't go through with it and that if someone would tell William, she would very much appreciate it."

I took this in. "And has Mr. William been told?"

"Of course!"

"And he's spoken to Miss Louise?"

"She won't let him near her, the poor man. I keep hoping her father will come and talk sense to her, but he's in Washington, of all places!"

"Mrs. Benchley, where is Louise now?"

"Oh, I don't know. By the water, I expect. She seems to spend all her time there. Reading!" She uttered this last as if her daughter were one step from debauchery.

"I'll go to her."

A hand landed on mine. "Please, Jane. You may be the only one she'll listen to."

Walking down the hill to the edge of the water, I rehearsed what I hoped to say. The words "false" and "pretending" hinted that Louise might have discovered the . . . ambivalence I had heard in William's conversation with his mother. That wouldn't be welcome news for any bride, but especially not one as sensitive as Louise. Still, if the damage wasn't too great I felt I could persuade her that pre-wedding nerves were a perfectly understandable and forgivable error.

I found Louise sitting on the same bench Mr. Behan and I had shared. As I approached, I was met by Beatrice walking in the opposite direction. Catching my eye, she said only, "Good luck."

Louise smiled when she saw me. I said, "The latest petitioner has arrived."

The smile dropped. "Oh, then you're here to try and change my mind."

"That was my plan," I admitted. I looked at the ground. Louise indeed had been reading. *The House of Mirth*, as it happened.

I asked if I could sit down despite my plan and she said I could.

"Did you talk to Beatrice?" I asked.

"I did."

"Was she of any comfort?"

"She's not a very comforting person. But she listened." I felt the pinch of rebuke. "Do you know she loved Norrie very much?"

I did and said so.

"I didn't. Oh, I knew she expected to marry him and that she was disappointed, but I never thought of it as love. So, she and I have that in common. Loving someone even when you know you're going to lose them."

"Norrie Newsome and William Tyler are entirely different young men. There was nothing honorable about Norrie Newsome, and if Beatrice Tyler was deluded into thinking there was, it was an insult to her own intelligence."

Louise was silent a long while before saying, "And you think William Tyler is an honorable man."

"I do."

"Would you be surprised to hear that his sister disagrees?"

"No. She never had a very high opinion on anyone's character."

"Then would you be surprised to hear that I disagree?"

My silence spoke for itself.

Louise picked at her skirts, rearranged her feet on the ground. "That is, I think William is an honorable man. But I think he is also . . ." She frowned, trying to choose the right word. "Weak. He doesn't mean to be. And he's quick to admit his faults, almost too quick. But he has great faith in his ability to overcome those faults."

"And you do not have that faith."

"I would like to be clear-eyed. It's not pleasant, but far better than the shock that comes when you're not prepared for it."

"And have you had . . . a shock?"

"I have been made aware that William can disappoint."

This was impossibly priggish; all men—all women, for that matter—had the capacity to disappoint. Just as all men and women had the capacity to expect too much. I was about to say so, when Louise said, "William himself made me aware of it."

It seemed time for the bare truth. "What happened, Miss Louise?"

"I don't want to speak ill of him. He values your good opinion so much."

"Then he shouldn't do things that will lose it," I said. "What happened?"

She told me—and I realized that what I had on some level feared was true.

★ ★ ★

Banished from Louise's company, William had gone to stay with his mother at the Biddefords'. So I was denied the chance to tear his arm from its socket and slap him with his own hand, which was the activity that preoccupied my thoughts as I marched back to the house. His absence made me even angrier; the situation was dire, but not without remedy—if he tried. Fleeing to his mother was not trying.

It was a hot day, and I was panting slightly as I returned to the house after my unsuccessful talk with Louise. Alva Tyler sat on the porch, doing needlepoint. Dressed in a white linen gown, her hair high and proud, she looked more at ease. "Restored"—that was the word that came to mind. Here, I thought, was an unorthodox woman, who was also married and a mother. She lived with fears and anxieties, but she had not given in to them. Approaching, I said, "Mrs. Tyler?"

"Jane. Welcome back. Is it dreadful in the city?" She fanned herself with her straw hat. "It's stifling here."

"The air is better here," I said, walking up the steps. Alva Tyler appeared to be wrestling with a stitch in her needlepoint. She ran the needle through, realized it was still wrong, pulled it out, slid it back in. Her hand grew shaky with frustration as she failed time and again. She began pulling senselessly on the needle, as if that would make the thread behave. One hand clenched into a fist and her fingers curled around the edge of the frame.

"Can I help?" I asked. "Sometimes you just need a fresh hand."

Exhaling, she passed the frame to me. "I never have and never will be any good at needlework."

Untangling the thread, I saw that it was a circlet of flowers around the words "My darling."

"But this is so pretty. You must have some skill."

"Thank you. It's for Mabel. I feel so dreadful sending her and Freddy away. She doesn't understand why, and I thought perhaps if—"

"She must understand that it's for their safety."

"Perhaps what she doesn't understand is why they are in danger in the first place. But then, neither do I."

Then shaking herself out of her bitterness, she said, "Oh, look how you've fixed it, thank you." She took it back from me. "I shall set it aside before I do any more harm. Now, you didn't come to fix my needlework disasters. Did you find Louise?"

"I did."

"And?"

I hesitated. "I was hoping you might talk to her."

Alva Tyler looked surprised. "I can't imagine she wants to hear my opinion. The poor girl must be positively fed up with other people's views."

"I thought you might talk to her about what it means to be married."

There was a long pause as the hoped-for offer of help failed to materialize.

"Mrs. Tyler, you have a courage that Miss Louise doesn't yet possess. If you could just—"

Alva Tyler turned her beautiful eyes on me. "Tell her she needn't be afraid of marriage? Why shouldn't she be? I think it argues great intelligence on her part."

"But you and Mr. Tyler are so well suited."

She paused the briefest moment, before nodding. "We are. But I would not tell any young woman that married life is something to be undertaken lightly. Especially if she has a personal income and needn't rely on a husband for her support."

"From what Miss Louise told me, it was a lapse, but not an unforgiveable one. Mr. William has told her how much he regrets it."

Alva Tyler was quiet, her needle poised over the taut linen. Without looking at me, she said, "I don't find regret a particularly satisfying admission. I always wonder if the person understands— truly—what it is they have to regret. Or if they simply offer up their regret instead of admitting the truth."

"But Mr. William admitted what he had done."

She gave me a curious look. "Did he?"

I did not know why she should ask such a question. And before I could find the words to ask, Alva Tyler observed that the snapdragons would bring some nice color to the dinner table and the conversation was over.

★ ★ ★

That night, I asked Mrs. Briggs if I might have the day's newspapers before they were thrown away. She gave them to me with a small smile and the observation, "I thought I was done with such requests now that Miss Mabel's in Saratoga."

Michael Behan's article was nowhere to be found. Clearly, he was still working on it.

16

Emily Tyler arrived the next day, giddy and full of herself in her second semester at Vassar College. With the women assembled—Mrs. Benchley, the two Mrs. Tylers, Beatrice, and Emily—a picnic on the beach was proposed. "Picnic," of course, being the polite term for what was to be a full-scale intervention. Such a frank encounter could not take place near the house, and Emily was keen to see the ocean. So the ladies were driven to the southern shore.

When I first met Louise Benchley, she had described herself as a girl who hung back terrified as her bolder sister flung herself into the waves on summer vacations. That memory came back to me as I packed her swim costume and she sat on a wicker chair, tense and watchful.

"You have to be there," she told me. "Someone has to be on my side."

And so, with sewing as my cover, I took my place on the blanket, slightly apart from the larger party. The older ladies had not bothered with swim costumes, each attired in white linen dresses and large hats, which blew back in the strong ocean wind. The younger women had changed into blue swim costumes with white piping and stockings to hide their legs. During the polite chatter that made up the preliminaries, I gazed out at the expanse of water, wondering at what lay on the other end if one swam straight into the horizon. It felt at once impossible and imperative; no wonder people had been driven to cross oceans from the very first. Vikings in their longboats. Columbus, searching for the Indies. Today, the waves were high, gathering into a towering height before falling with a crash. The sound was tremendous, violent; it put me in mind of vengeful gods. Poseidon, Neptune . . . the Titans, offspring of the earth and sea, for whom the *Titanic* had been named. The sea was adventure, opportunity—and graveyard. My mother lay out there somewhere. And my sister.

But this was all loss, and turning away from these thoughts, I listened for the sounds of persuasion. The intervention had been delayed by Emily, who had either not gotten the message as to the purpose of this picnic or had decided to ignore it in favor of something far more interesting: namely, herself. Somehow between making daisy chains and dancing with the young men at West Point, she had gotten hold of something called sociology and someone called Durkheim, who, from her mother's expression, was not the sort of man she had hoped to be hearing about.

"You see," said Emily, as Alva Tyler passed her a small plate, "it's all about society and culture and a collective consciousness."

"Collective," said Beatrice, biting into a sandwich. "Isn't that a bit . . . socialist?"

"No." Emily was scornful, but I had the feeling that if asked to explain the difference between sociology and socialism, she would be hard pressed to answer. "What I'm learning about is what holds societies together, how we can be both ourselves as individuals and part of a larger thing as well."

"And how do we do that, dear?" asked Mrs. Benchley politely.

"Well, it's . . . shared beliefs and everyone agreeing that while we all want different things because we are individuals, we all want the same things as well and we all have a function in the group, a role to play."

"That's *pre-posterous*," drawled Beatrice.

"No, it's not. When something happens, you can't simply say oh, that's good or bad, you have to look at it in terms of society. What's normal in, say . . . Africa, might be horrible here. But the reverse is also true. And what we consider deviant now might be completely normal in a hundred years."

Alva Tyler's needlepoint became quite focused. Mrs. Benchley's smile rather strained. Beatrice reached for a biscuit. Louise dug in the sand with her toes. Mrs. Tyler was just about to open her mouth, no doubt to tell her daughter to close hers, when Emily announced, "He even says that crime is a good thing."

Gratified to see shocked looks all around, she added, "He says that crime can show us what's wrong with our society and force us to make changes. He says it's a way of challenging societal norms."

I was interested, but the other ladies clearly felt Emily had gone so far beyond the bounds of acceptable conversation that they were no longer obliged to even pretend to listen. Turning to me, Emily said, "Isn't it fascinating, Jane? To think even the worst crime could have some kind of societal benefit?"

"Benefit, Miss Tyler?"

"Yes. Because in an ideal society bound by common beliefs, everyone is happy with his—or *her*—function in the society. Aunt

Alva should be happy being a wife and mother, I should be happy to be a student, you should be happy to be a maid. But in a modern society like ours, people are forced to do work that does not make them happy."

It occurred to me to ask how happy the Israelites were building the pyramids in that "modern" society, but I didn't want to knock Emily off her stride.

"So, when someone commits a crime, it's an act against the social order that alerts us all that something is wrong. And that's how change happens."

Beatrice said, "So if Jane murders us in our beds, it means she wasn't being paid enough." She made a great show of removing the butter knife out of my reach.

"Maybe it means Mrs. Benchley ought to think about giving her a raise before it gets to that point," said Emily, smartly putting the butter knife back in its place.

Mrs. Benchley looked at me. "You're happy with your salary, aren't you, Jane?"

"Yes, Mrs. Benchley."

Beatrice argued, "So no one ever commits a crime for less than admirable reasons?"

This, as I understood it, had not been Emily—or Durkheim's—point, only that crime had a societal value. But Emily took the bait and answered airily, "Well, I can't say. What would cause you to commit a crime, Bea?"

"I'm sure nothing," said Alva Tyler.

"I'm not so sure," said Beatrice, glancing at Louise. "We all lose our heads now and then. Certain feelings are so big, you feel you must take action."

"I'm certain I've never had a feeling as big as that," said Mrs. Benchley.

"Really? How about anger? Envy. Or—jealousy. That feeling of being cheated. Someone taking what's yours."

As everyone could guess that Beatrice was referring to Charlotte's theft of Norrie Newsome, the silence was long and heavy.

Until Louise broke it, saying, "Jealousy is a terrible thing to feel."

Alva Tyler tied off a thread, breaking it neatly. "Which is why no woman should waste a moment on it."

Emily said, "Have you really never felt jealous, Aunt Alva? Uncle Charles is a handsome man. I've seen women fawn over him."

"No. I never have, and I never will." Mrs. Tyler kept her gaze down as she said this. "I don't believe in feeling emotions that can only do harm. Jealousy, anger, regret—what good do such feelings do? They just eat you up inside."

Rebuked, Beatrice said, "You may not want to feel such things, but you can't always help it."

"Yes, you can. If you want to." She looked at Louise. "If it's worth it."

I think Beatrice spoke for all of us when she said, "Well, I guess you're just cut from finer cloth than the rest of us, Aunt Alva."

"Aunt Alva for president!" said Emily. "Are you going to the suffrage parade, Aunt Alva?" she asked eagerly. "A lot of us from Vassar are going."

Alva Tyler shook her head. "I don't seem to have much energy these days. Certainly not for marching."

Emily's bright expression dimmed at her aunt's dismissal. Hugging her knees to herself, she turned and stared out at the ocean.

In the meantime, Mrs. Benchley had grown restless. Now she burst out with, "Louise, you simply must reconsider."

Almost immediately, Mrs. Tyler weighed in with, "You must remember that men are different from us. They're weak."

This was an uncomfortable reference to the girls' father. Beatrice flinched. "I thought we were supposed to be the weaker sex."

"Hogwash," said her mother crisply. "When it comes to women, men can be utter fools and it's just as well Louise learns this now."

Everyone looked to see how Louise was taking her "education." Thus far, with silence and flushed cheeks.

Now she said quietly, "I can learn it, but I don't have to like it. Or live with it."

Her mother gasped. The rest were quiet. No one knew what to do with this new Louise who had embraced the unorthodox position that her life was her own.

I said, "May I . . . ?"

A chorus of "Yes, please," and "By all means, Jane."

"I think perhaps Miss Louise is speaking with the wrong people." Remembering something Anna had said long ago, I added, "After all, she's not marrying any of us. What we think doesn't really matter."

Louise went pale. "I don't want to talk to William Tyler ever again."

"I think you have to," I told her. "I think you owe him that. It would be . . ." I tried to think of a word that might be compelling to this new Louise. "Dishonest not to. You don't have to marry him. But you do have to hear him out. That way, whatever you do, you'll know you . . ."

An odd phrase came to mind: "have all the evidence."

For a long while, we sat, each lost in her thoughts. Then Emily said, "The Babylonians believed the ocean was female. A goddess who gave birth to everything that exists." She smiled, her nose wrinkling. "She had a bad temper, though. Her children annoyed her, so she tried to destroy them."

Alva Tyler's needle missed its target. "That's dreadful."

"Is it? In revenge, her son chopped her in half. One half became the sky, the other the earth." She gazed up at the clouds, then stood up, brushing the sand from her legs. "I say do what you want, Louise. There's no need to marry if you don't want to. I'm going for a swim."

Her mother said, "Surely it's too early. The water's far too cold."

But Emily had already started to walk down the beach. After a moment, Louise got up and followed her. Beatrice looked at her mother, aunt, and Mrs. Benchley. Then she joined her sister.

★ ★ ★

That afternoon, Louise made a point of staying in her room, far beyond the reach of argument. I offered to keep her company, but she dismissed me. Which left me on my own to ponder the life and death of Sofia Bernardi. Or Rosalba Salvio. Other people seemed so certain about who she had been. What had happened to her. Time after time, I put all the pieces of what I knew together and hoped to see the picture they saw. And time after time, all I saw were the gaps and ill-fitting pieces. I needed more parts of the picture.

As I left my room, I told myself I was being ridiculous. I might not know her full story, but we knew who had killed the poor girl; as Michael Behan had said, just because people enjoyed reading about the Black Hand didn't make it fiction. And yet I kept walking, finally climbing the small, narrow stairs that led to the nursery wing. All the doors were shut; the quiet was mournful rather than peaceful. The silence of absence. The children's rooms were to be moved to a different part of the house entirely; there was even talk of Mrs. Tyler moving herself and them to her mother's in Saratoga, although Mr. Tyler was said to vehemently oppose that plan.

I went to what had been Sofia's room and turned the knob.

Servants' rooms were always interesting to me, as they were to most people who worked in service, as they were a sign of importance and prestige. When I had started at Mrs. Armslow's, I had shared a room with two other parlor maids. When I began attending Mrs. Armslow personally, I had been allowed only one other roommate; Mrs. Armslow's official ladies' maid had her own quarters and was addressed as Miss, as I was now. It was only at the Benchleys' that I had my own room. The space people made for others in their home said a great deal.

Sofia had been given her own room, but it was by far the smallest room on the floor; three of her rooms could fit into Frederick's, two into Mabel's. I noted there was only one small, round window; I tried to open it, found it sealed. I wondered if Sofia had preferred sleeping in Frederick's larger room with its two windows that opened.

Still, it was a simple, pleasing space. Snug rather than cramped, it was dominated by a large bed with a plain white coverlet. Nearby, an armchair covered in a rose-pattern slipcover. A sturdy dresser with a bowl and water jug stood to the right of the door. Opening the drawers, I saw that Sofia's things had already been removed. What lay here now were faded clothes—children's rompers, maids' aprons—somewhere between repair and ragbag. In another drawer, a wooden box of singularly hideous silverware, in another, cracked frames and abandoned needlework pieces. A search of the closet yielded the same sort of thing: out-of-date dresses, yellowing, watermarked papers, dingy shoes. Sofia's room had become a storage space for things the family didn't want, but could not yet get rid of. It told me nothing. Frustrated, I sat down on the bed and tried to remember the young woman I had walked with. She had been afraid, I saw that clearly now. At first I thought she was afraid of Aldo Grimaldi. Now I wondered. What had she said? All of a sudden, I could hear her voice so clearly.

"'*Oh, he is one of my people, I trust him, he's a good man. Good woman.*' *Once, I try to tell him, I say, Mr. Tyler, you want to trust this person, but—*"

Good woman. Had she meant herself? Had she been trying to tell Mr. Tyler that he shouldn't trust her?

I almost didn't hear the creak of stairs, but I became suddenly aware that someone was at the door. I stood up from the bed and the door opened.

"William," I said. "What are you doing here?"

★ ★ ★

He stepped inside the room and closed the door. "I don't know." His gaze fell on the bureau. "I suppose I wanted to see if there was anything of her left. I suppose Aunt Alva got rid of it all."

I asked, "Why did you do it, William?"

He met my eye, then looked away.

"I don't know," he said finally. "Why does anyone do anything?"

"That's not an answer."

He leaned against the wall, arms folded. "It was only—"

"Only?" Then I reminded myself people could not confess if you insisted on interrupting them.

He took a deep breath. "A few weeks ago, Sofia had put Freddy to bed and was walking outside on the lawn. She did that sometimes."

I had a memory of my first night here, the shadow in the moonlight. So, that was who the midnight walker had been.

"I was having a walk because I'd just had an argument with my mother about starting at the firm and I was feeling, well—"

I nodded to say I understood.

"Sofia said something like, what a beautiful night, and I said yes. Then she said she was having trouble sleeping because Aunt Alva didn't like the windows open and there was no air. She admitted sometimes she felt a bit trapped in the house and I said I knew how she felt. And we started talking. It was nice. Like talking to you, Jane. I told her I didn't really want to practice law and she asked why I had to, if I was—"

Here he went red.

"Marrying a wealthy woman?" I guessed.

"Yes. Then she said, Oh, but maybe you don't want to marry this woman. I told her that was not the case, that I loved Louise very much. Only—"

"Only" was fast becoming my least favorite word. Why did men not understand that the moment you tell another woman you love someone very much, *only*—the other woman sees an opportunity? Or did they understand that very well?

As if sensing my disapproval, William lifted himself off the wall, then fell against it in frustration. "I've never done anything, Jane! Nothing that *I* decided to do, nothing I wasn't supposed to do. Look at Uncle Charles. He hasn't done a single thing he was supposed to and has done loads of things he wasn't, and he's a genuine success, his own man. When I was a boy, I wanted to be just like him."

He dropped his head. "I guess I'm not quite ready to give that up yet."

"You don't have to," I said.

"Don't I? What sort of husband am I if I go flying across the country or join a polar expedition? If I say, No, sorry, I'm not going to be a lawyer, I'm going out west and shooting buffalo instead."

William was never going to do those things and Louise was not the reason. But now was not the time to tell him that. "Then what happened?"

"So, then I was an idiot and said, Do you know, Louise is the only girl I've ever kissed? And she said, Well, that's not right, kiss me, I'll tell you if you're doing it right."

William's shoe made a long progress along the floor.

"So . . . I did."

I didn't want to ask the extent of the experiment; I could guess it was somewhere between a friendly peck and full-blown indecency on the Tylers' lawn. I wasn't surprised. Men often gave up their freedom with a last dalliance. We had never expected it of William because he had always been the safe, dutiful—and poor— Tyler boy. Despite more romantic inclinations, he had done exactly as his family wanted, followed his uncle's prescriptions on how to behave as a proper gentleman, and stayed unfailingly courteous in the face of provocation and foolishness. At parties, he was a great favorite of women over fifty and avoided by girls under twenty-one. A word often used to describe him was "kind"; I used it myself.

And just as I had wished to be more like Alva Tyler, he yearned to be a heroic man of action like his uncle. Those men and women don't always think of others. And those men and women break rules; it was part of what made them so wonderful and daring.

But I wished with all my heart William had joined the rodeo rather than make love to Sofia.

"I see," I said, aware that I was absolving him with those two words. "But why tell Miss Louise?"

"I didn't. Someone must have seen us—or guessed—and decided Louise deserved to know the truth."

I would have to ask Louise who had been so kind as to deliver the news. And then, if possible, wring that person's neck.

"Your trip to the city, the one you decided not to take—it wasn't to meet Sofia, was it?"

"No!" He looked genuinely shocked, then sheepish. "I was

supposed to have lunch with one of the partners at the firm. Mother arranged it, even though I told her I wasn't certain I wanted to go into law. Said my personal sentiments didn't matter. Then when Sofia . . . died, I told myself, Well, with everything that's happened and Louise needing me so much, I certainly can't leave now. The partner phoned Mother and told her I hadn't shown up. She wasn't happy with me."

Remembering the argument, I felt a wave of relief that William had not been balking at marriage to Louise, but at a future as a lawyer. Still, I reminded myself, he had given her grounds for doubt.

"William, do you want to marry Louise?"

"Of course."

"Don't say of course, tell me why."

"Because . . . she's lovely and . . . kind. . . ."

"No, tell me why. Truly. You can say it's the money."

He looked at me curiously. Then said, "Well, that helps. But I don't feel alone when I'm with Louise. I feel she's on my side. Even if she doesn't say anything, I feel it. And I feel, well, I can't be so useless if such a person thinks well of me."

"She thinks the world of you."

"Then why won't she talk to me? I've told her I'm sorry for what I did."

Did he? Alva Tyler's odd little question drifted through my mind. She doubted . . . what? Should I also doubt?

"I know I've hurt her, badly, but she must know it would never happen again."

He sounded sincere, was sincere. Uneasy, I thought there was a chance Louise knew him better than he knew himself. But he wanted to make it right. And didn't he deserve a chance to try?

I said, "You'll tell Louise it was only the one lapse? That she's the only girl in the world that you care for?"

There was a fraction of hesitation. "Yes, of course."

"Let me talk to her."

★ ★ ★

I intended to talk to Louise after dinner that night. But early that evening, she announced she would be returning to the city. To think, she said.

17

The next morning, Mrs. Benchley announced she was not yet ready to leave. The reasons for delay were unclear. I had packed her trunk, but she felt certain something was missing. Then she felt unwell, either the head or stomach, she wasn't sure. Then she worried that the train would arrive at midday and the streets were crowded at midday, would it not be better to arrive later in the afternoon? But before people left work . . . oh, perhaps it would be best to simply travel the next day.

To which Louise replied that she understood her mother's worry. But she herself would be leaving as planned.

Louise's lack of compliance upset her mother's sense of the universal order to a degree that she had to lie down and it was agreed she would travel tomorrow. In the meantime, Louise and I left for the station.

"Good," she said on the drive. "Now you can have Mother's seat."

As I settled her case on the train, it was hard not to remember the way William had taken charge on the journey out. Louise must have been thinking the same thing because as the train lurched into motion, she said, "William wanted to accompany us to the station. I said I would rather he didn't. It would just make it more difficult."

The difficulty remained unspecified, and I asked, "To end the engagement?"

"To . . . decide." She looked troubled. "Has William said anything to you?"

"He has."

"And?"

She listened to my report without speaking, her eyes averted, her thoughts her own. I finished by saying, "I believe he loves you. And means it when he says he would not hurt you again."

She looked at me, hopeful, and I had to add, "But I also believe he is young and possibly naïve. About the world and himself. You have to ask yourself: can you bear to see him fail again?"

I had asked the right, cruel question. Louise's face creased with misery. "I don't know."

"Then can you bear to give him up?"

"I don't know."

"Well, then." I hesitated. "My apologies for being crass—but the marriage would give you a firm place in society. You would be Mrs. William Tyler."

"And who is that?" She settled back in her seat restlessly. "Who is Louise Benchley, except the girl who married William Tyler? William thinks he hasn't done enough. Well, I haven't done anything."

Stunned by this display of ambition, I said, "What do you want to do?"

"That's the problem: I can't think of anything to do and it's so horrible for women if they're not married."

I looked out the window at the world rushing past. Turning back to Louise, I said, "Well, why should it be horrible? We can't be the only ones not to marry. We should look at this differently. We could do all sorts of things married women can't. We could sail down the Amazon River. Or go on a trek to the South Pole. I think there's one leaving in May. Or we could study forensic science in Paris or . . ." My imagination was failing me. "Break wind!" I finished triumphantly.

Louise gave a shocked scream of laughter. Several passengers glanced at us.

Lowering my voice, I said, "The point is, you are a woman of great means . . ."

"But small intelligence."

I pretended to glare. "And even though I am a woman of small means . . ."

"But great intelligence."

"There are many, many things we might do, Miss Louise. Many things."

She smiled. "I like that."

For a while, she gazed out the window as if it offered a view of her future. At one point, she said, "Jane?"

"Yes, Miss Louise?"

But she decided the question wasn't worth asking and she shook her head. I thought to ask her how she had found out about William's dalliance. But I didn't want to plunge her back into unhappy memories.

I did notice that in all our talk of the future, Louise hadn't once asked me to stay with her. What would I do if she decided to marry William—but did not ask me to join their household staff? Would I stay with Charlotte? That didn't feel like a secure position. The murkiest question of all: What did I want?

If she does not ask me, I thought, I will go back to my uncle's house. I will work for him. I will not be paid. And that will be my life. I tried to persuade myself this was a good future, a safe future. It felt like defeat.

Mrs. Benchley had been right to worry about the noonday crowds. We had to struggle through the station out to the street, where O'Hara waited with the car, and it was a slow journey to the Benchley house. Louise looked weary by the time we arrived; I was trying to decide between recommendations for various forms of oblivion—a nap, tea, bath—when the front door opened and Charlotte appeared.

"You ninny," was how she greeted her sister.

★ ★ ★

I was dismissed—only for the rest of the day, but the chill in Charlotte's tone suggested that if she had her way, I would be out the door and on the street. In contravention of legal procedure, I was not informed as to the nature of my crime, but I guessed it was either the failure to shepherd Louise to the altar or setting her on the path to begin with. In short, I was a free woman for the afternoon. It didn't make me happy. Charlotte's displeasure reminded me what future employment with her would be like. I wandered downstairs where I heard the drag, thump, drag, thump of the cleaner and the increasingly aggressive sighs that went with it. Then a crash. Then a curse. Bernadette had done battle with the vacuum cleaner—and lost, from the sound of it.

Going to the parlor, I saw Bernadette breathing heavily and glaring at a broken plate as she nursed a cut on her thumb. In words eloquent and profane, she assessed the situation.

I was about to suggest a new cleaner or reverting to the old practice of sweeping and beating, when I realized something. Bernadette's problems went beyond method.

"You should quit."

Still sucking the blood from her thumb, she looked at me, astonished.

"You're too smart for this job. You shouldn't be doing it." Kneeling, I began picking up the pieces of the shattered plate. "You're bored and it makes you destructive. Do something else."

I was being very blunt with a woman I might have to work with for years. And Bernadette relished insult as a soldier relishes the clarion call of the trumpet to battle. I braced myself.

But Bernadette slowly released her grip on the cleaner and sat down on Mrs. Benchley's hassock. "Who would hire me?" she said. "And to do what? I stopped school at ten."

"You're smart, Bernadette. You'd find something. My uncle trains lots of women for new work."

"I'm not the same as them," she said, appalled that I would compare her to women who had once been prostitutes.

"You need new work, don't you? Well, don't you? If they can become secretaries and telephone operators, why can't you?"

I stood up with the broken pieces. "I'll throw these away in the kitchen."

I went to the kitchen, where I found Mrs. Mueller scrubbing pots. Nodding to a collection of envelopes on the table, she said, "Pay day." I gathered my envelope, put it in my pocket.

The day's newspapers were also on the table. Among them, the *Herald*. Michael Behan's article. It must be printed by now. Maybe it had taken him a day longer, but he was a quick writer with a good story. I picked up the paper, expecting to see a scorching headline: BLACK HAND WHORE DIES IN CHARLES TYLER'S HOME!

The front page, it would be on the front page. Or . . . perhaps not, I thought as I studied the headlines and found no mention of Charles Tyler or the Black Hand. I turned several more pages. And breathed a sigh of relief. It seemed Michael Behan was still writing his story.

Which meant there might be time to change his mind.

"Mrs. Mueller," I said, "I'm going out."

* * *

I didn't know what Sandro's regular delivery route was, or if he even had one. But Mulberry Street was the most likely place for it to start. If anyone remembered me as the girl with the eggplant, they were much too busy to notice me this time. I went back to the Banca Stabile but did not find him there. But I did find the young man he had been talking to and he told me Sandro was doing a job on Broome. Going there, I saw him loading things onto a wagon. Someone, it seemed, was moving. I wondered how many of their possessions would make it to their new home. When Sandro spotted me, he was holding a large crate. Otherwise he might have run again. As it was, his shoulders slumped as he shoved the crate onto the back of the wagon. Then he fastened the back gate and went around to the front and climbed onto the front seat.

"Sandro."

He ignored me, taking up the reins and setting the wagon in motion. I put myself in his path. He pulled the horse up short and the wagon bumped to a halt. He sat facing front, refusing to look at me, his hands white-knuckled on the reins.

"You need to get out of the way."

"I need to talk to you."

"I got nothing to tell you."

I put my foot on the step and climbed up. "I'll just take the ride then."

I could feel him watching as I settled onto the seat beside him. He could have pushed me off or threatened me. But he didn't. Instead he glanced around the street to see who was watching, saw no one was especially interested, then took up the reins and moved us along. It was a bumpy ride over the cobblestones and I had to hold on.

When we were well away from Broome, he said, "You're Anna's friend. The girl from the . . ."

"*Not* whorehouse," I said, using a word I would never have uttered in the company of the Benchleys. Or Tylers. Or even Michael Behan.

"I wasn't going to say that."

"Yes, you were."

"I was going to say *bagnio*." He smiled. "Means the same thing, but sounds a little better. Can mean bathhouse, too. Just in case you get invited to one and you're worried."

We were out of Little Italy now, drawing close to Houston. Sandro stayed on the smaller streets, and as we passed a ramshackle house, I heard pigs squealing in a nearby pen. They were the property of one Jim Brodie, who set them loose to clean the streets. Many objected to this approach to urban sanitation, but the pigs were deeply committed to their work and devoured everything in their path, be it moldy bread, cigarette ends, or—in more than one instance—a severed finger. The city's incinerators had cut into their share of the garbage market considerably; most pigs now found their employment as people's dinner. But these particular pigs were the descendants of Brodie's original herd and he refused to give them up.

It seemed wise to talk of the old days, so I said, "How are your aunts?"

"They're aunts. They're fine." He glanced at me. "I don't think I ever said thank you for not ratting me out. About that time in the alley."

We pulled up to let another wagon cross our path. When he started the horse moving again, I asked, "Why did you attack your sister?"

"Because my older brother said he would beat the . . . daylights out of me if I didn't. Besides, I didn't like Anna in those days. She was always yelling at me."

"But you like her now."

He grinned. "Not really." I laughed. "I never see her and when I do, everything I do and say is wrong."

"Oh, we're all wrong. She tells me, too."

"I bet she doesn't hit you in the head."

"No. But I never hit her."

He nodded, conceding the point. We drove for several more blocks until we reached Houston. Here the traffic was busy, the crowds and buildings big enough for some measure of privacy. Sandro said, "So, what happened to her?"

His neck was strained with the effort not to show emotion and I understood we weren't talking about Anna. "Just what I told you."

"She was killed in the city?"

"Long Island." He shook his head, bewildered and disgusted. "You knew she was coming to the city. You were going to meet her."

"Yes."

"Why?"

He shook his head.

"If you know something about her, even if it's something bad, it could be helpful to the police."

"I don't care about being helpful to the police."

"Oh. Well, I want to know who killed her, and it would be help-ful to me."

He shook his head. "It's no good knowing something if you can't do anything about it."

"Maybe I could give the information to someone who could do something with it."

"Oh, yeah? Like Charles Tyler? He sure kept her safe."

"What do you mean?"

"Nothing, forget it. He's . . . Mr. Protect the People, you'd think working for him, she would have been all right."

It was a reasonable thought, but there had been something else behind his sneer at Charles Tyler.

"Do you know how she started working for the Tylers?" He didn't answer. "Was it to keep her safe?"

He shifted in his seat. "Didn't turn out that way, did it?"

"But you knew her before she worked for the Tylers." He stared straight ahead. "You knew Rosalba Salvio."

"Maybe. Why do you care?"

"Because *I* want to know Rosalba Salvio. I want to know the woman she was, what she did. Why she did it. Because she's dead and lying unclaimed in a morgue and I think she deserves to have people at least know that she existed."

He stared hard at the road ahead, then said in hoarse voice, "She was real sweet with that kid."

"Emilio Forti?"

He glanced at me. "How'd you know that?"

"How did you know it?"

Sandro exhaled. "Look, I just drove the kid there. I had nothing to do with grabbing him. Rosalba's father's store was up on Eleventh. She worked behind the counter. The cops were so busy sniffing around Mulberry, they didn't think to go uptown."

"Why did they hide the boy there?"

"Her father paid the Morettis to take care of problems for him."

"What kind of problems?"

He shrugged. "You know." I didn't. And neither did he. There were no such problems, it was just the veneer of a business transaction for an act of extortion.

"But she and her father had nothing to do with the kidnapping itself?"

"No, they were good people. But Alberto Salvio's weak,

frightened. Does what he's told. Rosalba never liked me much 'cause I . . . took the payments from her father. But when I turned up with the kid, she gave me this look like I was—"

He dropped his head and I heard the unspoken words: *Animal. Scum. Filth.*

"But I felt bad. I would go around every once in a while, check in on them. The kid was scared out of his mind. And his family wasn't paying up. I didn't know what they were going to do to him."

"How much did Rosalba know?"

"Well, she knew right away he wasn't some kid straight off the boat without papers, which is what she was told. Once she found out he was the kidnapped kid everyone was talking about, it was hard to keep her calm. She kept asking me, 'What will they do if the family can't pay? What happens to him?' She wanted me to tell her they wouldn't hurt him. I couldn't tell her that."

"So she went to the police."

He sighed heavily. "Yeah, she went to the police."

I made a show of picking at my skirts so I wouldn't have to look at him as I asked, "The police think she was seeing Dante Moretti."

He rolled his eyes and for a moment looked very much like his sister. "Yeah—seeing. Like I'm seeing this horse's ass right now. Sometimes, when I would go to the store, Dante would come with me, try to talk to her. He tells everybody, 'Oh, that girl, she's crazy about me. She'll do anything I ask. Sometimes, she pretends to be nice, because'—but no. So when she calls the police, everyone says, Dante, I thought that girl loved you so much, what happened? You know, insulting him. So he makes up the story about her being jealous over the other girl."

I nodded. "And Charles Tyler gave her a job to get her out of the city."

"You think Sirrino didn't figure out who turned in his boy? If he'd known I went back there all those times, you'd find me in a barrel, too."

"But she came back to the city. Why?" He shook his head. "For you?"

He looked away, his neck and cheek flushed. Whatever there had been between them, he didn't want to discuss it. We rode in silence for several blocks, the air humming between us.

Then he said, "I had heard they sent her out west somewhere. Then one time, she was here with the mother and the little girl. I saw her going into the park . . ."

"And she remembered you." He nodded. "And came back to see you."

"Yeah, I guess she decided I wasn't so bad. We did the newspaper ads so no one else would know. She told me to use Bible quotes so she'd know it was me."

"But if it was so dangerous . . ."

He slapped the reins in frustration. "She needed to see people, talk to people who knew her. Spoke her language, you know? She was lonely. Out there with the Tylers, that wasn't home. She—"

He broke off. "What?"

"Never mind. She's dead, it doesn't matter now."

"Did she like the Tylers?" I found myself asking.

"She loved the kids. Talked about them all the time." He smiled his crooked smile.

"Who do you think killed her, Sandro?"

"You know who killed her." His mouth tightened. "Sometimes when I went to see her and Emilio, we would talk about leaving. Maybe going west. She wanted to see California. I'd get another job—"

He broke off, probably remembering the stories they'd spun together. Their fantasies of the future. I felt desperately sad for both of them.

"You should go to California, Sandro. Get another job."

"Sure, that's easy."

"Your uncle has the restaurant, he could hire you."

"He tried. You know how long that lasted? A week. I couldn't remember the orders. Then he had me washing dishes, but I thought, I'm not going to wash dishes my whole life. So one day I didn't come to work and he fired me. Now he won't even talk to me because of who I work for.

"You know in Italy, they have signs: Come to America, there's work in America, they want you there. But they don't want us. From the day I got here, people let me know I was a problem. Coming home from school, we went through an Irish neighborhood. The mothers shut their windows as we passed, didn't want our filth getting in their nice homes. I'd get to the end of the block, their kids punch me in the head for good measure. In church on Sunday, they put you in the basement. People tell you you smell. You're dirty. Maybe your English isn't good, the teacher decides you're stupid. Well, she's the teacher, she must be right, you sure feel stupid most of the time. So you leave school. You try shining shoes. Which means you got to pay for your corner—and shine every policeman's shoes for free—or you get a broken head. You start digging ditches. You get cut out of that job when the German foreman brings in his pals. Get a job hauling boxes for a friend of your uncle's, the friend says, Sorry, I got a cousin coming over, he needs the job.

"Then one day, your brother says, Hey, stupid, come work for a guy I know. It's easy. Even you can do it. Deliver groceries to these addresses. When they open the door, look inside. If it's a nice house, with nice things, let us know."

That was how Moretti has the names and addresses of people doing well enough to extort or rob, I realized.

"And you do it. And this guy your brother knows, he says, Thanks, good job. Pays you more than you thought he would, says he's got more work. You move a family's things to a new house; maybe some silver gets lost. But you tell yourself your boss probably helped them find the apartment, so it's probably a thank-you."

Staring straight ahead, he almost whispered, "Then one day, they hand you a heavy bag and the next thing you know, you're hauling a little kid screaming for his mother into a cellar. And you realize you just moved up from stealing rugs and hassling shop-keepers to a whole new game. And if that family doesn't pay . . . you know what your next job is going to be."

He held the reins tight and the horse stopped. "You should get off. Tell Anna I say hello. Tell her . . . I don't know, tell her I'm sorry."

Then he turned the wagon around the corner and soon he was swallowed up in the traffic of cars, pedestrians, and other wagons. With Anna not here to be furious with him, I took it as my job. Why had he ever done that first job when nothing his brother ever told him to do turned out well? Why hadn't he and Sofia run? They could have taken the child, told the police where to find him. . . .

Except they had no money. No family to run to outside the city. They had made choices—or had them made for them—and now they were stuck. *You are here, but you don't belong. You are in between. Not here, not there. Nobody.* I thought of her little room with its sealed window. No wonder she had come to the city at such risk, just to see someone who knew her, really knew her, to speak her language, feel like herself. And no wonder she had flirted with William. Just for a moment to feel the free of the past, just a pretty girl with a life of possibility. Not a dirty Italian or an accomplice of the Black Hand or a dark-skinned agent of death. Just a nice woman who loved children and had dreams of seeing California. Not a very exciting story, perhaps. No one would want to read about it. . . .

Slightly dazed, I looked up at the street sign to see where we had ended. Thirtieth Street. Close to Herald Square. Called Herald Square because the *New York Herald* office stood at the center.

Picking up my skirts, I started to run.

18

The New York Herald had come to life as a four-page sheet, smaller than some papers but promising to serve readers of all levels of society and stay clear of "faction." In the vision of its creator, its value lay in its "industry, good taste, brevity, variety, point, piquancy, and cheapness." It took a breezy approach to its coverage of the wealthy and did not hesitate to chronicle the lurid. One critic had dubbed it "The Whore's Daily Guide and Handy Compendium."

Fittingly, its offices on Thirty-fifth Street and Sixth Avenue were colorful, almost garish. Styled to resemble a Venetian palazzo, the building was a long, two-story structure with roman arches all around, two clocks peering like eyes at the shoppers and passing trolleys. It stood on a triangle of land in the center of the square. The newspaper's publisher was fond of hoot owls, and several perched at different spots in the building. Over the entrance, Minerva stood proudly, an owl on her arm, to symbolize the infinite wisdom of the newspaper itself.

It was dark by the time I reached the building. But I was in luck.

Michael Behan was just coming out onto the street. He was alone, thankfully; most of the other reporters, I realized, would have already left.

Running up to him, I said, "You can't write that story."

"Miss Prescott. Still trying to put me in the poorhouse."

"You can't write it. It's not true. I—" I struggled to think of a quick way to sum up everything Sandro had told me. There was none. "I want to tell you a different story."

"All right."

"I can't on the street. . . ."

The clock overhead started to chime and Behan took the opportunity to note that it was dinnertime. Frustrated, I thought, How had Behan gotten Sullivan to talk to him? Money. He had spent money . . .

I put a hand to my purse. I had money.

"Mr. Behan, may I invite you to dinner?"

★ ★ ★

I took him to a restaurant called Lanza's. It was on the cellar level, down a flight of wrought-iron stairs. It was small, with only eight tables. A waiter pushed a cloth along the bar. A single man sat in the back consuming a plate of veal with great concentration. A family of five was just finishing their meal.

"I don't like Italian food," Behan had said when he saw our destination.

"Maybe it's time you became better acquainted with it."

The waiter was happy to seat us at one of the white-and-red-cloth-covered tables. He turned to Behan to take the order, but I ordered the things least likely to outrage an Irish stomach. Gnocchi, polenta, ziti marinara, and escarole, because I liked it. It was said the sauce of garlic, oil, and tomato was called marinara because sailors' wives could make it quickly once they spotted the boats returning to shore. Thinking of wives, aware that I had caused Mrs. Behan irritation, I asked, "How is Mrs. Behan?"

Settling back in his chair, he said, "Mrs. Behan is . . . tired. Mrs. Behan's head aches, as do her feet. Mrs. Behan would like to see something of me occasionally. Mrs. Behan also cannot stand the sight of me. At least, she couldn't when she last saw me. Perhaps having established beyond a reasonable doubt the existence of Mrs. Behan, we could drop the subject."

The waiter set several plates on the table, as well as two glasses of wine. Tucking his napkin into his collar, Behan said, "My wife is very well, thank you."

He started with the escarole, lifting a forkful to his mouth. Then coughing violently, he spat it into his napkin and gasped, "Jesus, that's every garlic clove that came across the ocean in a Sicilian's arse."

I looked at him.

"I'm sorry." He took a long swallow of wine. "Sorry. It's just a little strong on the seasoning for me."

I waited.

"And I apologize for the profanity."

I stayed as I was.

Behan lowered his voice. "Am I to apologize to the waiter and our friends in the corner as well?"

I nodded.

Behan looked toward the bar and raised a hand in contrition. The waiter pointedly ignored him and—in truth—the other diner remained focused on his veal. One of the children had spilled water on the table and the family was distracted.

"You're very partial to the Italians, aren't you, Miss Prescott?"

"I'm partial to not insulting people when I'm eating their food." I hesitated, then said, "When I was young, Anna's family welcomed me into their home. That might sound like nothing to you, but no one else was interested in a girl who lived with 'fallen women.' They fed me, were kind to me. They let me wash the dishes." I smiled, thinking of that funny honor. "Anna wasn't allowed to, but I was because I was *premuroso*. It means you pay attention to people, you're careful." The words caught in my throat and I took up the escarole. "So, it feels odd to me when people say shut the doors to people capable of that generosity." I ate some of the escarole. "And it's exactly the right amount of garlic."

Behan was quiet. Then he slid one of the plates in front of him and said, "What's this then?"

"Polenta."

He ate the smallest forkful conceivable. But the next forkful was larger. For a while, we were content to eat.

Then I said, "I want to thank you for not writing about Sofia."

Behan drank his wine. "Oh, but I did. Yesterday. Page seventeen."

"But—"

"Did you not see it? 'Woman Found Dead in Oyster Bay.' About two inches near the bottom right of the page. Right near 'Dead Dog in Tiny Coffin.'"

"Your headlines are usually more dramatic than that."

"It wasn't my finest effort."

"Everyone has their bad days, I suppose."

"Sure."

"May I ask what caused your bad day?"

"Remember how I said I didn't like being fed stories?" I nodded. "Well, let's say when I started writing up Sullivan's account, I felt a little full. Nauseous, in fact. So I checked with some of my fellow parishioners—did you know Sullivan and Charles Tyler were colleagues? They work in the same precinct. For a time, Sullivan was even on the Dag—"

The family got up to leave and Behan amended his statement

to, "Served on the squad that focused on crime in a particular area."

"I didn't know that."

"And furthermore, I heard that while Mr. Tyler has many fans, Sullivan is not one of them. Thinks Tyler's a little too friendly to the nonnatives, wastes too many resources better spent on real Americans. An attitude that not surprisingly got Sullivan kicked off the squad. So, I thought maybe I'd wait a bit. See what else came up. Has something else come up, Miss Prescott?"

"Maybe."

In careful language, making no mention of last names—Moretti, Forti, or Tyler—I told him what Sandro had told me.

"He's not brilliant, but he's smarter than his sister gives him credit for," I said. "And since he admits he was involved, I think we can consider him the highest authority on Rosalba's innocence."

Michael Behan had started the meal unhappy, but was eating more naturally with each bite. Now he signaled for another glass of wine and ran a piece of bread around the plate and asked, "What about the open window?"

"What I thought; she wanted air. They think the killers were watching the house before the kidnapping. They probably noticed she had a tendency to leave it open. But you can see that Charles Tyler shouldn't be publicly mocked for trying to help a woman who saved a six-year-old boy."

He chewed, a frown on his face.

"What?"

He pointed to a plate. "What's this again?"

"Ziti marinara."

"It's good."

"And?"

"And I think I'm feeling fonder of the Italian people, Miss

Prescott." He sat back. "What if Sofia's death isn't the work of the—" He wiggled his fingers to indicate "hand."

"I don't understand."

"Well, you said yourself, she was pleasing to the eye."

I almost laughed. "Mr. Tyler has many flaws, but he loves his wife."

"Didn't Mrs. Tyler just have a baby?"

"Yes, but—"

"Wife is tired, getting over the birth. Pretty, buxom addition to the household."

"I'm telling you, you're wrong."

"Your faith in men is touching, Miss Prescott."

"My faith in men is exactly what it should be, Mr. Behan. Charles Tyler wasn't having an affair with Sofia, because if he has eyes for anyone other than his wife, it's Charles Tyler. Why seduce the nanny when you have the press at your feet? And why kill her if they were having such a convenient little affair?"

"She made it inconvenient?"

"And he sleeps on the other side of the house. That's why Mabel came to get me instead of her father. Charles Tyler was nowhere near the nursery that night."

"And where does William Tyler sleep?"

The sudden switch threw me and it took me a moment to say, "That's ridiculous."

"Why?"

"Because . . ." Because it simply was. "He's getting married in a matter of weeks."

"I don't know what you think matrimony is, Miss Prescott—it's not blinders you put on a horse."

No, it certainly hadn't been in William's case. And yet, to be blunt, he was a horse in need of a fine stable, the kind that Louise was going to provide for him. *If* she decided to forgive him. And if the romp on the lawn was all she needed to forgive him for . . .

No. This was ridiculous. To jump from . . . a wander to murder was wild speculation. Why would he even do such a thing?

"William Tyler is a good man." I spoke slowly so he might understand these simple words. "Just because he's a well-known, good-looking young man—"

"You think he's good-looking?"

"Yes, because he is."

"Did Sofia think he was good-looking?"

I felt caught.

"She did, didn't she?"

She had. And she had shown interest in the woman William was going to marry. *Mr. William, he's verynice. I do not want him having a killer in his family.* And perhaps she had been a little . . . disinterested in the feelings of others; her callousness toward Alva Tyler. I took it as the natural antipathy for a critical employer. She was a kind woman, I thought, struggling to recall Sandro's stories of her. Not the type to threaten a young man with the destruction of his hopes . . .

Resolved, I said, "She thought he was a nice man, which he is. Which was my very point to you. I know I took a good story away from you, Mr. Behan, but don't build another one on William Tyler. Not if you ever want to speak with me again. The unsung heroine of the Forti kidnapping—that's your story. Although if you could put off writing it until after the wedding, I'd be extremely grateful."

The waiter brought Behan the check. Taking it with a flourish, I took my purse out of my pocket and started counting out bills. Behan watched me, uncomfortable.

"Miss Prescott." I kept counting. "Jane."

"I asked you to dinner, Mr. Behan." Despite the emptiness of my purse, I took great pleasure in laying the money on the table. Let Michael Behan try and write the wrong story after being fed gnocchi and polenta.

As we left the restaurant, Behan said, "By the way, your friend Anna was right about *mano nera*. Well, the name anyway. A reporter did make it up."

"Really?"

"*Herald* reporter. A woman, as it happens. She saw one of the extortion letters, how someone had drawn a black hand, and she started calling it a *mano nera* letter. The gangs liked the sound of it and took it up."

Behan began walking to the train with me without comment. Near the station, we passed by a poster that read MARCH FOR WOMEN'S SUFFRAGE, MAY 6TH! It was tattered and someone had scrawled an obscenity on it.

Wanting to change the subject from murder and adultery, I said, "Tell me why you support Mr. Roosevelt."

"I never said I did."

We reached the station and started making our way down the stairs.

"On the train, you said, 'Fine,' when I asked if you were voting for him." He shrugged. "You will vote, won't you?"

Startled to be challenged, Behan said, "I'm not sure that that's any of your business."

"Well, if you're going to say I can't, then you certainly should." Irritation growing, I continued, "If it's such a complicated and intricate process well beyond my understanding, then as someone granted the privilege—because *you* have the mind and wherewithal to distinguish a good candidate from a poor one—you have a responsibility to exercise it."

We pushed our way into the crowds already waiting on the platform. Behan said, "I didn't say you can't have the vote."

Emboldened by his equivocation, I said, "Then you're a supporter of the suffrage movement."

The train rolled into the station and we stepped on. The train was packed with people and we both had to stand. Swaying from a handle, a gentleman's elbow in my back, the feather of a woman's hat brushing my neck, a foot that threatened to tromp mine with every jolt, I thought of the jaunty new song, "The Subway Glide." *"Ev'rybody you rub when you're doing the sub . . . doing the subway gli-ide."*

His voice roiling with sarcasm, Behan said, "Just remind me, how does you having the vote help you sew a better hem?"

For a moment I was stumped—I hadn't realized voting was meant to support you in your profession. Then I said, "How does having the vote help you write about heads in barrels?"

Angry now, he said, "There are differences between men and women, Miss Prescott." The train took a sharp curve, throwing us all off our feet. My foot was stomped, I tasted feathers, and what little space there was between me and Mr. Behan vanished as we crashed into each other. For a strange, brief moment, my forehead rested on his chest, my fingers on his coat, and I was keenly aware that his heart was pounding. I say aware, but it was more a confusion. He had reached out to steady me, and his hand was at my waist.

I stepped back. "I am well aware of them, Mr. Behan."

Returning to the argument, he said, "Men do things women do not do. We fight in wars, we are policemen, we protect—"

"So only soldiers and policemen should have the vote." The man behind me turned the page of his paper, his elbow making its presence felt in my ribs.

Behan lowered his voice to say, "Men are . . . *in* the world, Miss Prescott. We face the realities of life in ways that women—"

I thought of Mrs. Tyler, weary from motherhood and childbearing, of Louise, so fearful at the thought of taking on those challenges, of Sofia, who would never have the chance now. Jabbing at the gentleman's soft midsection with my own elbow, I said, "Do you honestly think women don't face the realities of life? Isn't *birth* the first reality of life?"

As the doors slid open at Fiftieth Street, the rumble of the train died and the word "birth" seemed to reverberate in the silence. I was aware of being stared at. Behan said quietly, "Miss Prescott," and gestured ahead to indicate we should be going. Feeling both chagrined and elated that I had come through the argument and had the final word—even if it had been uttered a little too loudly—I went ahead.

As we turned onto Fifth Avenue, Behan said, "I'm guessing you'll be marching on the sixth then."

"It's a few days after the wedding. I intend to be asleep."

"I tell you what, you have my vote. I'll sleep in on Election Day."

"Fine. But I might vote for Wilson."

"You can't waste my vote on Wilson."

"It's not your vote, Mr. Behan."

"Oh, right." He smiled.

As we arrived at the Benchleys', Behan nodded solemnly. "Thank you for dinner."

"Thank you for page seventeen."

I started walking up the back stairs. Then stopped.

"By the way—the dress."

Behan looked up, eyes bright under the derby brim.

"Is by Worth. Cream silk charmeuse, with handmade Brussels lace at the neck and shoulder flounces. At the sleeves, dangling tassels finished in pearl. The veil is full length with a headdress of wax orange blossom. Good night, Mr. Behan."

And I went inside, feeling just the tiniest bit like Mrs. Langtry sweeping through the doors at Keens in her feather boa.

★ ★ ★

The next morning, the Benchley sisters shared a quiet breakfast. Their mother was to arrive by lunchtime. As I came down, I saw Bernadette idly pushing the vacuum an inch or two across the hall rug, her head cocked toward the closed doors of the dining room. In the kitchen, Elsie stood by the swinging door, tray in hand, ostensibly waiting to be called in. Only Mrs. Mueller was fully engrossed in her duties, carefully tending the eggs while adjusting the bacon's position in the pan. I sat down at the table and complimented her on the meal. Then I looked toward Elsie, who shook her head. A moment later, Bernadette, also frustrated, came through the door and viciously bit into a piece of toast.

Coming to the table, Elsie whispered, "Is she calling it off or not?"

"She's thinking," I told her.

"What's she want to call it off for?" Bernadette asked. "All I heard last night was her crying about trust and respect. Miss Charlotte said she'd be Mrs. William Tyler, and she could trust people would respect *that*." She drank her coffee.

"Do you know why, Miss Prescott?" I shook my head. "Well, my guess is it's another woman."

"It's not always about that, Elsie," I said, more sharply than I meant to.

"Almost always," she insisted. "Almost always, it's a love story."

Just then the front doorbell rang. "Oh, Lord, it's Missus. She's early," said Elsie, smoothing her skirts and setting her cap straight.

She left to answer the door. I waited for the explosion of fretfulness that always accompanied Mrs. Benchley's return. But it didn't come. I glanced at the clock. She would have had to leave early to arrive this long before noon. And she was not one for early arrivals . . .

Then I heard Elsie open the dining-room door and announce, "Mr. William Tyler is here, Miss Louise."

There was a gasp, followed by Charlotte saying, "Tell him to wait in the parlor, Elsie."

Louise whispered, "No!"

"Tell him to *wait*."

I got out of my chair and opened the kitchen door, pausing to gesture to Elsie that she should stay where she was. Then I went as quietly as possible down the hallway to find William standing at the door. I hurried him into the parlor and said, "Why are you here?"

"To speak with Louise." He turned his hat in his hand; Elsie should have taken it. I held out my hand and he gave it to me. No, I thought, reassured. This is . . . William. Awkward, over-tall, well-meaning, and yes, *kind*, William Tyler.

"What will you say to her?" I asked him.

"What I said last summer. That I want her to be my wife."

"And?"

Before he could reassure me that he had more planned, Louise appeared at the door.

"I was just taking Mr. William's hat," I explained.

"That won't be necessary," said Louise.

Courtesy dictated I return William's hat to him and escort him out. I held it uncertainly in the space between him and Louise. After a moment, William took it.

But he did not leave, saying to Louise, "I thought we might walk in the park? Perhaps we'll run into Mrs. Abernathy and Wallace."

Louise smiled ever so slightly. "I do miss Wallace."

"Then . . . for Wallace's sake?"

We heard the creak of floorboard and I smelled lily of the valley. Her sister approaching, Louise took matters into her own hands and said, "Jane, would you get my coat and hat?"

"Of course."

For a moment, it seemed she would ask me to come as well, as she so often had. William glanced anxiously at me. I prepared an excuse.

But then Louise said, "Thank you, Jane."

William and Louise were gone quite some time. They took their luncheon elsewhere and so missed Mrs. Benchley's arrival home. But they returned just in time to find her in tears in the parlor.

"Mother, what on earth is wrong?" said Louise.

Mrs. Benchley was weeping by the fireplace, a newspaper in her lap. She paused for a brief moment to register the presence of her newly reinstated son-in-law-to-be, then cried, "It's a disaster!"

"What is?" asked William.

"There," she cried, pointing. "There, there, there . . ."

GOWN WORN IN WEDDING OF THE YEAR
TO BE DESIGNED BY WORTH!
All details revealed, down to the last pearl!

I swallowed sharply. Michael Behan had an excellent memory. He hadn't forgotten a thing. Last night, giving him the dress details had seemed like an excellent way to thank him for his discretion. Now it did indeed seem a potential disaster. I looked to Louise, worried as to how she would react.

She was smiling, a finger curled at her lips. Then a giggle escaped. Then a guffaw.

"Louise!" cried her mother.

"I know, I know. It's . . . terrible. Just . . . awful. It's . . ."

But laughter overtook her and she fell sideways into a chair, laughing uproariously. William had a hand over his mouth; you could read his expression as concerned, but I could see he was laughing as well.

That evening, Louise announced that the wedding would take place as planned. We would return to Pleasant Meadows the next day.

★ ★ ★

Despite having to repack Mrs. Benchley's things as well as Charlotte's, who, despite protest, was returning to Philadelphia, it was an easy trip back. I couldn't help but marvel at the difference between our first journey and our second. William assisted only one elderly woman and Louise did not retreat into silence at any point. And of course, Mr. Grimaldi met us at the train.

I assisted him in taking the cases off the charabanc, despite his objections. I asked how his spirits were. He smiled sadly but didn't answer beyond that. When we had settled Louise's cases in her room, I went back to get my own. The chauffeur insisted on taking my case down himself. Then he said, "Miss Prescott?"

"Yes, Mr. Grimaldi?"

"You remember that night?"

"It's difficult to forget."

"Yes." He pressed his lips together, then said on a sigh, "I don't know if this is right, to tell you this."

Oh, Lord, I thought, not something else about William. Still I said, "It is."

"One thing bothers me. That night, I look at the house and I see . . ."

"The window open at eleven, yes."

I had interrupted him and he looked puzzled. "No—I didn't say that."

"But you did. Mr. William said you told the police that."

"I never spoke to the police." He saw my astonishment. "I talk to Mr. Tyler. I don't . . . trust regular police. And I was upset, so he says, Aldo, you tell me and I tell them. No need for you to go through that."

And no one, I thought, would dare question the deputy commissioner. "So, you never saw the window open before the murder?"

"No. But I saw the light was on."

"In the nursery?"

He shook his head. Pointed. It took me a few moments to understand.

"And it was almost midnight. I am sure because at the time, I think, No, they should be asleep."

I thought back over the events of that night, when I had been awoken, when Mabel said she first heard her brother crying. "But Mabel . . ."

"Yes," he said. "That's why I tell you."

19

As *a child*, I said my prayers before bed. I never liked saying the words "And if I die before I wake," feeling it was somehow giving permission to God to cut my life short. But when I got up the nerve to complain to my uncle, he said gently, "He doesn't need your permission."

I had fallen out of the habit of nightly prayers. But that night, I made a strange request of the Almighty: *Please, God, let Mrs. Briggs not be troubled with insomnia. Amen.*

The steps I took from my room and down the hall of the servants' quarters seemed endless and no matter how lightly I set my foot down, the floor creaked with protest. But there was no sound of bedclothes pushed back, no sudden lamplight gleaming under the doors, no call of "Who's there?" And once I was at the end of the corridor, I exhaled in relief.

Now I only had to hope that Charles Tyler did not lock the door to his study.

Wrapping my hand in the sleeve of my robe, I twisted the knob.

It turned easily and the door opened. I heard the squeal of old hinges and slipped inside as soon as there was enough room. Then for a few minutes, I stood in a dark corner, just in case I had been heard and Mr. Tyler came to explore.

But he did not.

Darkness and silence let the imagination loose, freeing it of the mundane realities that are so clear in daytime. In the moonlight, the elk head with its long, curled horns looked uncomfortably like a biblical demon, the bear seemed ready to roar back to life, and I gave the vulture with its cruel beak and raised wings a wide berth as I passed. There would be only one place I might find what I was looking for, and that was Mr. Tyler's desk.

Creeping behind his desk, carefully moving the chair back, I tugged first at the center drawer. It was locked. As were the three side drawers. And I strongly suspected Mr. Tyler carried the key with him. No wonder he did not bother to lock the door. Disappointed, I sat on the desk chair, clasped my hands, and looked.

Mr. Tyler's desk reflected his character: busy—and disorganized. Clearly Mrs. Briggs was not allowed to tidy here. Books and papers crowded every inch of the desk's surface. An inkwell sat open, a pen lay on an unfinished letter; it had dripped, leaving a blot. Mr. Tyler would have to rewrite that one, I thought. The days since the murder had been so frenetic, he probably had not had time to attend to his affairs.

Then, puzzled, I looked closer. People didn't suddenly drop pens dripping with ink—not even someone as boisterous as Mr. Tyler.

> *My dear Graves,*
> *It is late as I write this, well past midnight. The*
> *household has gone to bed. Perhaps that is why I*
> *can confess that the recent statements by Moretti's*

lawyers concern me. I refuse to hide. I will not be
cowed. But I wonder: should I send Alva and the
children abroad? That plan presents some difficulties,
which I will not go into here. But I worry . . .

Here the letter trailed off in a rivulet of ink. Had Mr. Tyler grown disgusted with what he might have seen as cowardice on his part and tossed the pen aside? Or had something interrupted him?

I had told Michael Behan that Charles Tyler was nowhere near the nursery the night of the murder; he had been asleep in his bed clear on the other side of the house. Now I knew otherwise. He had been in his study—well within earshot of his son's crying. Of course, no man would pay attention to that. But surely Sofia had called for help. Why hadn't he answered that call?

Or had he?

And why had he lied to the police about where he was and what he must have heard? To protect himself? Or . . . someone close to him?

Heart pounding, I told myself for the hundredth time that William could not have killed Sofia. No matter if their . . . encounter . . . had been repeated, no matter if she threatened to tell Louise. At any rate, what would he have used? William was not in the habit of traveling with weapons. He had no knife. Yes, he might have gotten one from the kitchen, but to kill a woman, then calmly clean the knife, go quietly back downstairs, and put it in its exact place, so that the all-seeing Mrs. Briggs noticed nothing amiss? William simply wasn't that cold-blooded. Or that efficient. His mother was, but she would never have seen a servant as a genuine threat to her security. Dismiss them, pay them off, make sure your friends knew never to hire them—yes. Murder? More trouble than they were worth.

Charles Tyler thought more of his staff. More important, he had lied. More important still, he owned weapons.

Well, he owned guns. But it wasn't easy to cut a throat so cleanly. You needed a particular kind of knife for that. Behan had said so when he looked at the blood spray in the room. I looked around the moonlit study. For all the grotesque remnants of death, I saw no knife. Just animal heads, framed newspaper articles, and family photos. One framed portrait showed a young Charles Tyler in uniform, standing alongside other men in front of a large pit. He held high a feathered headdress as he beamed at the camera. At the bottom of the picture, he had written, *7th Cavalry, Wounded Knee, 1891.* Clearly Mabel was not the only ardent chronicler of Charles Tyler's career.

That made me think of Mabel's scrapbook, the one she had shown us the night of the murder. Image upon image of her celebrated parents, ending with the most recent, most splendid, to use Charles Tyler's words, episode: the rescue of the Forti boy. Little Emilio sitting happily on the great man's lap, brandishing a knife recovered from the foul Black Hand.

★ ★ ★

If you did not have a telephone, you headed over to Snouder's Drug Store, which had installed the area's very first telephone. Realizing that telephones brought young people, the far-seeing owners built a soda fountain, making the store a popular gathering spot. Charles Tyler had his own telephones. But none where I could be sure I wouldn't be overheard. And so the next day, to Snouder's I went.

I told the operator whom I was calling and waited while we were connected. When I heard, "Behan," I said, "It's Jane." Then added, "Prescott."

There was a pause. Then he said, "It was all right about the article, wasn't it? You still have a job?"

"Yes, that was fine." I had to talk fast. "Do you remember the child in the Forti kidnapping?"

"Little Emilio of the dark eyes and gap-toothed grin? Sure."

"Do you think the family's still in New York?"

"I can find out. If I find them, then what?"

"I need you to ask them something about the kidnapping."

"His parents might not like that. Poor kid's been through a lot."

"I know. But it's important."

"What's your question?"

I told him.

"That's all?"

"That's all."

"And . . . hold off on the headline?"

"I'm afraid so."

* * *

It was William's mother who had the idea for a garden party. Alva Tyler seemed unenthused by the notion of dozens of people on her front lawn, just two weeks before it was to be trampled again by the wedding party; her husband even went so far as to indicate mild disapproval of his sister-in-law's proposal. But she promised that it would be a small gathering of friends and neighbors and that she and the estimable Mrs. Briggs would be solely responsible for its execution. Alva Tyler's energies would not be taxed in the least. And, she said, perhaps the children might be brought back from Saratoga. The danger was past, and it would be pleasant for them to return to a festive occasion. The boys could even come home for the weekend. At that, Charles Tyler—who had never liked sending the children away—gave his full and noisy support.

And so it was a week after my return that tables were set outside, a light luncheon prepared, and croquet competitions organized on a day of blue skies and sunshine. I had worried that a demanding social event might wilt Louise's good spirits, but she had a new confidence these days. As I watched her walking arm in arm with her fiancé, I couldn't help thinking that oddly, facing her worst fears had achieved what William's smiling support had not: she was now . . . rather splendid.

When I asked Louise why she had decided to become Mrs. William Tyler after all, she said that she had always felt on some level that William had been pushed into courting her, that it had not been his idea to begin with. (Here, I kept silent.) Taking the initiative to follow her into the city had shown her he was now more his own man—and that that man wanted to marry her very much indeed. Besides, they had Wallace to think of.

"And," she said, "I can still go to the South Pole or down the Amazon as Mrs. William Tyler. William's very excited by the idea, in fact."

The Tylers being allergic to anything "grand," the style for the afternoon was informal. I dressed Louise in a simple but lovely dress of blue-green silk. The V-neck broadened her shoulders, giving her the appearance of a waist; the folded collar was embroidered with violets, and there was a row of beaded violets at the point where the bodice gave way to the skirt. The sleeves met her white gloves at the elbow. The final touch was a gorgeous straw hat, circled with pink silk roses. The entire effect was fresh, lively, and hopeful. More hopeful than I felt.

As I straightened the back, she said, "You should come, too, Jane. I'm sure the Tylers wouldn't mind. In fact, Mabel asked me this morning if she might see you. Poor thing. I think she misses Sofia. Alva Tyler doesn't seem to know quite what to do with her."

"I'll make sure to see her," I promised.

Before joining the party, I went to my room to fix my own hair. Peering into the mirror, I thought of the last time I had thought of my appearance. It wasn't such a bad appearance; maybe I ought to pay more attention to it.

There was a knock. I said, "Come in," and Mrs. Briggs opened the door, a piece of folded paper in her hand.

"Message for you," she said, and handed it to me.

"Thank you, Mrs. Briggs."

When she had gone, I opened it. The message was brief, lacking Mr. Behan's usual style. But it was illuminating. Tragically so.

20

I took a walk. I had things to think about, and I wanted to be away from the house. As I wandered the grounds, I stared into the stretch of woods that surrounded the property and thought back to that indistinct figure making its way in the dark. And that open window, the intruder who'd crept into the house . . .

Or so I'd thought. But the danger had been inside the house all along.

Charles Tyler had indeed given little Emilio the knife taken from the Black Hand. But whether because his parents thought it dangerous or wanted no reminders of their ordeal, the knife had been returned to the police. Who, according to Mr. Behan's message, had no idea of its current whereabouts.

I had at least one idea. One of those three locked doors in Charles Tyler's desk.

And yet I could think of no earthly reason for Charles Tyler to murder the young woman responsible for his greatest triumph. A woman he had saved from danger. I thought of Michael Behan's point about horses and blinders. But Charles Tyler did not just love his wife, he adored her. And he loved the image of himself as his family's protector almost as much. Had he been on the *Titanic*, he would have lifted Alva and the children into the boats, smoked a cigar, and gone down laughing. Of that I was sure.

But it was impossible that he had not heard the struggle in the nursery just one floor above. And he had lied to the police, saying that the window was open before the murder. Yes, the window had been open when I found Sofia, but in all likelihood, he himself had used it as an exit. No doubt his nephew, wanting to impress him, had told him how to use the windows and ledges as footholds.

But why? What was happening in this house?

Kicking the grass in frustration as I went, I found myself at the tree where I had sat with Sofia that warm spring day. In the distance, I saw the makeshift family graveyard. Approaching, I saw a clumsily built wooden cross sticking out of the ground, with the name "Bunkum" in blue paint. A wilted bouquet of daisies lay at the foot of the cross. This must be the dog Mabel had talked about. No doubt she had left the daisies. I hadn't gone much farther down the hill when I came across the second grave marker, very different from the first. This one was a small solitary cube of marble, about the size of a box you might stand on to make a speech. The inscription was:

> Beloved Son
> John Algernon Tyler
> Born March 14, 1910
> Died April 17, 1911

It was impossible not to look at these pitiful dates and not feel the breath-catching spasm of grief. So small a span, so brief a life.

He had barely begun to live. And if tears came to my eyes at the thought of a happy toddler whose ambling explorations were cut so painfully short, what must his mother feel? Perhaps that was why the gravestone was placed so far from the house. Easily visited, but not in plain, everyday view.

And yet someone had been here recently. A bunch of bluebells tied with a black ribbon rested on top of the grave.

That visit, which from the look of the flowers would have happened a week ago, pulled at my thoughts. With everything that had happened, someone had made a point to come to this grave. Of course, I realized, it was the one-year anniversary. But so close to Sofia's death—

No, the *day* she died.

I stopped walking. Reviewed in my head everything that had happened the day of our arrival, our welcome. Charles Tyler saying, "This is a happy house." Smiles, hearty laughter, toasts to the couple, sly inquiries as to when a new arrival might make an appearance.

And tears, yes, some tears, over a petty household problem. Not so strange, except when you considered that there must have been other tears to shed on the eve of the anniversary of their son's death. But there had been no mention of it at all. Not even from the staff. It was as if any reference to the event were forbidden. What must it be like to have your heart bleed inside you while you smile and discuss the endless possibilities of orange blossom?

It was time, I decided, to make my appearance at the party.

★ ★ ★

I saw Mabel wandering on the outskirts of the gathering. She was dressed in a lingerie dress with a wide yellow sash and short sleeves. It was a sweet, cheerful outfit, and Mabel was a sweet girl. But she was not cheerful. Her head was down and she swung her arms in an aimless, unhappy way as she made her way around the tree, slapping its bark in a halfhearted attempt at play.

I approached. "Hello, Miss Mabel. Can I get you something?"

"No. Thank you."

It was my inclination to leave people alone when they gave no indication of wanting company. But isolation wasn't usually Mabel's preference.

"Is it nice, having your brothers home?"

She nodded. "I told them about Sofia."

"They didn't know?"

"They said they did, but . . ." She frowned. "They didn't talk about it, so I thought perhaps they didn't. Nobody talks about it."

"I know."

"My grandmother didn't want to talk about it either. She kept telling me to smile. I told her I didn't feel like it, but she said that didn't matter. I feel like everyone's forgotten Sofia was ever here."

I leaned against the tree. "I'll talk about her if you want. What's the first thing you remember about her?"

She stood beside me, keeping her hands behind her back to protect her dress from the tree bark. "I liked when she sang."

"Me, too. How did it go? *'Fi la ninna . . .'*"

"*Fa*," Mabel corrected me.

"*Fa la ninna, fa la nanna—*"

Mabel lowered her voice to basso levels. "Ninn-oh, ninn-oh."

"That's it. Ninn-oh . . ." I went too deep and coughed.

Mabel laughed. "You can't sing at all."

"No. Sofia could sing."

"And she laughed. And she told you things, real things. One day she said straight out, Oh, Miss Mabel, I am having a terrible day. Today, I hate everyone except you. And she didn't really mean she hated Frederick. Just that sometimes you want to . . . yell. Even if it is rude."

"Aha—" All of a sudden, we were in the whirlwind of Charles Tyler's personality as he came out from behind the tree to snatch his daughter up. I smiled, expecting to hear Mabel laugh as her father pretended to be an elephant and swung her as if she were his trunk. "Here he is, the African pachyderm seeking out a drink. Is there water here?" He set her feet on the ground briefly before pulling her up. "There is not. Is there water here?" Again he set her down. "Wait, wait, I think I have it . . ."

But Mabel pushed her father's hands away and stepped out of reach.

"Too old for the elephant game?" he said. "Poor old elephant. Well, maybe you'll come have a dance, then."

"No, thank you, Father." She kept her gaze on the ground. "I'm not feeling very well."

"Oh." Charles Tyler was nonplussed at the combined oddities of rejection and ill health. "Then under this tree in the shade is probably the best place for you. Maybe Jane could get you some lemonade . . ."

"I don't want lemonade," said Mabel.

"All right," said her father after a moment. Touching her hair, he said gently, "If my girl doesn't want lemonade, it shall be against the law to give it to her."

He caressed her hair a little longer, watching the top of her bowed head with disquiet. I smiled at him—*Well, children*—and he offered me a quick smile back before saying to Mabel, "I'll leave you be."

When he had gone, I asked, "Are you angry with your father, Mabel?"

"No." She leaned against the tree, looked off into the distance.

"Is that what Sofia would say?"

There was a long pause. Then I heard from around the tree, "He didn't save her."

"Oh, Mabel."

"He saves people, that's his job. He saved that little boy and he didn't even know that little boy. He should have saved Sofia. She kept calling for him but he never came."

"She called for your father?"

Mabel nodded.

"Can you . . . I know it's strange, but can you say it exactly the way you heard it?"

She did. My heart stopped for a long moment.

"Why didn't he?" Now there were tears in her voice. "Men are supposed to save people."

"Mabel."

"Yes, Miss Prescott?"

"Can I tell you something that I really think?"

"Yes."

"People don't always save you. They—men—don't come to your rescue. Maybe they try, but they don't always make it in time. Sometimes they can't. And sometimes, they don't even try. It's not . . ." My voice caught. "It's not something you can count on. You have to take care of yourself. Not now, but later when you're older. And it's not something to be afraid of. You're very smart. And you're strong. Remember what Mr. Behan said? You saved Freddy. That's how strong you are."

I was no longer sure that Freddy had ever needed saving—at least, not in the way we'd all been told. But I needed to make Mabel understand that she shouldn't make herself weak because others were supposed to be strong. In the distance, I heard Charles Tyler regale a rapt audience with his hunting stories. ". . . tiger—charged straight at me. Eyes flashing, fangs bared. Must have weighed more than five hundred pounds. Stood my ground, shot him square between the eyes. Wretched to have to kill such a splendid creature. I hated it. But it's the only thing. Look the danger in the face and destroy it."

I heard Mabel say, "I like Mr. Behan. Can we visit him at his newspaper, like he said?"

"I'm sure someone can take you. Maybe—"

"No, I want you to come. I'll see you, won't I? At Cousin William's?"

I didn't know how to tell this little girl that her world and everyone in it was about to change and there was very little that I could promise her.

But then I wondered if perhaps she already knew that.

★ ★ ★

I went into the house in search of the courage to do what I knew I had to. Which was no less than to destroy the happiness of several people. Wanting to put Sofia firmly in mind, I went to the nursery floor. Reaching the landing, I thought for an awful, slippery moment, *No. Leave it. What's to be gained? No one really needs to know.*

But then I remembered Sofia's hand, the few feet that formed a chasm between her and the baby she loved so much, between her and help. And that song, that silly song that I struggled to remember. I remembered her as pretty, but could not say what it was about her face that had made me think so. Her voice was low, I knew that. But . . . perhaps not? People fade so quickly, we lose them so easily.

I turned the doorknob, pushed the door open. The nursery was now simply a room. Someone had removed the rug and done a halfhearted scrub of the walls. They had taken the blankets and toys, removed the crib.

And of course they had shut the window. The curtains hung straight and still on either side. With the vague idea that perhaps I would discover that it did indeed open from the outside, or that there was a broken pane someone had missed, I approached. I looked up, I looked down. I looked side to side. But I saw nothing I had not seen before. It was simply a closed window. Look beyond and there was the stretch of lawn far below. In the distance, the ring of trees that hid the kidnapper.

Sighing in frustration, I sat on the window seat. And that was when I saw it. Right below the window. A glint of gemstone and the glitter of gold.

Sliding off the seat, I crouched down to get a better look. Too small for a necklace, it had to be a bracelet. It was a fragile piece, designed not to overwhelm a lady's slender wrist, but the jewels— they looked to be sapphires—would slide alluringly on her arm as she made a languid gesture. If she happened to have blue eyes, you would have to guard against the boringly obvious match . . .

But blue-green eyes.

The nursery, she never comes there . . .

I heard the door close behind me and scrambled to my feet. Alva Tyler stared at me, stricken. Then she gripped her stomach and put her hand over her mouth as if she were going to be sick.

"Oh, God," she whispered. "Oh, God, Jane . . ."

She wheeled blindly toward the door, but finding it shut, groped her way to the changing table. Leaning heavily on it with one hand, she doubled over and cried out. A woman so desperate did not feel threatening, and I helped her to the rocker.

"I'll get you a glass of water," I said.

"No!" Her grip tightened on my wrist. "No, don't leave me, please. Just . . . just let's . . ."

"We can be quiet," I assured her. "Stay as we are. We don't have to do anything."

Her mouth trembled into almost a smile. Then tears began to run down her cheeks.

I kept my promise to stay, kneeling beside her as she wept. And I managed to keep my face open and calm when she said, "It sounds so terrible—it is so terrible—taking a life. But truly, truly, it seemed the only thing I could do at the time, the only way to make it . . . right. I didn't feel I had a choice."

She turned her gaze to the window. "I tell myself now, Oh, you wouldn't have really done it. But I would have." She gripped my hand again. "I was going to go after, I wouldn't have left him to go on his own. I would have been a good mother at the end, I swear it."

Her words were coming so fast, the truth behind them so unspeakable, it took some time for me to understand that we were now talking about a very different murder.

She whispered, "Not like Johnny. He wouldn't have died alone. I would never have left him."

I had one word and I barely breathed it. "Why?"

She blinked into the distance and for a moment I thought I'd lost her. Then she said, "I never wanted a nanny, you know. I don't like . . . people in the house. Mrs. Briggs is fine, she understands, but I don't like being watched."

Yes, I thought, privacy would be essential to someone so fragile.

"And I wanted Mabel for myself, you see. People told me I was wrong, told me I had far too much to do being Mrs. Charles Tyler and a mother of two boys. They all said, You'll be exhausted, and I thought, Nonsense, I'm Alva Tyler. Even when Johnny came along and I was going to have Frederick, I thought, No, I'm fine. Mabel was five that spring, and you know, five . . . they're very strong at five, children, strong-willed, and Johnny had just started walking."

Just started walking. A phrase I had heard from other mothers with such fondness and nostalgia. Now I thought I had never heard anything so ominous.

"We loved to have them play on the grass, just . . . run wherever they wanted. It was a warm day. One of the kitchen girls, I don't remember her name anymore, was doing the wash outdoors. She had a tub full of water. She went inside to get something. I was . . ." Her eyes closed as she remembered. "I was with Mabel on the front lawn. I was feeling a little . . . sick. She was having a tantrum over something, and I was trying very hard not to scream. I can't remember what I said, or even what she was upset about. I just remember standing on the lawn, with a fist to my mouth, the world swaying and feeling it was all going to come out, the sick and the screaming and the . . ."

She turned her eyes on me. "And I forgot. I forgot Johnny. It was only when the girl came back from the house and she found him . . ."

Her voice twisted like a rag caught in two fists. "He . . ."

"It's all right, Mrs. Tyler, I know."

"I wasn't there," she exhaled in a rush of anguish. "I wasn't there, and he died. He died alone. I am not a mother, Jane. These poor children have no mother. I tried to tell Charles, but he wouldn't listen. When Frederick came, he said, 'Another baby, that's what we need Alva, another baby to love.' But I don't. I can't. Is there anything worse than a mother who does not love her children? Who has nothing to give them except . . . weakness? And despair?"

"You have much more than that, Mrs. Tyler."

"I used to think so. When I had Mabel"—she broke into a true smile—"oh, I thought, my girl, my daughter, all the things I'll show you. So many things we'll do together. I saw us riding horses, scrambling over rocks, or just sitting together, making silly dreams about the future, but real ones, too. I thought for her, the dreams will be real. She'll do things, she'll break free—"

"And she will, Mrs. Tyler."

"But then I was so tired. Not like before, but . . . bone tired. Like my blood had turned to lead. I couldn't get up. For almost a year, I just lay in bed. The boys were fine with Charles and school. But poor Mabel! She would come to the door, ask me to read or braid her hair or play cards, and I couldn't. I wanted to do so much, but I was so tired and I couldn't. The sound of her voice made my head ache. The pull of her *wanting* all the time, I felt I would come apart."

"She loves you very much," I said, thinking that would comfort her.

"I know," she said fretfully. "But—you're not a mother, you can't understand, but sometimes you feel, oh, it's not really me they want, they don't know *me*. They only know this thing called Mother who's meant to do this and that and whatever else they want." She pressed her fists to her temples. "You see? This is how awful I've become."

She was silent a long while. Then, still bent and gazing at the floor, she said in a lower voice, "I thought of not having him. I thought of . . . I don't want to say, but . . . you're an intelligent woman, Jane, you know what I thought." Her mouth twisted in disgust. "But I didn't. I brought that poor child into the world when no one wanted him."

Mabel loved him, I thought. And Sofia. But perhaps that was what Mrs. Tyler had meant when she called Sofia a thief. She had stolen that place in Frederick's life that belonged to her. No matter that Mrs. Tyler was unable to claim it.

"Surely Mr. Tyler loves him."

"Charles?" She smiled sadly. "Oh, Jane, really."

I wasn't sure what she meant by that, but clearly to her it was so obvious it didn't require explanation.

"What happened that night, Mrs. Tyler?"

"That night, I couldn't sleep. It was . . ."

"The anniversary, I saw."

"I couldn't stop thinking about Johnny. He was such a fat, handsome boy. So gurgling and happy. Everyone said he was Charles without the mustache. I hadn't"—she swallowed—"I hadn't slept for days. Sometimes it feels like I haven't slept since it happened. Sometimes I walk around the grounds. If the guards have ever seen me, lord knows what they think. I try to stay at the back."

I remembered the shadow figure I saw that first night we arrived.

"That night I was at the back of the house and I heard Freddy crying. My heart just tore at the sound. I was convinced that he felt it, how I hadn't wanted him. And I thought, I can't let him endure this, it's better if we go. I'll take him out of all this and . . . end myself at the same time. I know it sounds horrible, but you can't imagine how relieved I was. I thought we'll just fly away. Somewhere quiet and I'll hold him . . ."

The footprint under the window, I thought, the too-small-for-a-man footprint. Of course, it was Alva's foot.

"I practically ran up to the nursery. Of course *she* was already there by the time I got there. I said, Let me have him, I'll calm him. She wouldn't give him to me, kept saying everything was fine and I should go back to bed."

I could imagine the state poor Mrs. Tyler had been in. No wonder Sofia had been reluctant to hand over the baby. I remembered our talk under the tree. All her questions about how well I knew the Tylers. She was trying to see if anyone but her realized how sick Alva Tyler was. She had tried to tell Charles Tyler not to trust someone—this man, that woman. I thought she meant

Mr. Grimaldi or herself. But she was talking about his wife. No wonder he had been so angry.

"I finally had to shout at her, He is my child and you will give him to me right now! She did, but she wouldn't leave the room. She refused to leave us alone. I tried to be nice, saying, You know, you're right, it really is too warm in here for him. And I opened the window . . ."

Here her expression began to crack again. Her lip trembled and tears began to course down her face. "She asked me what I was doing, and I said, I am just opening this window. And . . . I don't know . . . She stood in front of it, told me to give her the baby. I told her to get out of my way, I suppose I even tried to push my way through. We struggled, Freddy landed on the floor. He was screaming . . ."

"Alva."

I jumped to see Charles Tyler standing at the door. In that moment, I had a flash of understanding, although it was not clear to me what I had learned.

In a measured voice, he said, "Alva, come with me."

For a long moment, she stared at him. "Charles, there's no point."

"You're tired. Stop talking to Jane and come with me now."

"I cannot do this any longer. We have to tell the truth. You must tell the truth . . ."

He had, I realized. Simply by standing there, Charles Tyler had revealed the final truth about that night.

Standing up, I said, "Mrs. Tyler, I think Mr. Tyler is right. You should rest." I gave Mr. Tyler a pointed look to indicate he and I were now allies, then told his wife, "You've done so much, it's only natural to feel you can't go on a minute longer."

"That's right, dearest." Charles Tyler stepped into the room to take Alva Tyler's arm. Raising her out of the chair, he said, "To bed.

We'll put you to bed. I'll say goodbye to our guests, don't you worry about them."

She gave me a despairing look, certain I had betrayed her, and it occurred to me that she should not be left alone. "Should I ask Mrs. Briggs to come stay? Just until you fall asleep?" Mrs. Tyler looked panicked, and I said, "She thinks so highly of you, Mrs. Tyler. I'm sure she'll want to help."

"Excellent idea," said Mr. Tyler. "Jane, you fetch Mrs. Briggs, I'll see Mrs. Tyler to her room."

As I raced downstairs to the kitchen, I realized I was gambling on an assumption and that if I were wrong, another life could be lost. Breathless as I entered the kitchen, I said, "Mrs. Briggs . . ."

She had been counting jars in the cupboard. But she heard something in my voice and said, "What's wrong?"

"Mrs. Tyler needs you, I think."

A look passed between us. Setting her list down, she wiped her hands on her apron and headed out of the kitchen with a determined look. "How bad?"

"Very. She shouldn't be left alone."

"Is Mr. Tyler aware of the situation?"

"Yes."

We were now at the bottom of the back stairs. Mrs. Briggs said, "You don't tell anyone about this. And you don't judge her. You don't know what that poor woman's been through."

"I have some idea," I said. "But no—I don't judge her."

21

I waited for Mr. Tyler at the foot of the stairs. I could hear the noise of the garden party, happy laughter and chatter. I thought of the poor woman upstairs. I thought of Mabel and hoped someone was looking after her. I both dreaded hearing Mr. Tyler's footstep and was terrified to leave this spot in case I missed him.

But Charles Tyler was never a man who missed being noticed. When he saw me, he flashed his famous smile and clapped his hands as if all had been taken care of.

Then he tried to walk past me as if I were not there.

"Mr. Tyler?"

"Not now, Jane."

"I'm afraid I have to speak with you."

"I'm very sure you don't. Excuse me—"

He was going, leaving the house, escaping . . .

I called after him. "You should finish that letter."

A good hunter has sharp instincts. They feel threat before they know what the danger is. Charles Tyler was an excellent hunter. He knew he was in danger.

Half turning, he said, "Have you been reading my private correspondence?"

"Only one letter. And then only the first line and the date. In the first line, you note the lateness of the hour—well past midnight. Do I need to tell you the date?"

He was silent.

"You weren't in bed that night. You were in your study."

Abruptly, he grabbed me by the arm and pulled me down the hall and into his study. It was a violent act from a desperate man, and it occurred to me that I was not safe. But the thrill of being proved right is potent, and all I could feel was rampant curiosity as to what he would say. As he shut the door behind us, I marked the wide windows that looked out onto the party. There were at least fifty people present nearby. And, I noticed, an oar from Mr. Tyler's Harvard days hung on a wall, well within my reach. It was not a broom, but it would serve.

Charles Tyler took refuge behind his massive oak desk. Placing his hands flat on the leather blotter, he said, "And if I was?"

"The study is close to the nursery. When Sofia screamed for help, you heard her, didn't you?"

He was silent.

"She called for you when she was fighting with Mrs. Tyler. Trying to stop her from what she was about to do. The baby was on the floor, she knew it wasn't safe for him there, especially in the middle of . . . well, let's face it, a fight to the death. But if she got free of Mrs. Tyler, she couldn't be sure of getting to him first. Or preventing Mrs. Tyler from jumping."

He closed his eyes.

"That was what she meant to do, isn't it? Take the baby and jump? Kill herself and him?"

"My wife was not in her right mind. Who knows what she meant to do? She doesn't know herself."

"Yes, she does, Mr. Tyler. And it's destroying her. Guilt and grief are eating away at a fine mind and a great spirit. She needs help."

The hand formed a fist. "Don't you think I know that?"

"Yes, I do. I do, Mr. Tyler. I think you've been trying to help her for years. Even as you insisted she was fine, just fine. 'Just needs rest,' isn't that what you said? I imagine you said it to her when you hired Sofia. 'This way you can rest. Get your strength back.'"

"She needed it. After what happened . . ."

"Yes, after Johnny died. But she hadn't felt strong even before his death. And she blamed herself for his loss." I paused. "Needlessly, I think?"

This was a point of which I was not certain. But Charles Tyler said wearily, "Of course needlessly. Alva was at the front of the house when it happened. She was nowhere near Johnny. That's how it happened. No one was watching. It was an accident. An awful, tragic accident. But she blamed herself, God, how she blamed herself. I wanted to move back to the city, away from memories. She wouldn't hear of it. Couldn't leave him again, was how she put it. When Frederick was born, I insisted she have help. Get a nanny, take some of the burden off her . . ."

But every time she saw Sofia, it must have been a reminder that she had not been strong enough to care for her own child. Never mind that most women of her stature employed nannies. Sofia was there because Alva Tyler was . . . tired. Not well. Unfit. In a house where you were not allowed to be tired or weak. Unable to cope? Not Alva Tyler.

"She doesn't like to be coddled," said Charles Tyler with sudden vehemence. "Won't have it."

"If she broke her leg, would you let her walk on it? It's not coddling, Mr. Tyler. She's ill."

Then, painfully, I asked, "You liked Sofia. You were kind to her, she said so. Why?"

"I was kind to her. When she was in danger, I moved her from that sewer of a neighborhood, got her a job someplace safe."

"Your home."

"That's right," he said, not recognizing the irony. "You think anyone else would have hired a girl with ties to the Black Hand to care for their children? I could see she was a good girl. Good heart. At least, she used to be."

"Then how could you cut her throat?"

He blinked rapidly, almost a twitch.

"I was . . . as you said . . . in my study that night. Writing a letter. When I heard it. Heard her. Sofia. Screaming for me to come. I, ah . . ." He dropped his head, stared down at his desk for several moments. "I went upstairs to find Alva hysterical and Sofia holding her by the arms. Frederick was on the floor. I suppose I had known Alva was feeling some distress. She gets moods sometimes, spells . . ."

Moods. Had that been what Alva Tyler meant when she worried "they" would come back? That she wouldn't be able to stop them? And the children would be harmed? That was why she had sent them away, I realized. Not to protect them from kidnappers, but herself.

I said, "It was the anniversary of John's death."

"Yes." He acknowledged this briefly. "I said, 'Alva, you come with me now, we'll see Frederick tomorrow when you're better.' I brought her back to our bedroom, gave her . . . something to help her sleep. She kept saying, 'I was going to free him, Charles, that's all, I was going to set him free.' Then she said something about setting me free and herself. I told her to stop talking nonsense."

"And then?"

He hesitated, stretching his jaw to its full length. "I naturally

went to check on the baby. Sofia was soothing him. Right off, she
started accusing Alva of . . . horrendous things, terrible things. She
claimed to be frightened of her. Frightened for the baby."

"She'd tried to tell you before, hadn't she?"

"I told her she had no business making those accusations and
that if she breathed a word of it outside this room, I'd make sure
she was on the next boat back to Italy. But this time she was hysterical. Said if I didn't do something, she'd tell the authorities."

Perhaps remembering that he was the authorities, he laughed
soundlessly.

"I suppose I lost my temper at that point. I might as well admit,
I've been under some strain lately as well. The trial. Alva's . . .
worries. It went wrong. Badly wrong."

"All in an instant."

"Yes."

"A moment of rage and poor judgment."

"I was afraid for my wife," he said through clenched teeth.

"I know you were. So afraid that when you left her in her room,
you went to your study and got the knife before returning to the
nursery. You knew about the threats against your family. You'd
saved a kidnapped boy—why not make it look like a kidnapping
attempt? You even had their kind of knife. Where is that knife now,
Mr. Tyler?" I nodded to the desk. "The center drawer? Bottom?"

"Middle." He smiled thinly. "Quite clean, I assure you."

"A Black Hand kidnapping that became a Black Hand murder.
People would believe it. I believed it. I think the minute you saw
that open window you knew very well what Mrs. Tyler meant to
do. And that if people ever found out, it would be the end of her.
It wasn't a moment of rage and poor judgment. You had time. Time
to realize that Sofia was serious about telling the world about
Mrs. Tyler's illness. And that there was only one way to stop her."

How strange—I had thought Sofia had been killed in revenge

for her going to the police to protect a child. In fact, she was killed to stop her from going to the police again, to protect a child.

"Alva's suffering is no one's concern but our own. I let that young woman into my home. I gave her a job. I trusted her—and asked nothing in return. She'd have been dead if not for me, and she tried to repay me by destroying my family."

"Perhaps she saw it as saving your son's life," I said quietly. "Why was Frederick on the floor?"

"Sofia was holding him, you see. Wouldn't let go. If I'd insisted on taking him, she might have been suspicious. So I . . . acted from behind. She dropped him as she fell. I left him because . . ."

Because Frederick on the floor supported the kidnapping theory. It came to me that I was alone in a room with a man who had cut a woman's throat as she held his child. What would those mothers who swooned over the hero of the Forti kidnapping think when the truth came out?

"Does Mrs. Tyler know . . . what you did for her?"

"Alva knows: there are times in life when you must take action to protect yourself. Waffling about it afterward does no good."

"Was it you or she who brought the details of Mr. William's indiscretion to Miss Louise?"

Because whoever had done so had possibly hoped to implicate William in Sofia's murder. I didn't think Charles Tyler would have done such a thing to his nephew and his befuddled expression told me I was right. It would have been Alva, I thought. Concerned, practical. "My dear, marriage is a difficult road." Or Mrs. Briggs. Sensing threat to the family she was devoted to, loathing Sofia, wanting it clear that no one of any value had died.

"What are we going to do, Mr. Tyler?"

He looked at me, pleading. But he had enough self-possession not to ask me to forget.

"Even if I never tell a soul, your wife cannot bear this any longer. She knows what happened that night. She will protect you, but I think it would destroy her."

He was silent, fists on the desk, head down. Then nodded in exhausted acknowledgment.

In a hoarse voice, he said, "My children will live with such shame."

"They will remember other things, too. Mabel's scrapbook—"

He shook his head violently. When he was able, he said, "I see what it has done to my brother's family. I always thought myself better, stronger . . ."

And you wanted strong people around you. Strong, healthy, sane people who never experienced fear or doubt, never faltered or struggled, just strode boldly forth into the bright future. But Charles Tyler didn't need more reason to reproach himself.

"You are stronger than your brother. You have acknowledged responsibility. You did what you did, not out of malice, but to protect your wife."

I did not add that had he been truly strong, he would have been able to admit his wife's illness, not felt he had to take a life in order to shield her—and himself—from the scandal.

"They can't know." The finger was drawn and pointed at me. "No one can ever know of Alva's affliction. What I did, I did in a moment of madness. I shall never say why. Let the world draw its own conclusions."

So it would, I thought, and it would not be kind.

"You protected Aldo Grimaldi. You could have laid the blame at his door. I said you should. But you didn't. That does you great credit."

If Mr. Tyler accepted my paltry absolution, he gave no sign of it.

"But you also tried to blacken Rosalba's name. You called Officer Sullivan the day I left for the city, didn't you?" He nodded. "You often have him feed stories to the press for you, don't you? Heroic stories about a brave deputy commissioner. This one was about a stupid girl in love with a criminal who helped him kidnap a small boy—then turned him in when he jilted her. Why did you say all that, Mr. Tyler? Why damage her reputation?"

"I knew Sofia was going into the city. I didn't know who she was talking to. I thought if Alva's . . . pain ever came out, it would discredit her."

There was a burst of laughter from outside the window, and Charles Tyler gazed out at the party. "The wedding will proceed," he said. "Afterward, I shall present myself to the police."

Uneasy, I said, "The wedding is not for another three days."

"And?" He thrust out his jaw.

I thought of Charles Tyler's friends all over the world, the remote places he might flee to and hide. "I think it cannot wait."

"*You* think it cannot wait," he echoed, almost amused.

"No, I don't."

"Are you threatening me with the police?" he asked.

"I'm not threatening you with anything," I said. "That would be highly inappropriate."

I moved to the library door. "But three days is too long. Rosalba Salvio has waited long enough for justice. She saved your son, Mr. Tyler. Even if the world never knows how or who she saved him from. She deserves to be remembered as a heroine. Not another shabby Italian"—how did William's mother put it?—"killed in a tawdry scandal."

★ ★ ★

In the end, it did not take three days. Charles Tyler emerged from his study perhaps fifteen minutes after I left it. No one who spoke with him that afternoon would have guessed he had just confessed to the brutal murder of a young woman in his own home. No one who had seen him laugh with his beloved wife would have any sense of the misery that had hung like a lead chain around their necks for the past few years. No one who saw him dance with his daughter standing on his feet, her tiny hands in his large ones, would suspect his life was over.

And so when the world learned that Charles Tyler had been killed in a hunting accident the following day, it was shocked. Charles Tyler, the man who had shot game in Africa, faced down black bears in the Rockies, and knew more about guns than any American since Bat Masterson—killed when his own rifle misfired?

Some noted in private that the new Winchester was more volatile than previous models. Charles Tyler was no longer a young man. Maybe the gun had been too much for him. He had been walking in his woods, perhaps he had tripped. Easy to get a shot off with the new pump. Several of the obituaries—while unanimously fawning—referred to his bombastic personality, his penchant for the grand gesture, implying a slight unsteadiness of temperament without casting outright aspersions. One paper saw fit to remind its readers of his brother's tragic history. But that article was pulled by the afternoon edition.

Charles Tyler's grief-stricken widow and her children were under the care of her sister-in-law and her daughter, Beatrice, who would be staying at Pleasant Meadows for the foreseeable future. In light of the tragedy, the family announced that the nuptials for William Tyler and Louise Benchley would now be celebrated quietly at the Benchley home.

22

It was Louise's idea to invite Mabel to serve as flower girl. Mrs. Benchley was dubious at first—"But my dear, she'll be in mourning, dressed in black. Won't it seem a bit odd?"

To which Louise answered, "Mother, sometimes there are things more important than what a young lady is wearing."

★ ★ ★

Charles Tyler's funeral was also private—and smaller than might have been expected. That no one questioned this showed that the city was sensitive to the shadow that had fallen over the family, even if no one knew its source. The police commissioner and the mayor were in attendance, but the governor sent regrets. The commissioner gave the eulogy, remembering Charles Tyler as a true example of American manhood, bold, selfless, always putting country and family first. Charles Tyler was buried near his son at Pleasant Meadows, his funeral service held at First Presbyterian Church of

Oyster Bay. His two older sons made the journey from school. But his widow was too ill to attend, the other children too young.

The older Tyler boys—ten and twelve—did not look like their father. One resembled William to a startling degree, and the younger one had his mother's auburn hair and blue-green eyes. Both were wide-eyed with shock and while they strove to sound like the young men their father would have expected them to be, they felt no older than Mabel as they sat stiffly in church, hands trembling as they held the prayer book. The older one's lip shook with the effort not to cry, and at one point, the younger one gave up mouthing prayers, dropped his head, and sobbed quietly. William made a point of taking them both by the shoulder as we headed to the cars that would take us to the gravesite. He drove with them. Louise and I followed.

"William's devastated," said Louise. "To see them go through what he went through as a child. We're hoping they'll stay with us for the summer break."

At the site, the two boys were joined by William, Louise, Mr. Grimaldi—and myself. As we observed the hideous ritual of dropping earth on the coffin, I could not help expecting Charles Tyler to leap from the grave, large as life, roaring that it had all been a ridiculous mistake. But the coffin stayed meek and closed, the dirt landing with a hollow thud.

It was William's idea that we all walk after the burial. His uncle loved nature and was never still. Vigorous activity seemed the best way to remember him, far closer to his spirit than hymns. William and Louise walked with the boys. Mr. Grimaldi and I followed at a distance.

"And how are you today, Mr. Grimaldi?" I asked.

"I am confused, Miss Prescott." He gazed up the hill at the boys. "How is a man great and terrible at the same time?"

"'Fire both gives life and destroys,'" I said, quoting something my uncle had said. "I am very sorry that you have lost two people you cared for. But thankful that you told me where he was the night of the murder. May I ask you a personal question?"

He nodded.

"How did you come to work for Charles Tyler?"

For the first time since Charles Tyler's death, Aldo Grimaldi smiled. "You can't guess?" I shook my head. "I was a policeman. I worked for Charles Tyler in the city. He was good to me, promoted me."

"To the Italian Squad?"

"Before he started the squad, they were trying to stop the Black Hand with Irish cops." He snorted to underscore the idiocy of that approach. "Charles Tyler knows I am Italian and he also knows I am honest and there are many who are not. So he said to me, 'Aldo, you watch and you tell me who these men are.' I do. I give him the names of the men who are always around the corner when the crime happens. Or when they're going to arrest someone, they make a lot of noise, let the whole neighborhood know, the cops are here, give the criminals time to get away.

"One time, we see a couple of guys on the corner. Now, everybody knows, these guys stop women on their way home from work, and they take a cut of their pay. One woman finally says she'll testify. So, I say to this cop, You going to arrest him? He says, You do it, I don't speak Italian. I tell Mr. Tyler, Either they're lazy or they're bought."

"What happened?"

"What happens is, they framed me. You remember the bomb in his car?"

One of Charles Tyler's greatest moments, the narrow escape from death, played so insouciantly for the papers.

"It was my job to watch his car, so this cop and his friends, they make it seem like I did it. That day, I'm standing by the car outside the mayor's office. Two of the 'we don't see nothing' cops are with me. One of them says, 'Hey, take a look across the street, something's going on.' I say, I don't move from Mr. Tyler's car. But he keeps arguing, until I start to think, This makes no sense. And I know something's going to happen. I can feel it. When Charles Tyler comes out of the mayor's office, I say to him, You don't get in the car, we go around the back, I get you another car. A minute later—boom.

"Right away, the two cops say it's me—the guinea did it. We saw him. He looked under the hood, put something in. Mr. Tyler knows it's not true, he says he'll go to the papers if they charge me, but his boss says, Get rid of him. Charles Tyler says, Aldo, you come work for me for a while."

He pulled a handkerchief from his pocket and mopped his forehead. "When Sofia was killed, I think, That foolish girl, she went back to the city, she gave herself away and they found her. I am upset, not thinking right. It's only a few days later when Charles Tyler says, Aldo, I feel terrible. I was in my bedroom, I didn't hear that poor girl—that's when I remember the light in his study, and I know he is lying. But I don't want to believe . . . what the lie means. I go to the city to find proof it's someone else. But inside, my gut tells me. And I also know nothing will be right for Charles Tyler now. He can't live with this. He is a murderer who has also been very good to me. So, I tell you and not him, because I'm a coward."

"Your gut sounds very intelligent," I said. "Maybe you should go back to work for the police."

A shadow fell over his face. "It's not good to say, but I don't trust them."

"Then maybe the Pinkertons. I'm sure Mr. William would be happy to recommend you."

When we returned to the house, Louise took the boys inside

for tea. William lingered on the lawn, his attention drawn by the nursery tower—its flag still bravely waving. I was about to leave him to his thoughts when he said, "He killed her, didn't he?"

From the tone of his voice, he hoped I would say, No, no, it wasn't him.

"Yes. He took her life."

"I didn't know him at all, did I? He was just a figment of my imagination . . . this hero." He looked at me. "Why?"

Part of me felt it was not my place to reveal his aunt's sorrow. But it was also unkind to let William wander in darkness. And so I told him the full truth, as much as I understood it. I did not exonerate Charles Tyler. But when I was done, William could at least feel that he was not wrong in what he had seen in his uncle—but that he had not seen everything.

He was silent for a long while after I finished. Then he surprised me by asking, "Tell me honestly. Should I let Louise go?"

"Let her go?"

"Call off the wedding. After what's happened, no one could blame her. My half of the bargain was my family line." He shrugged painfully. "Not much of a bargain. Some might say bad blood."

I thought of the woman who had given me my first job, William's great-aunt, Lavinia Armslow. Vastly rich, she had given a good deal of her money to charity, once saying to me, "Tiaras pall after a time." She had fought through the after-effects of two strokes and had managed her financial affairs into the last week of her life. I thought of William's mother, who had made a success of her family despite her husband's collapse.

And of Charles Tyler, who did much good in this world and no small amount of evil. Strangely enough, when he thought he was doing good.

I rolled up my sleeve and examined the inside of my wrist. William said, "What are you doing?"

I traced my veins with one finger. "Trying to judge the quality." I held up my arm. "What do you think? Good or bad?"

"Jane . . ."

"I don't even know my parents. I can't tell you a single thing about them. I have to look to myself, no one else. Maybe you should do the same."

As we walked back to the house, he asked who else knew about the identity of Sofia's killer. I said myself, his aunt, and Aldo Grimaldi.

"That's not enough, is it?"

"It is for the children," I said, having thought about this a lot over the past few days. "Though Rosalba Salvio's father might feel differently."

Thinking of Rosalba's family and how they might never learn the truth of what happened to their daughter, I visited Anna at the Labor Hall. I found her at a desk, making notes on a typed speech. As she scribbled, she said, "Sit. I'm almost done." Then to the paper, "Ah, why does he *always*—?" She wrote furiously in the margins, then set the pencil down. "Yes."

"I saw Sandro."

Her hand went back to the pencil, rolling it between thumb and forefinger. "And?"

"He's—" I was about to call him a good man, but he wasn't a man quite, not yet. "I liked him. He's not such a fool."

"People learn, I suppose."

"You should get him away from Moretti."

"So he can do what?"

"He wants to go to California."

"Oh, well then." She nodded as if I had said her brother wanted to go to China.

"Maybe you know people out there. I have a little money . . ."

She snapped, "That's all it costs to go to California, a little money."

Then she raised her hand, stopping herself. "I'm sorry. I apologize. For things to change for Sandro, he needs brains he doesn't have or money I don't have. I don't know what to do for him and it makes me sick."

". . . Your uncle?"

"He has both my aunts to care for. And the people who work for him."

She rubbed at her forehead, the other arm tight around her stomach. It was true, her helplessness was physically painful to her, and to change the subject, I said, "I imagine you won't be going to the suffrage march."

She laughed and the arm around her middle relaxed. "No, I will not be marching beside Mrs. Belmont. I have a previous engagement with some women at the Smithfield cannery. Why? Will you?"

I shrugged: *probably not.*

Then Anna said, "Don't worry. They'll give women the vote. As long as they pick the five people we get to vote for, it's meaningless. So, why not?"

I thought to say, if it is so meaningless, why are they fighting so hard to keep us from doing it? But I knew what Anna would say. And I knew what I would say in return. We were old friends.

Standing, I said, "For Sandro. If you need . . ."

She looked up. Smiled. "I know."

"Tell Maria and Theresa I think of them."

"They think of you."

★ ★ ★

The next day, William went into the city and met with a representative of Commissioner Rhinelander Waldo. He said later that he had the sense they expected him to discuss a tribute to his uncle, some memorial honor that might be bestowed. But he was there to discuss something quite different. The representative found his story deeply disturbing and told William he would have to give a full report to the commissioner and that charges might be brought. William said that was the precise reason he had come. But out of respect for the deceased, it was agreed that no one would say anything until it was decided how best to proceed—especially as Charles Tyler had already suffered the highest possible penalty for his crimes. They would, they said, be in touch.

The call never came. Rhinelander Waldo resigned the following year, his career damaged when one of the heroic officers in charge of the anti-vice "Strong Arm" squads was discovered to have collected nearly two million dollars from gangsters, in exchange for losing evidence and alerting them to upcoming raids. One of the cases where the evidence went mysteriously missing was the Forti kidnapping. As one of the key witnesses was dead, the prosecution's case foundered. Dante Moretti was found not guilty and set free. His father told the newspapers he was very happy to have his son home.

★ ★ ★

Boys who are troublesome are sometimes sent off to experience what's called "two years before the mast as a common sailor," employment so arduous and unpleasant it makes men of them—or at least more appreciative of the blessings life has bestowed upon them. Clearly, caring for her aunt in Philadelphia had provided Charlotte with similar insight. The morning of the wedding, as I tried to arrange Louise's dress—it was a great deal of silk to drape elegantly in the smaller space of her own room—there was a knock at the door, and Charlotte came in.

"Say thank you," she told her sister. "I've just introduced Mother to the duchess of Chelmsford. No one will be able to pry her away until the I dos."

Then Charlotte laid her critical eye on her sister, and I braced myself.

Finally, she said, "No—you look perfect." And both sisters smiled.

Then Charlotte said briskly, "By the way, I've decided something: Jane should go with you. That's my wedding present."

Louise glanced at me. "That's marvelous, but . . . shouldn't we ask Jane?"

I hesitated, looking from one Benchley sister to the other. Then said, "I'm sure we can work something out."

★ ★ ★

And so Louise got her quiet wedding at home.

Even minus many of the guests, it was a crowded affair. Mabel dropped her rose petals with great dedication and expert precision. Louise's smile as she came down the stairs on her father's arm was not captured by the photographer, but it lives in my memory to this day.

Surprisingly, the wedding was even something of a social success. Having sailed all the way from England, William's cousin decided to attend the wedding, no matter where it was held. And she was particularly taken with Charlotte.

"Such a glorious, glorious girl," she told Mrs. Benchley. "You must let me take her to Europe. I could do so much for her."

★ ★ ★

A week after Louise and William left for their honeymoon in London, John Jacob Astor was buried at Trinity Church Cemetery. Two days later I took Mabel to *The New York Herald*, where she was given a lively tour of the city room. Whether Michael

Behan had alerted his colleagues that the little girl was to be treated with special kindness or whether her black dress and famous name provided the clue, reporters, editors, and pressmen alike went out of their way to answer her questions and consider her points. There was one disappointment when the child asked to meet Emma Bugbee. The men glanced at one another, puzzled, until one snapped his fingers and explained that Miss Bugbee's desk was on another floor. Women reporters were not allowed in the city room.

At the end of the visit, Michael Behan presented Mabel with a piece of metal type stamped with an *M*. His father had given it to him, perhaps she would like to have it for a while. But he said, "Your first day at the *Herald*, you'll give it back, right?" She promised.

As we waited for Mr. Grimaldi to bring the car around the street, Mabel looked up at me, her eyes anxious under the straw brim of her black hat, and said, "Mother wants to go to France. But she says Freddy and I are to stay with Aunt Florence."

I could understand Alva Tyler's desire to leave Pleasant Meadows and its dark memories behind. Of course, it was harder for her daughter. "Perhaps that's best. With Frederick so young and your brothers in school."

"She says we'll visit her in summer. But that means she'll be gone a long time, doesn't it?" I had no answer for her. "What if she doesn't come back?"

"Why on earth wouldn't she come back?"

Mabel's small, sharp eyes fixed on me and while I knew it was impossible for her to know what had really happened to Sofia, I had the sorrowful sense that she understood that her death, her father's disappearance, and her mother's desire to abandon her life in America were somehow tangled in one miserable snarl of loss. Kneeling, I gave her a hug. It was a poor substitute for her happiness. But she put her thin arms around my neck and pressed her head hard to mine.

Swallowing to gain control of my voice, I adjusted the collar of her coat and said, "Now, if you do go to France, you must write to me all about the Paris fashions. Since Miss Louise is married to your cousin, I'll have to be informed of the latest styles. We can't have her looking like a frump."

Mabel both smiled and wrinkled her nose with distaste. "Can I write about other things, too?"

"Of course."

She brightened at the sight of Mr. Grimaldi, who opened the car door and guided Mabel inside. His manner with her was gentle, almost clucking, and he spoke to her in a mix of English and Italian as he asked about her visit and admired the piece of type. As we shook hands goodbye, I had the odd thought that Aldo Grimaldi would see to it that Mabel Tyler got to where she needed to go. As would her aunt and cousins.

When they had left, Michael Behan asked if I would like to enjoy the beauties of Herald Square Park, a miserable patch of grass with a semicircle of a bench, squeezed between the elevated and the trolley line. I said I would like that very much.

He had sandwiches, cold beef on brown bread with butter and Worcestershire sauce, and a thermos of coffee. "First Keens, now this," I said. But the sandwich was very good and I complimented Mrs. Behan.

A newsboy passed, calling out the latest details of the Astor funeral. I turned my head to listen. Noticing, Behan said, "Strange, you don't seem like one of those women who suck up the details of other people's tragedy as entertainment—"

"Is that a different breed than the people who read about slit throats and severed heads?" I wondered.

"Possibly related, but there's something odd about the way we weep over the death of certain individuals"—he waved a hand at the picture of Astor on the cover—"when hundreds of people die every day, and they're lucky if they make it onto the back pages."

"Like Rosalba Salvio."

"For example."

He waited. I made him wait.

Finally, I said, "She shouldn't be famous because of the man who killed her. She should be famous for what she did."

He raised a finger. "Speaking of that. I saw Officer Sullivan the other day. I gave him your regards, of course. He says William Tyler visited recently. They didn't arrest him, though. And they let him leave the country. So, I'll assume they don't think he's guilty."

"He's not."

"But he's related to someone who is. Or . . . he was."

"Remember Mabel," I said.

"I will," he promised. Then asked, "Why'd he do it?"

"That's a strange question, isn't it? We always ask it when someone is killed—why? As if there should be a reasonable explanation."

"I didn't say reasonable. Just that men don't usually wake up one morning and decide to take someone's life and destroy their own if they're not in the habit of doing so. Why?" He repeated the question as if it were a chess move.

I looked at the paper. "'One of the world's wealthiest men, he sacrificed himself for the sake of others.' Charles Tyler loved his wife," I said. "He felt it was his job to protect her—at all costs."

"So, it *was* an affair."

I shook my head, unsure as to how to explain the Tylers' pain and Charles Tyler's ruthless, disastrous quest to keep it secret.

Finally, I said, "Think of the arrogance of the *Titanic*, the hubris of the men who built it. They think, What we have made is so colossal, so magnificent, it defies nature. We have no need of life-boats, the ocean cannot best us." I thought of Alexander Cassatt blasting his way through the riverbed. "It is splendid, this arrogance, it takes us forward. But it's also ignorant. It won't tolerate weakness. And when nature—human or otherwise—does not comply, it can be savage."

"But this isn't the story of a ship," said Behan gently.

"No, it's the story of a woman. And children. And birth. Those soft, foolish things—of no concern to anyone of consequence."

He frowned. "What are you telling me, Miss Prescott?"

"That maybe it's a story no one needs to hear. At least, not from *The New York Herald.*"

He was silent a long time. "All right. But tell me at least."

So I told him what I knew. When I explained why the window had been opened, he interrupted, "Wait a minute. Are you saying—?"

"You have to imagine how guilty she felt, Mr. Behan. For the death of her son, her failure to mother her daughter, her frantic desire not to be a mother again. She was exhausted, not in her right mind. And on that night, at that moment, she thought death was better for Frederick than to live with her as a mother. In killing herself, she would atone for John's death and free Charles Tyler from the unhappy woman she had become. Free herself from his expectation that one day, she would again be the brave, bold young woman he had married. That girl who could go anywhere with him, dare anything. Imagine a husband who wants you to climb Kilimanjaro when you don't have the strength to get out of bed. You're Alva Tyler, the woman who can do anything. But you couldn't save your own son from drowning."

Michael Behan's breath was harsh, his eyes hard as he stared into traffic. "No," he said. "You can't excuse . . ."

"I don't excuse. But remember that she didn't kill anyone."

"Sofia might say different." Then recovering his professional demeanor, he said, "So, Tyler killed Sofia to stop her talking?"

"Yes. I also think he killed her because she told him what he didn't want to hear: that his wife's illness was real. His brother suffered from melancholy and he committed suicide, I think that left Mr. Tyler with a horror of unsound people. A lesser man might have been able to accept his wife's struggles. Not Charles Tyler. That's why he destroyed himself when his life fell apart. Better death than failure.

"So, there's the truth. The only people you can punish now are his widow and children. And some might say they've suffered enough."

Behan said, "From what I've seen of Mabel Tyler, she'd want the truth."

"Maybe. But it's not my job to give it to her, and not yours either. Not when she's only six years old."

He exhaled, shook his head. "Nice family your Miss Benchley's married into."

There was no answer to that, and so for a long time we sat, supervising the pigeons in their battles and wanderings. I found myself preoccupied by the memory of that night, sitting numbed through shock and liquor, while the Tylers wrestled with the question of what to do. I had been offended by their obsession with their own safety, their lack of outrage on Sofia's behalf. I had understood it as the vanity of the wealthy. When it was simply that the murderers were present in the room and did not care to focus on justice for the dead woman.

Rather, it was the open window they were obsessed with, the break in the defenses, the unreliable watchman. Someone had let the wrong person in—and violence and misery had followed. How easily we had all believed it was someone from outside. Of course, it had to be. Nothing like this ever happened before *they* came. I found myself wondering if I had ever made it clear to Mr. Grimaldi just how sorry I was.

Then I heard Michael Behan say, "So you're a woman of leisure these days, Miss Prescott."

"No woman who works for the Benchleys is that, Mr. Behan." I looked at him. "And you? Now that you're not listening to Officer Sullivan, what will you write about next?"

He stretched his legs, scattering a few complacent pigeons. "Oh, I'll find something, Miss Prescott."

"I'm sure."

It was then I decided to say something that had been on my mind since Behan first turned up at Pleasant Meadows.

"I'm sorry I didn't answer your last letter."

"Didn't you?" He looked at me. "No, I suppose you didn't. I didn't honestly remember . . . anyway. Nothing to be sorry for."

He half smiled, and I realized he was embarrassed for me. I had built up the importance of those letters in my mind, not understanding that they were nothing at all to him. Possibly something he scribbled for fun while waiting for an interview. A way to pass the time. If a reply came, lovely, another time filler. If not, well, there was always tobacco.

And, I thought, I worked for a wealthy family that had made its way into the news once already. Behan probably wrote to lots of people like me, hotel staff, waiters, hansom cab drivers. Anyone who could give him a bit of information, a new story.

"I'm glad to hear it," I said, aware that I was putting words in a row without being sure of their meaning. "Now that this is over, your wife will have you back at dinnertime."

"That might not be good news to her. For Mrs. Behan, preparing the evening meal is an undertaking similar in scope to the Erie Canal. Leaves her quite exhausted. Some might say ill-tempered."

It was a funny remark, and I smiled. But then I thought of the empty thermos cup, and the wax paper that had been wrapped around the sandwiches I'd just eaten. I thought of Mrs. Briggs, her arm stiff with exertion, Mrs. Mueller pounding the dough, Bernadette trudging the cleaner she so hated up and down stairs, Elsie struggling with a basket of heavy wet sheets. I thought of Maria and Theresa, preserving their family's traditions, painstakingly, one plate at a time. And of Alva Tyler, soothing her daughter's tantrum, even as, at the back of her mind, she felt the ominous absence of her other, more vulnerable child . . .

"Well, perhaps if Mrs. Behan is tired, you should hire a day girl to help her. It needn't be every day, it wouldn't cost much. It's no small amount of labor to keep people fed, provided of clean clothes and linens, and living in a well-ordered house. You might find her more welcoming of your company."

"'A man may work from sun to sun. But a woman's work is never done.'"

"Well, mine is. But I'm not married, so I get paid. Hire a day girl, Mr. Behan." I stood and held out my hand. "Goodbye."

He shook it. "Goodbye, Miss Prescott."

As I walked away, I heard him call, "When Signor Caruso is next in town, I'll ask the music critic if he can get you a ticket. He's in Russia right now, though. Publisher told him to cut his hair and he refused, so off to Moscow he went. Or it might have been Siberia."

I smiled. And kept walking. As I did, I made a list in my head. I would read the newspaper every day, not rely on what was talked about at the breakfast table. I would ask Elsie if she wished to attend a lecture or go to the pictures or one of those municipal dances. On my days off, I would take secretarial classes at the refuge. Perhaps I might even learn French.

And I would tell William and Louise that I wanted a raise in salary.

★ ★ ★

It being a pleasant day, I walked from Herald Square to the Benchley house—although it was currently devoid of Benchleys. Louise was on her honeymoon and Charlotte was dining at the Waldorf with the duchess. Mr. Benchley being out on business, Mrs. Benchley was attending a meeting of the Ladies' Auxiliary for the *Titanic* Memorial. The staff ate in the kitchen as usual, but there was a giddy, almost truant mood. The Benchley house was quiet—and to me, who would be leaving soon—almost abandoned. There was a sense of change in the air, and we found ourselves ignoring our traditional roles in the house, all cooking, serving, and clearing the table.

"When do you move to the new house?" Elsie asked as we washed the dishes.

"I suppose when they get back in a few weeks. Although they'll be staying at Mr. William's mother's home in the city while it's finished." Louise's dowry had included a townhouse in the East Twenties—and a job for William with the Benchley firm. Mrs. Benchley had been distressed to learn her daughter would be more than a mile away, but Louise had hurried to her father's side and kissed his cheek once, then twice. And then again.

Bernadette, having sharp ears, heard it first. But the instant she looked up, I heard it, too, the rising cry of an excited crowd. And in the distance, the officious clop of horse hooves and the thud of drums. Seated in the kitchen at the back of the house, we had been unaware there was anything happening outside. The suffrage march. I had forgotten all about it.

Without speaking, we all went out the back door to be confronted by a mass of people gathered on the street. The traffic police were having difficulty holding the crowds; people kept breaking through the cordons and spilling onto the streets to get a better view of the approaching parade.

"I see it!" cried Elsie, who was the tallest among us. "I see it!"

I stood on my toes and gazed where she was pointing. Bernadette was looking, too, although she was trying to appear uninterested. Mrs. Mueller was wiping her hands on her apron, her mind clearly on the dishes in the sink and whether she had turned off the stove. But she, too, was craning her neck for a better view. Up and down the street, people leaned out of windows, waving handkerchiefs.

The happy chatter of the spectators around us turned into a roar as the first marchers appeared. A phalanx of women on horseback carrying American flags and wearing black straw hats with the cockade of the Women's Political Union led the march. They ranged in age from Mrs. Charles Knoblauch, whose husband had ridden with the Rough Riders, to fourteen-year-old Miss Phyllis Mueller. Also among the leaders was Miss Mabel Lee, or "little Miss Mabel Lee," as *The New York Tribune* had called her in a profile titled "Chinese Girl Wants Vote."

The horsewomen were followed by a blare of brass as the Old Guard Band announced itself. After them, for blocks and blocks, a seemingly unending flood of women in white. At the sound of trumpets, several young women pushed their way through the front of the crowd to join the parade.

"It ends at Carnegie Hall," said Bernadette cynically. "I don't know how much marching they'll be doing."

And yet she stayed. And I stayed. We all did, transfixed by the sight before us. For myself, I could only think, There are so many of us.

I had lived my life among women. First at my uncle's refuge, then in the Armslow and Benchley homes. I had spent my time in countless rooms with only other women in them. And yet staring at the river of humanity passing before me, I began to have my first comprehension of how many women there were. Not just here on this street and stretching as far as the eye could see up and down the avenue. But in the city. In the nation. In the world. It was like seeing the ocean for the first time, to be confronted with a glimpse of what the word "vast" truly means.

Wave upon wave, they came. There were society women in all white, factory workers who could afford only a white shirtwaist. Mrs. Belmont, once Mrs. Vanderbilt, marched in a white silk suit with a black ribbon with members of her Political Equality Association, while the eighty-seven-year-old Rev. Antoinette Brown Blackwell rode on a chariot covered in lilac and dogwood. Other elderly women made their way with canes, while the youngest marchers were pushed by their mothers in carriages. They had divided the women according to profession, and I stood amazed to see all that we did and were. We were doctors, lawyers, clerks, milliners, stenographers, bookkeepers, actresses, unionists, investigators, and students. Nurses, all dressed in uniform, came bearing a banner with the names of Florence Nightingale and Clara Barton. They were followed by doctors whose banner honored Dr. Mary Putnam Jacobi. Then came the writers, marching behind a standard that bore the names of Louisa May Alcott and Harriet Beecher Stowe. The Theatrical Brigade was led by Mrs. Maria Stewart, dressed as Joan of Arc in full armor and riding astride a white horse. Miss Fola La Follette held a banner with the names Modjeska, Siddons, and Kemble. Dressmakers carried a banner emblazoned with a sewing machine. The cooks marched behind a kettle. The enormity of the march was matched by the crowds on sidewalks; women and men—eyes fixed on the marchers as if they were the most important people doing the only thing that mattered in the city that day. Which, I realized, they were. As the socialists marched past singing "La Marseillaise," I found myself grinning without quite knowing why.

There was some hissing and some boos, but they sounded churlish and pathetic. At some points, rowdies rushed onto the parade route, trying to spook the horses or scatter the marchers— and the police did not stop them. But the marchers refused to be scattered. There were many children, carrying hand-lettered signs that read WE WISH OUR MA COULD VOTE! Other signs read MORE BALLOT, LESS BULLETS! And THE FEEDERS OF THE WORLD WANT VOTES TO LOWER THE COST OF FOOD! There were delegations of men as well, representatives from the League of Men for Women's Suffrage. Younger men came representing their universities. I thought this was touching and rather brave. They were greeted on some blocks with jeers but with clapping on others.

A great cheer went up as the scholars came into view, several of them wearing academic robes and mortar boards. Girls in the crowd became giddy when they spotted teachers they knew, calling out, "Mrs. Ackerly!," "Miss Lourdes!" Behind them came their students, carrying banners from their schools. As the rose-and-gray banner of Vassar passed, I caught sight of Emily Tyler, who, seeing the house, and then me, called out, "Jane!" and beckoned me over.

I smiled my apologies, but then Elsie said, "Let's do it. Let's march."

Mrs. Mueller held up a demurring hand, and Bernadette said, "Oh, no."

Elsie turned to me. "Miss Prescott, will you? I don't want to do it alone."

I was about to say no out of habit, then realized I could not think of a single good reason not to.

"Why not? We all should. Come on, Bernadette. Mrs. Mueller?"

The older woman gestured anxiously. "The house . . ."

"The door locks when you close it and you turned off the oven, don't worry. Come. It'll be something to tell your grandchildren about."

The very mention of the longed-for grandchildren was enough for Mrs. Mueller, who began hesitantly following Elsie as she made her way through the throng. Bernadette, being Bernadette, held out the longest, but finally even she shrugged her way forward.

I had the terrible fear that the moment we stepped foot in the street, someone would shout at us to get back on the pavement, what did we think we were doing? We were too late, we hadn't signed up, we weren't wearing white—and we had no thirty-nine-cent hats. And our place, where did we belong? Finally, we found a spot in a section that seemed to be women who worked with their hands, professions ranging from industrial to domestic. It was a lively group. One woman immediately linked arms with a startled Bernadette. Mrs. Mueller, kitchen forgotten, was smiling broadly and humming along with a band a little ahead of us, swishing her apron as she went. Elsie practically skipped down the street, pausing every so often to grab me by the arm and say, "Isn't it wonderful? Isn't it?"

I looked up at the sea of women before us and then behind at all who came after. I thought of Berthe Froehlich, her strong, scarred arms swinging that broom, of that woman on Mulberry, eggplant and good humor raised high. I thought of Louise, who was now learning to be Mrs. William Tyler. I thought of Anna, who was working as hard today as she always did, too busy to join something as frivolous as a march. I thought of Sofia, who would never see another day. Of Mabel, her sturdy little legs stepping into the car as she held fast to her piece of type. And her mother, that brave, marvelous, broken woman who would—I hoped, I prayed—laugh again one day.

"Yes," I said. "It really is."

Epilogue

The other day, I went with my daughter to the Metropolitan Museum, where we had not been since she was little, and I took her to see the Greek statues. She was a very practical child and did not care for art. She doesn't care much for it as an adult, and after a few rooms, she said she was going to the café and would meet me in the Impressionists.

That left me free to wander among the Eakinses and Sargents. Today I paused by Sargent's portrait of the Stokeses, whom I remembered as friends of the Armslows. Isaac Newton Phelps Stokes married Edith Minturn, and it is Edith who stands out in the portrait, the vision of the new woman, a straw hat held on cocked hip, a raised eyebrow, frank smile. She is a study in white and black, the crisp snowfall of the skirt contrasting with her vivid black jacket, handsomely accessorized by a black bow tie and white collar. Her husband, a last-moment replacement for a Great Dane who was supposed to partner Edith in the portrait, stands behind in relative shadow.

Gazing at Edith, I thought of Alva Tyler, who had not occupied my thoughts for many decades. She did move to France soon after the events I have related. Her children did not go with her, remaining in the care of their aunt and Mrs. Briggs. When war came, Alva was told to leave by the American embassy. But she stayed, working with the American Hostels for Refugees; after, she made her life at a hospital for men crippled physically and mentally by the war. Some found it astonishing that a woman who had lost her husband to suicide would take refuge among the ill and unbalanced, but a few of us understood it very well. Alva Tyler's was a nature that was at its best in extremes; physical danger held far less terror for her than domesticity. And I think after the events of 1912, it gave her some solace to live with the mentally anguished. The hospital was a realm where the truth of mental illness was frankly acknowledged and understood; here she could ease her own mind in service to others. She was awarded the Cross of Honor before her death in 1936.

I stared at the Stokes portrait so long, I found myself slightly disoriented to turn and see a large man in shorts and sandals snap a photograph of the painting.

Exploring the adjoining galleries, I found myself face-to-face with a vibrant image of a mother and child. The woman is sewing, head lowered in concentration. A small girl, maybe five, leans on her mother's knee, gazing back at the viewer, chin resting on one hand, pudgy fingers dug into her rosy cheeks. She wears a white smock dress and a curious expression. Who is this person who has come into the room where her mother is sewing? What do they want? Have they brought her a present?

I had seen the portrait before, but I had never noticed until today that she is actually leaning on her mother's work, which flows over the lap the child might view as her rightful place. And yet the two look quite easy in their separate interests, the mother in her work, the child in the viewer. At the bottom right, you can see the signature of the painter, Mary Cassatt. And if you cared to look at the information card provided by the museum, you would see that the painting is a gift of Mabel Tyler Forbes. Sometimes I wonder who she thought of when she looked at the painting: her own mother—or Rosalba Salvio, whom I see in the woman's high, dark hair, the strong nose, and air of gentle preoccupation.

The murder of Rosalba Salvio remained a small item on page seventeen in the minds of most people: easily ignored and soon forgotten. It was only when people began to write the history of the Tyler family that the story attracted any attention. It was treated as a macabre incident in the life of a branch of the family that was celebrated in its own time, but had since faded from prominence. In the '50s, a Long Island writer became obsessed with the case and became convinced that Charles Tyler had murdered the Italian girl shortly before his own suicide. In his book, he drew elaborate diagrams of the house to show how the accepted story of the unknown kidnapper could not be true. But he never came up with a motive, and as no one cared about Charles Tyler except as the relation of other more famous members of the family, his book was not a success.

"That's pretty, I guess," said my daughter, coming up behind me.

"Is pretty something you admire?" I asked her.

"Not especially."

"Then maybe choose another word." I looked back at the painting.

"Am I supposed to say it's important, groundbreaking, momentous?"

"What would you say about the Sistine Chapel? The vision of God giving life to Adam? It's a similar endeavor." My daughter's expression told me I had been clever, but not persuasive. "Did you know her brother built Pennsylvania Station?"

"The old station?" Now my daughter looked interested. "No."

"Alexander Cassatt. His statue used to stand in the grand hall. It was ten feet tall and glared down at you from a pedestal. I felt like arguing with it every time I passed."

"I suppose they melted it down after they tore down the station."

"Not quite. I think it lives in a museum in Philadelphia."

As we moved on to the next room, we found ourselves in front of a very different Sargent. On loan from England, it depicted a row of soldiers, each with his hand on the next man's shoulder. Blindfolded, the soldiers are unable to see the many men who lie at their feet, dead or dying. The painting was called *Gassed*. My daughter had little patience with art, but great respect for the power of witness, and she lingered.

"Did you know anyone who fought in that war?"

"A few people." One of whom had been Sandro Ardito, who lost his life at Meuse-Argonne, fighting for a country he never felt was his, perhaps because he saw it as his only escape. His body was not returned to his sister, who had begged him not to fight the businessman's war. Another had been Charles Tyler Jr., who joined as soon as he turned eighteen. He was killed in the Second Battle of the Marne; a reporter said of the American forces in that fight, "I never saw men charge to their death with finer spirit." His father might have relished the compliment; I do not think his mother would. I hardly need remind people of the splendid life and career of Frederick Tyler. I have not seen him for many years, but his sister keeps me informed.

President Wilson, for whom I was not permitted to vote, had promised the United States would stay out of the war. But as is so often the case, that promise was broken and men—tens of millions of gallant, chivalric men—turned the world into a charnel house.

As we left the gallery, a towering statue caught my daughter's eye and she said, "I don't like to be maudlin, but it really was a crime that they tore down the old station. Particularly when you consider the monstrosity that replaced it."

In the bright, airy hall, surrounded by the statues of the heroic and departed, I thought of Penn Station—and the *Titanic*. (Michael Behan was right about many things, but the short-lived appeal of that story was not one of them.) I thought of the dead who had no monuments to them. Of Alexander Cassatt, so certain that the station would be his lasting monument, while now he gathered dust in a museum. I remembered its destruction, the wrecking balls that smashed through the walls, shattered windows, reducing that architectural marvel to rubble to be hauled away by garbage trucks.

Before leaving we passed again by the pretty Cassatt, and I caught the child's eye. "That's the thing," I said. "Buildings fall. But people go on."

My daughter observed that was perhaps a mixed blessing. And then we went to lunch.